The Cor

Fion

CLOCH**O**DERICK

The Consolation Prize was first published in 2018
by Clochoderick Press.

www.clochoderickpress.co.uk

Clochoderick Press
27 Newton Street,
Paisley,
Renfrewshire,
Scotland,
PA1 2RN

A CIP catalogue record for this book is available from the British Library.
ISBN: 978-1-912345-07-6

Typeset by R.K. Wallace in Garamond

Printed and bound by:
Imprint Academic
Seychelles Farm, Upton Pyne, Exeter, Devon EX5 5HY

Funded by:

Photo by Lynn Holmes

Fiona Lindsay studied English Literature at the University of Glasgow. She is an active member of Johnstone Writers' Group and the Romantic Novelists' Association. This is her first novel.

Acknowledgements

I would like to thank the following people who have assisted me whilst I was writing the Kirklochy Chronicles:

The idea initially came from a conversation – not entirely serious – with a writer friend, Mo Blake.

I completed the first draft whilst attending a novel writing group which met in the Mitchell Library and I thank Merle Brown, Colin Donnelly, Margot McCuaig, Sheila McLachlan, Marianne Morrison, Gerry Stewart and Steven Tobin for their invaluable feedback.

I must also thank the members of Johnstone Writers' Group for their advice and constructive comments.

I have benefitted greatly from the support of the Romantic Novelists' Association, especially Janet Gover and Alison May, who run inspiring novel writing retreats.

Thanks also to my friends and colleagues within Renfrewshire House for helping me out with advice, suggestions and funny lines: Kerri-Ann Bishop, Wendy Bolt, Nicola Cameron, Amanda Colvin, Wendy Davidson, Maggie McAleer, Pamela Mulholland, Lynnette Sibley, Vanessa Stevenson, Lisa Sweeney and Linda Watson.

I also thank my mum, Margaret, and my brother, Duncan, for helping me to brainstorm ideas at the dinner table.

Thanks to Kathryn Metcalfe for her enthusiasm and editing skills.

I thank Shaun Moore for the joke about the taxi driver and Elspeth McLachlan for the story about the talcum powder.

Thanks also to my friends, Lynn Holmes, Eileen McDonald, Sheila McLachlan and Karen Pittis for their expert advice and unceasing support and encouragement.

Finally, thanks to Robert Kerr, without whose vision, expertise and hard work this book would not have been published.

This book is dedicated to Sheila and Eileen,
with love and gratitude.

1. *Other Side of the World*

Heather drove slowly along a narrow, winding road in her ancient, purple Fiat 500. Huge mountains loomed over her and a forest of dark trees cast shadows across the land. The loch rippled, deep and iron grey. Tufts of white, waving in the chill wind, indicated a bog, just in front of a ruined croft. She shivered. She was totally lost. What if the car was to suddenly stop, and refuse to go any further? All around her was deserted and eerily silent, apart from the occasional bleating of sheep, the sudden, plaintive call of a bird and, in the distance, the crash of the waves. Her mobile phone, clipped to the dashboard, had died. Fortunately, she'd managed to speak to her boss before she lost her signal, but now her sat nav app had stopped working. As irritating as the tinny American voice had been, mispronouncing all the Scottish place names, she really missed it. She was lost without her phone: completely cut off from civilisation. She parked in a lay-by, leaned back in her seat, and wondered what to do next. She must get to Thistle Cottage before it got dark. She didn't exactly relish the idea of sleeping in her car in the middle of nowhere, and the only rations she had left were half a Mars Bar and some tepid coffee in a flask.

Suddenly, reflected in her driving mirror, a young man turned the corner and strode along the grass track at the edge of the road. Quickly, she switched off her iPod and wound down the window.

'Excuse me,' she called.

The man approached her car. Dressed in a leather jacket, jeans and boots, he didn't conform to her advertising agency's image of Highland men – no sign of either a sporran, red hair or a beard. He bent down, his head framed in the window, so that he could talk to her.

'Oh, my God!' she cried in shock and disbelief. 'Euan Buchanan! I've never been so glad to see anyone in my life. I'm utterly lost,' she added, red faced, but beaming.

'Heather McAndrew! How long's it been?' Euan smiled. 'Wait there. I'll get in.'

'Thanks,' Heather breathed. At this moment in time, she would gladly give him her hand in marriage. Scratch that. She intended never to marry anyone.

Euan disappeared round the back of her car, and climbed into the passenger seat, hunching up his long legs. He was still smiling.

As a teenager, long before she'd met Aidan, (A.K.A. The Bastard) she'd had a bit of a crush on Euan. He must be twenty-five now, and was even better looking than he had been back then – he'd grown tall and filled out. He had deep-set dark eyes and hair of a rich brown.

'So – are you just here on holiday, or are you staying a while?' Euan asked.

'Staying for a while. Treeny needs me now.'

'Good. I mean, good to have you back, but really sorry about Treeny. I heard she'd had to go into Twilight House. How is she?'

'Not brilliant. She's putting a brave face on it, but she just wishes she could come home. And she absolutely hated losing her independence; it was her greatest fear.'

'You were always really close, weren't you?' Euan asked.

Heather nodded.

'We used to love coming to Aunt Treeny's every summer,' she said. 'We'd look forward to it for weeks. I'd sit in school and daydream about the picnics on the beach, swimming in the sea and running across the fields.' She sighed. 'We'd go hill walking, bird watching with my grandpa – oh, and I loved Aunt Treeny's homemade tablet. Nothing like it. I even learned to like porridge with salt.'

She paused for a moment, memories flooding back.

'Then there was Jamie's Cove,' Euan said. 'I don't think anyone else ever went there except our crew. God, just about every night turned into a party.'

'Yeah – our own private beach,' Heather said. 'No parents on our case. Burgers never tasted as good as when we barbecued them and ate them in the open air. I used to love it when Lewis would bring his guitar and we'd have a sing-song. I still love that acoustic sound. I remember it was light until nearly midnight some nights.'

'Those were the days,' Euan joked, in a creaky, old-man voice.

'I never painted as much as I did in when I stayed in the village,' Heather said.

'Yeah, I remember. Mum's still got that sunset painting you did for her fortieth up in the living room.'

'She has?'

'Yeah. She really loved it. And to think me and Cal only asked you to do it because we were too skint to buy her something decent.'

Heather gave a shout of laughter.

'You absolute bastard! You're lucky I'm driving, mate, or I'd give you a slap.'

'Only joking. It's brilliant.'

The chat with Euan had cheered her up momentarily, distracting her from her thoughts of Aidan, but then they came crashing back in and she felt a stab of homesickness for the anonymity of London, where no one even spoke to their near neighbours. Despite the name inherited from her Scottish father, her beloved Great Aunt Catriona and her Jamie's Cove friends, she suspected that, among many of the villagers, she would never fully shake off the reputation of the outsider from the big city. The *English* big city.

'Euan, do you think the villagers can accept me, and not keep thinking of me as an in-comer?'

'Sure they can. Just give them about three hundred years.' He frowned. 'But, Heather, what about your job back in London?'

'The boss says I can work remotely for a few months.'

Not wanting to dwell on this subject, she switched her iPod back on, turning it up. Euan sang along, tapping his chunky boots, to Paolo Nutini's *New Shoes*, pausing now and again to give directions. She could appreciate the scenery now – mist hovering around the top of mountains, the tallness and straightness and darkness of the trees. She puttered along, praying that her car wouldn't pack up so close to her destination. They passed a farm and a bothy, then, round a corner, the road that led down to Kirklochy. Heather gasped; she'd forgotten how terrifying it was. Euan grinned at the incredibly steep gradient, as if he was just about to go on a rollercoaster ride.

Heather winced. 'If we don't make it, it's been nice knowing you.'

She switched her engine to neutral to save precious petrol, took a deep breath, and began the descent. Her car plunged at speed until finally, after what seemed like forever, it came to rest in the main street of Kirklochy.

'Dread to think what the cottage'll be like, now that it's been empty for so long,' Heather said, with a slight shiver. 'Cold and dusty, probably. Plus, since Treeny broke her hip, she hasn't been able to keep it like she used to. Mrs Gillies and Mrs Peden would help her if they could, but they're both pretty frail now, too.'

Euan touched her arm, his eyes, warm and chocolate brown, fixed on hers. He'd always been a kind boy, even as a teenager, she remembered. A memory unwound of him comforting her when her grandpa's Labrador, Paddy, had had to be put down and she'd cried for two days solid.

'Why don't you unpack and get settled in, then, tomorrow night, we'll get together for a catch-up?'

Heather smiled, although she was exhausted from the ordeal. 'That would be brilliant.'

'Will we say 7 o'clock in the Claymore?' Euan suggested. If Heather hadn't totally given up on romance, she might have found him somewhat attractive.

'Great. I'll look forward to it,' she said.

'It really is good to have you back.' He touched her hand before releasing his seatbelt and opening the door.

'Lovely to see you again.'

Heather thought it extremely likely that she'd run into more of her old friends before long, given that the population of Kirklochy was about 47. She started up the car again, watching Euan march off down the street and go into the Claymore Inn, which would be her local – everyone's local, come to that, being the only pub within a thirty mile radius.

Having always travelled to Kirklochy by train and bus before, Heather knew exactly where she was when she saw the bus shelter. Thistle Cottage was just round the bend, perched a few hundred yards up a hillside. She drove round the corner, and, after a whole day on the road, she'd reached her destination. There it was: white painted, low roofed, with ivy not just round the door, but covering every wall as well.

The key was hidden where it always had been, under a stone pig.

She let herself in, switching on the hall light. The cottage was as chilly as she'd expected, and much more neglected looking than she remembered. Feeling shattered with all the travelling, she decided not to unpack anything other than the essentials. As she dragged her case towards the bedroom, she caught sight of a postcard lying on the linoleum of the hall.

In the kitchen, she plugged in the kettle and found an aged teabag in the cupboard above the sink. Since there was no milk, she added a splash of whisky from a dusty bottle half full of the amber liquid. *Glenmorangie*, she said aloud, liking the sound of the name. She curled up in the armchair by the window, wrapping a tartan travelling rug round her, and sipped her drink, feeling the whisky warming her right through, and reading the postcard, with its spindly handwriting, which was addressed to herself.

When are you coming to visit? Bring a cake with a file in it! T xxx

She found herself smiling slightly at Treeny's spirit, then a tear ran down her cheek at how shaky her aunt's handwriting was, evidence of her increasing frailty. Suddenly she was sobbing – she'd never felt so lonely in her life, or needed a Tweed and Elnett scented hug from Treeny so badly. She'd been able to talk to her great aunt about anything, but now the roles were reversed and Treeny needed her support. She almost winced as, yet again, she relived thoughts of Aidan's betrayal, finally admitting to herself that he didn't really love her. After crying for a while, she felt slightly more at peace. With a tiny spark of hope, she remembered her arrangement to meet Euan the next day. It was as if they'd never been apart; they'd just slipped back into easy banter. She now needed her friends around her more than ever before.

Outside, it was growing dark. All she could see from the window was a patchwork of fields stretching back to where the mountains started, and the lit-up windows of one other cottage a couple of hundred yards up the hill. In London, there was the constant rumble of traffic out on the main road; the throb of taxis; the thump of music from passing cars; the shouts of people coming out of The Grapes or The Bombay Ruby Curry House down the road. What was she doing here? Good question. She'd loved London.

Advantages of London:

- Whole Foods
- MAC lipstick
- Night buses
- Matilda and Lucie
- Harvey Nicks
- Camden Market
- Sundried tomatoes

This was to name only a few. So what *was* she doing here? It was all down to Aidan.

She looked at her phone, finally found a signal, and speed-dialled her sister.

'Kirsty?'

'Hey, babe.' Her sister's voice was shrill. In the background, she could hear jangling guitars and a quavery baritone.

'Where are you?' Heather found herself shouting above the noise.

'We're in the Bear and Barrel in Camden Town.'

Kirsty favoured "authentic" dingy and sawdusty pubs where indie bands played.

'Listen, I'll just –' Kirsty's voice became muffled for a moment. 'Shut up, Auburn.'

Her sister's friends, mostly fashion and media types, tended to have outlandish names, but that had to be the best yet.

'That's better.' Kirsty's voice came through strong and clear again. 'I'm outside.'

The background noise had now changed to the swish of traffic punctuated by the occasional siren. 'Tax-ay,' shouted a man's voice from nearby.

'Just phoning to let you know I got here safely,' Heather said, 'about an hour and a half ago.'

Really, she was phoning just to chat, to hear her sister's voice. But maybe it wasn't such a good idea as she was suddenly nearly winded by another wave of misery and homesickness. How could Aidan have cheated on her? They'd been so happy – or she thought they had, anyway.

'Heather, are you still there? How is the old place?'

'Quiet.' In one ear was the sound of London, in the other, the static surge of surf on sand.

'Is the cottage still the same as ever? Is the Ghost still on the ceiling?'

'Yup,' Heather said of the dampness. 'The Ghost is still here.'

'Wish I was with you,' said Kirsty, almost drowned out by a barrage of voices.

'So do I.' Heather was close to tears again.

'How are you, anyway?' Kirsty's voice assumed the tone of solicitous enquiry that everyone's did since The Break-Up.

'Fine,' said Heather. She hoped she soon would be, now that she'd put six hundred miles between herself and Aidan. 'Oh, God, Kirst, actually I'm not, I –' Her voice came out high pitched with pain.

'Kirsty, I've been looking for you.' Heather recognised the mockney drawl of Blakey, Kirsty's current boyfriend.

'I'm talking to… stop it –'

From the muffled noises, Heather gathered that Kirsty and Blakey were kissing.

'Babe, I'll call you back,' said Kirsty, at length, and the line went dead. Heather pulled on a long flannelette nightie in blue-grey belonging to Treeny, a garment that Lizzy Bennett herself would reject as being too unsexy – but who cared; Heather now had no use for sexiness. It was very cold – Treeny didn't run to central heating. In the bathroom, she looked at her face in the mirror. Her freckles stood out against her pallor, her eyes were bruised with exhaustion. Was she right to come here, hundreds of miles from home?

She hurried into the bedroom, the wooden floorboards chilly under her bare feet, then paused, alert, at the creak of the gate opening. Then she heard the sound of a twig cracking and saw a dark shadow on the windowpane.

There was someone outside.

For a moment she stood, frozen with terror – she was all alone and surrounded by dark fields. There was a local policeman, Philth, but who knew how long it would take him to get here? Her thoughts raced as she found herself imagining the headlines:

BODY OF YOUNG WOMAN
FOUND IN REMOTE HIGHLAND COTTAGE

Maybe she'd make it onto *News at Ten* – when she was eventually discovered. Aidan would be deeply sorry then. A cheering image of him weeping at her funeral flashed into her mind. Matilda and Lucie back in London would be sobbing, too, clinging to each other. Jessica Lomax would rock up late, wearing a black pill-box hat with a sequinned veil. Wildly, she ran into Treeny's bedroom, grabbed an Elnett hairspray and pointed it like a gun.

There was a banging on the door.

2. Smells Like White Spirit

Did murderers or burglars knock on your door? Probably not, Heather decided, letting out a long, quavering breath. Heart still thumping, she hurried across the hall and opened the latch, her hands shaking. Facing her was a tall man, his dark hair tousled, his grey eyes cold as winter seas, his face and tee-shirt bloodstained.

'Oh, my God,' she gasped, clapping her hand over her mouth, her heart now beating wildly.

'What?' asked the man, looking at her as if she were the mad one.

She should slam the door in his face, but, somehow, she was rooted to the spot, unable to move. 'Look, I'm sorry if I frightened you, but when I saw the light on I came to see what was going on. I knew Treeny was in Twilight House, so I couldn't think why anyone would be here.'

He didn't sound like a mad axe-murderer – his voice was soft and his tone reasonable, but, then again, maybe you could say that about most of them.

'It's just… your face. Your tee-shirt -'

The man glanced down at his stained chest, tugging at the tee-shirt for a better look.

'Yeah – I was working on a commission tonight. Only just got it finished. It's oil paint. Carmine.'

'Oh.' Heather glanced at her feet.

'What did you think it was?'

'Er… blood.'

'Shit. No wonder you were freaking out. Anyway, what're you doing here?'

'I live here.'

Heather faced her would-be attacker defiantly. *Take that*, she thought.

'Who even *are* you?' Her unwelcome visitor's voice was marginally more friendly.

'Heather McAndrew, Treeny's great-niece. Who the hell are *you?*'

'Sean McAllister. I live in the cottage further up the hill. Like I say, I came to check out why there was a light on -'

'And frightened me half to death.' Suddenly, she realised how undignified she must look, with uncombed hair and cream on her face, wearing a Waltons' nightie and clutching a can of hairspray as a weapon. She began to laugh.

'Sorry about that,' Sean muttered. In his answering smile, his face lit up and she realised that he was quite young - no more than thirty, she guessed. He ran his hand through his hair, ruffling it even more. His eyes, she now noticed, were a luminous, silvery grey.

'I suppose I did come here on a bit of an impulse, to be fair,' Heather admitted. 'There hasn't been time for the jungle drums to really get going.'

She'd burst into her boss's office only two days ago, still shaking from seeing Aidan and Savannah framed in the window of a nearby restaurant, engrossed in each other and holding hands across the table.

'I need to thank you, really, for looking out for Aunt Treeny's property,' she went on. Guiltily, she wondered how many Londoners would have been so neighbourly.

Sean shrugged.

'Well, my work here is done.'

'No. It's… *interesting* to meet you. Come in for a minute.'

Sean looked hesitant, but then he followed her down the hall and into the kitchen.

'I only got here this evening, so I haven't had time to get in any supplies,' she told him, as she again took out the bottle of Glenmorangie and held it up. 'This is all I've got.'

Sean gave a faint smile.

'Suppose it'll have to do.'

She poured out a generous measure each – a dram, she should learn to say now, and sat down with him at the table.

'Cheers.'

'Sláinte.'

They clinked glasses.

'So you're an artist?' she asked.

Sean nodded, his lips twitching in a you-don't-say gesture. Heather held her hands out.

'Okay, okay. You're covered in paint and I can smell turps.'

'That's my aftershave,' Sean said, completely deadpan.

'Actually, White Spirit would be a pretty good name for an aftershave,' Heather mused. 'White Spirit – the new fragrance from Davidoff,' she intoned. 'Sorry. I work in advertising, but really I'd rather be painting. That's partly why I've come here. The quality of light's so fantastic-'

After that, conversation was easy. Sean told her that he'd studied fine art and she explained how she'd studied graphic design but really wanted to be a serious artist. They talked about exhibitions they'd both seen in London and artists they admired, especially the Pre-Raphaelites.

'You know, you look like Miranda in the Waterhouse painting,' Sean said, as she was standing at the counter, refilling their glasses.

'The Tempest?' Heather squealed. 'God, I love that painting! It's my favourite. That and the Lady of Shalott – I've got a print of both of them in my bedroom at home.'

She'd studied the Miranda painting so often that she could easily visualise the girl, gazing out at a stormy sea, her dark blue dress, her long, wild hair tumbling down her back.

'Thanks for that,' she said, truly delighted. 'My flatmate reckons I look more like Sideshow Bob. You can come back.'

She rejoined him at the table, and they talked about favourite walks and the most scenic views around the village. Sean yawned suddenly.

'Look at the time. It's nearly midnight. I should go. 'Night, Heather.'

''Night, Sean. I've… I've enjoyed talking to you.'

After he'd gone, she realised that, one way and another, she hadn't thought of Aidan for a good half hour.

When she woke up the next morning, after a surprisingly good sleep, she stretched out in the, by now, wonderfully cosy bed, pointing her toes.

'Aid?' she murmured, rubbing her eyes. Then she recognised the leaf print of the curtains and the huge Victorian mahogany wardrobe and remembered that she was in the spare room in Treeny's cottage. She hated that, when she woke up, there were a few blissful seconds before the knowledge that Aidan was gone crashed into her consciousness, and she had to face up to it all over again.

She'd always shared this bedroom with Kirsty when they stayed here, and the familiarity, the old stain on the ceiling which resembled a ghost and the faded wallpaper brought a crumb of comfort. By the window was the bookshelf full of leather-bound classic novels where she'd first discovered *Wuthering Heights*, her all-time favourite book, as a teenager. She remembered sitting on this same bed, swathed in the patchwork quilt, so involved in the story that she'd stayed up half the night reading.

It was quiet outside but for the occasional bleating of sheep and the distant, unchanging sound of surf on shore. The sun shone in the window and, knowing that good weather in Kirklochy was almost as rare as a comet sighting, she pulled on jeans and a hooded fleecy, made a cup of coffee and took it out to the garden, breathing in the clear, pure air and looking at the patchwork of green and gold fields stretching back as far as the tall pines at the foot of the mountains. In London at this time, she'd be strap-hanging on the District Line, squashed between two equally fed up people and wearing uncomfortable high heels. Her heart might feel as if it had been through the office shredder, but at least there was zero chance of bumping into Aidan and Savannah here.

Back in the cottage, the *Kirklochy News* had been delivered and she sat down on Treeny's armchair, leafing through it. *Shocked onlookers watched in horror as three youths stampeded along the front at Inveralan,* the main story read. A Ewensay woman had been charged with possession of £7.50 worth of cannabis. The mobile cinema would visit Kirklochy village hall at the end of the month, as would ceilidh band the Drystane Dykes. Every article seemed to have been written by Euan. He'd always wanted to be a writer, she remembered – the reason they'd lost touch in the first place was that he'd gone off to uni in Edinburgh to study journalism. Marginally cheered up as she remembered that she'd arranged to meet her old buddy in the evening, she put the newspaper aside to take to Treeny this afternoon.

Shortly afterwards, she walked along the coast road, the wind ruffling her hair, looking at the gold curve of shell sand. Sun danced across the waves, glinting like diamonds. The village postman cycled by, calling out a greeting to everyone he passed. The beach was deserted, except for a man and a small figure in pink - from the height and the ruffled dark hair, she thought she recognised Sean. Good to meet another artist, she reflected, remembering their conversation last night, how engrossing it had been, how his luminous eyes had sparkled. She presumed the little girl must be his daughter. She felt a slight pang as she realised that Sean must have a partner also - but she squashed it down immediately.

Inhaling the fresh, salty air, she paused for a moment at the harbour, looking at the fishing boats moored there, the pile of lobster pots, the net of silvery fish. She was itching to start painting again. She'd been working as a graphic designer for Bright Sparks, a trendy, busy advertising agency in Charlotte Street, for three years. It was full of soft white leather sofas, abstract paintings, thick dove grey carpets, and bright, ambitious young people, especially Dave Sparks, her boss, with his bespoke suits, Rolex watches and six-figure salary. Dave was always on the move - visiting the gym every morning before work, swivelling in his chair, pacing up and down at meetings, as if he was so bursting with ideas that he couldn't keep still. Heather had enjoyed the buzz, the money, the partying, but sometimes she yearned to be an artist as she'd always planned.

∽

Ever since Heather could remember, the hairdressing salon had smelt strongly of perming solution, and had had, in the window, the same photo of a seventies' model, with hair flicked up à la Charlie's Angels, which was faded to blue. It had been the kind of place where you could still get a shampoo and set. Now, it had been freshly painted in the hot pink of a French bordello, with the windows adorned with black and white photos of sultry models sporting cuts "created" by the top London stylists. It also had a new name: *Sascha - Hair Artiste*.

Next door was Fratelli's, her favourite place when she was a child because of the Neapolitan ice creams, the knickerbocker glories and the huge, flashing, genuine 1950s' jukebox, giving her an enduring love of the music of Treeny's youth – rock 'n' roll and skiffle: Elvis, Buddy Holly, Chuck Berry, Johnny Ray. She passed its art deco frontage reluctantly, going instead into Maggie's Tearoom. Treeny's best friends, Mrs Gillies and Mrs Peden, aka "the girls", although they were touching eighty, sat at the window, sipping tea and nibbling homemade shortbread. The table covers were Flower of Scotland tartan and there were lace doilies aplenty and Spode china.

'Hi, ladies.'

'Pull up a chair, Heather,' said Mrs Gillies in her strong, deep voice. She'd been head teacher at Kirklochy Primary School - actually, the only teacher - for forty years.

'Misty,' called Mrs Gillies.

'Hi, Mist.' Heather jumped up like a jack-in-the-box to embrace her old friend, as, wearing a black dress and white frilly apron like something out of *Downton Abbey*, she approached their table. Heather grinned at her. Her name suited her - she was slim and ethereal with grey eyes and lots of pale hair tied back.

'Hey, Heather.' Misty's face lit up. 'Euan told me you were back.'

Heather hugged her tightly.

'Thank goodness I met your lovely cuz yesterday, or I might've been spending the night in my car in a lay-by.'

'Ooh – not nice,' said Misty, with a shudder. She squeezed Heather's arm. 'What can I get you?'

'Tea and toast, please,' Heather said. Not much chance of a tall, skinny, decaf latté and an artisan, fat free, gluten free, organic flapjack in here. Nor an £8 bowl of Shreddies.

'What's all this about spending the night in a lay-by?' Mrs Gillies demanded.

'I got lost. I couldn't get a signal on my phone, so my sat nav died on me.'

'Sat nav. What's wrong with a map? You wouldn't have lost your signal then. Sometimes the old ways are the best.'

Misty winked as she placed a tray on the table.

'Now, I thought we'd go in my car,' Mrs Gillies went on, as Heather bit into her toast. It was delicious: thick bread with masses of creamy butter.

'Er, don't you want me to drive, Chrissie?' said Heather, glancing at Mrs Gillies' pale blue 1960s' Morris Minor, which was parked outside.

'I may look decrepit to you, young lady, but I'm not dead yet, and I'm perfectly capable of driving a few miles,' sniffed Mrs Gillies. 'I've held a driving licence for fifty-seven years.'

'That's what I'm afraid of,' muttered Heather. Over Mrs Gillies' shoulder, she caught sight of Misty pulling terrified faces and tried not to laugh.

'I heard that,' snapped Mrs Gillies. 'Anyway, you don't know the way.'

This was true, Heather admitted to herself. She didn't dare mention her sat nav again. Also, she had form: the only time that she and Aidan had seriously fallen out – before he'd snogged another girl, obviously – had been when she'd got lost on the way to a Cotswolds hotel, where she'd booked a surprise romantic break. They hadn't got there until three in the morning, by which time the champagne was on water.

'I saw the hairdresser's was under new management,' she said, in a clumsy attempt to change the subject, as a teenager with a sleek pixie crop walked past. Behind her were Sean and the child she'd seen on the beach earlier. Close up, the girl looked about six or seven, with adorable bunches of curly dark hair like pompoms. She wore a pink jacket with a fur lined hood, pink mittens dangling on strings from the sleeves.

'Hair artiste,' scoffed Mrs Gillies. 'Sascha. Well, she'll always be Morag MacDougall to me.'

Still hungry, Heather ordered more tea and toast, remembering she hadn't eaten anything but half a Mars Bar since yesterday lunchtime.

'I'll pick you up at Treeny's at two,' threatened Mrs Gillies.

‿

'No one could accuse you of being a careless driver, Chrissie, that's for sure,' Heather said, as Mrs Gillies' Morris crawled along, being overtaken by a cyclist, two hill walkers and a black Labrador.

Round the next corner the road was blocked by a flock of sheep.

'Barley sugar, dear?' said Mrs Peden. She didn't talk much, which was probably due to not being able to get a word in edgeways between Treeny and Mrs Gillies.

'Thanks, Grace.' Heather popped the sweetie into her mouth.

When at last the blockade was cleared, they puttered off again, nearly touching ten miles an hour.

Eventually, they reached their destination. The door to Twilight Care Home was opened by a cheery looking black girl with short dreads, whose name, according to a badge fixed to her shirt, was Beaulah.

'Catriona McAndrew,' boomed Mrs Gillies.

'I'll just get you to sign in.'

'Don't be ridiculous, girl, you know perfectly well who we are. We were here the day before yesterday. Now, where is she?'

'She's in the conservatory.' Beaulah led the way down a corridor thickly carpeted in dove grey, to the strains of a Daniel O'Donnell CD. The main sitting room was carpeted in the same colour and furnished with chairs in pink. The curtains and cushions were a mixture of both colours. Several people were sitting in a half circle round a large TV screen, the volume turned up to deafening, watching *On the Buses.*

Treeny, eschewing the pastel cardigan, tweed skirt and slippers ensemble seemingly favoured by most of the other female residents, was sitting by the window, playing patience. Heather gazed at the view: the home overlooked a loch which, today, was smooth and calm, reflecting back trees and mountains as clearly as a mirror.

'Chrissie, Grace, Heather!' Treeny stood up with some difficulty, leaning heavily on her stick, a tall figure in a peacock blue trouser suit. Her poor old hip must still be causing her pain – not that she'd admit it. 'Take a seat, girls,' she invited, waving at a group of easy chairs. As soon as they were settled, Beaulah reappeared with cups of tea and cheese scones.

'Nerves shattered after your lift from David Coulthard over there?' Treeny asked, throwing a fond smile at her friend.

Heather giggled, munching her scone, which was buttery and light as a feather. And unbelievably calorific, added a voice – Matilda's – in her head.

'So, have you met some nice people?' she asked. She must try to put her own cares out of her mind; Treeny was the priority now.

'Very nice,' said Treeny. How sad was it that the older people here, moving slowly or leaning on zimmers or failing to recognise even their own families, must once have been vibrant youngsters, passionate about their children, their partners, their jobs.

'What about him?' whispered Heather, gesturing to a very good-looking man with a touch of Anthony Hopkins about him.

'Crashing bore!' barked Mrs Gillies, in a voice that could have been heard in Norway.

'It is lovely here, but it's just not my home,' said Treeny.

'Look, Treeny,' said Mrs Peden, in an attempt at distraction, indicating a poster on the wall. 'There's a beetle drive on tomorrow night.'

'That's for old people,' said Treeny. She lowered her voice. 'I'm trying to set up a few hands of poker for the weekend,' she muttered, looking sharply around in case any of the care assistants might be listening.

For a while, they drank more tea and Mrs Gillies and Mrs Peden brought Treeny up to date with village news, beginning with the latest gossip about Valissa Lavender, queen of the village Am Dram Society, whom Heather very much wanted to meet.

'She wants to stage *Brigadoon* later in the year. She's auditioning next week,' explained Mrs Peden. 'And she's starting Tai Chi classes in the village hall, whatever they may be.'

Treeny brightened at the news from home: the inexperienced climbers who'd had to be winched to safety by helicopter from the peak of Ben Lochy, the theft of two boxes of French fancies from the village shop and the scandalous goings-on at the B&B.

'Misty says this chap was drinking alone in the bar,' said Mrs Gillies, leaning forward. 'Hugh Grant type – English, posh, floppy hair, and after he'd had a few whiskies he went upstairs, and started banging on the door of the blue room, fit to wake the dead.' She paused, making sure her audience was paying rapt attention, then lowered her voice. 'He shouted, "Jeremy, I know you're in there. If you don't open the door, I'll break it down".'

She, Treeny and Mrs Peden exchanged knowing looks.

'And did he?' prompted Heather.

'Yes,' said Mrs Gillies. 'But he'd got the wrong room. He broke his elbow, and Misty's father made him pay for the door.'

'Well,' said Mrs Peden, with relish, folding her arms across her chest.

The final item of news was a punch up in the Claymore over a sheep dog trial.

'Dougal Galbraith accused Moray McManus of cheating,' explained Mrs Gillies. She turned to Heather. 'There's been a feud in the village between the Galbraiths and the McManuses for three generations.'

'And Rowan Galloway's back from university,' added Mrs Peden.

'There'll be trouble, mark my words,' said Mrs Gillies, spreading more butter on her scone.

'I've met your neighbour, Treeny. And I've seen him around with his daughter – I think it's his daughter, anyway. Bunches, pink jacket,' put in Heather.

'Yes, that's Sean and Katie. Poor wee soul,' said Treeny.

'Why –?' Heather began.

She was interrupted by a care assistant who'd paused by Treeny's chair.

'Time for your meds, Catriona.'

Heather's mind raced as she watched Treeny swallow her pills. Her aunt had had to move into the home because of mobility problems, but now Heather was here she could come back to Thistle Cottage to recuperate. Heather would learn how to look after her and supervise her medication...she began to plan Treeny's liberation.

'Nurse, nurse.' A sour faced old lady was shouting in a querulous voice. One of the care assistants hastened towards her.

'Hope I don't go on like that when I get old,' Mrs Peden said.

Heather again managed a smile at her uncharacteristic flash of humour.

∽

Back at the cottage, Heather cooked some pasta and put on Treeny's ancient "wireless", as she still called it, unaware that nowadays the word had a completely new interpretation.

She bobbed her head in time to the catchy tune.

'That was Amy MacDonald with *This is the Life* and this is the Drivetime show with Euan Buchanan, at Kirklochy FM –' came a familiar voice over the airwaves.

Heather turned the sound up.

'A big shout out for Morven and Mhairi on their twenty-first birthday, from all the family. See you at the party on Saturday –' continued Euan. 'And, Hamish Lockhart: a message from your mum – come home, you've gone out with the keys to the Land Rover in your pocket...And, Gus the Taxi, could you pick up Miss Munro outside the post office, going to the MacLeans'?'

'No way,' giggled Heather, clapping her hand over her mouth.

'And now, to take us up to the news, weather and traffic round-up at six o'clock, it's the High Flying Birds,' said Euan.

After listening to the rest of Euan's show, and giggling at the traffic news – a family of otters had blocked the road leading to Hermit's Point – Heather switched on the television. The hills were so high around Kirklochy that reception was poor, but, after several minutes of moving the aerial around, and finally putting it on top of an up-turned bucket, a Scrabble dictionary and a tin of shortbread, she managed to get a watchable picture. Earlier, she'd been buoyed up by seeing Treeny, but then her spirits had again plummeted as she began to think about Aidan. She'd been in the village store, buying her pasta. It was the most over-stocked shop she'd ever seen, piled to the roof and with narrow aisles. There was a small, but broad, selection of DVDs, intended to appeal to as many people as possible: a few Ealing comedies and some war films for the older people, some romcoms for the girls, the Godfather trilogy for the guys, a smattering of Disney films for the kids, plus *The Shining, Lord of the Rings, Trainspotting* and *Play it Again, Sam*. Aidan's and her favourite film.

Grimly, she threw some chocolate into her basket, catching sight of the magazines laid out on the counter. From the cover of *Hello!* smiled the gorgeous Chloé Marsden, whom Bright Sparks had recently used in a big campaign, equally as lovely in low-rise jeans and a sequinned vest as she had been the white dress she'd worn in the advert, with that must-have accessory, a premier division footballer. *Chloé Marsden and Ryan Wright tell of their romance and fairytale wedding plans,* she read. Ridiculous, she thought.

It was Monday night, and, on a Monday, she, Lucie and Matilda would go to the Bombay Ruby down her road for a curry, each always ordering the same food, and then onto The Grapes for a drink. She felt a stab of homesickness and wrapped the travelling rug, which smelled faintly of Treeny's perfume, more tightly round her for comfort. She was so glad Euan had suggested meeting. She thought about the kindness in his dark eyes and how he'd always managed to cheer her up.

Just starting on the TV was a Scottish soap in which a bunch of people yelled at each other in Gaelic against a background of sheep dotted fields, so she went to the sideboard and got out Treeny's photo albums. She'd looked through those scores of times before, but she opened them out again, leafing through the pages from sepia through black and white to coloured shots of herself, Jamie and Kirsty as children. There was her favourite picture of Treeny when she was young, standing against a backdrop of hills in a fifties' print dress with a flouncy skirt, smiling mysteriously, her long, dark curls lifting in the breeze. The photos evoked memories of carefree, happy times. Much as it pained her to admit it, Mrs Gillies had a point when she said that the old ways were sometimes the best – nowadays pictures were all on Facebook or Instagram and it just wasn't the same.

She replaced the photos, then it was time to go to meet Euan, so she slipped on a jacket and went out. The sky, peach and pink striped, was reflected on the water. One advantage of Kirklochy was that everywhere was within easy walking distance. On the way to the pub, she passed a girl on horseback, who threw down a haughty, unsmiling glance then clattered past, a sweep of shining auburn hair floating out behind her. Rowan Galloway, she guessed, the "spoiled little madam from the big house", as Mrs Gillies had described her.

She pushed open the door of the Claymore, which, probably in an attempt to seduce the many American tourists who visited Kirklochy, was carpeted in garish tartan, and had a roaring open fire at both ends. There were a couple of rooms for rent upstairs, but those were unbelievably "authentic" i.e. falling to pieces, the only air conditioning a broken windowpane. From the walls of dark wood, stags' heads with huge antlers and glassy eyes stared down. In one corner, a bunch of fishermen in rough sweaters were discussing the weather and their catches. In another two girls sipped red wine, engrossed in quiet conversation. Euan was sitting near the fire.

'Heather,' he called, gesturing to the seat opposite him. She pulled it out and sat down.

'Hi.' She smiled at him as the fire crackled.

'What can I get you to drink?'

'Er, what are you drinking?'

'Old Sheepshagger.'

'I'll have that, then. Thanks.'

'Slàinte mhath,' Euan said, when he'd returned with the drinks. They clinked glasses.

'Cheers, Euan,' said Heather. She sipped the beer, which was dark, rich and peaty – a far cry from the Japanese designer lagers favoured by the men who drank in The Grapes.

'So, how long are you here?' Euan asked.

'Until New Year. I'll be working remotely, just going to London now and again for meetings. The wonders of technology: it can all be done by Skype, email and conference calls. When I get broadband installed in the cottage, that is.'

'Good, good,' said Euan. He grinned suddenly. 'When did we all get so grown up? I remember when all we had to worry about was which box set to watch and whether we'd manage to get tickets for T in the Park.'

'So, you write and edit the *Kirklochy News*, take all the photographs, manage the website and present the Drivetime Show on the radio?' Heather asked, keen to be distracted from her own problems.

'And the lunchtime show,' said Euan. 'And take part in the mountain rescue team.'

'Wow. I must say, the *Kirklochy News* is a very impressive document.'

Heather had enjoyed reading the newspaper, which covered not just local and farming news and weather and the shipping forecast but also the shinty league, local gigs, gardening advice, film and book reviews, music, women's interest (written by a contributor called Sarah Michelle Cox), and horoscopes (almost certainly fictional).

'*Keep it Reel* are on at the Inveralan Arts Centre next weekend. I'm covering it. You should come,' said Euan.

'I'll hold you to that.'

'Great – it's a date.'

'So, you're quite settled here?' Heather asked. Euan looked so untroubled, tanned and healthy.

'I still love it. My ambition's to move to Glasgow and write for the *Herald* when I get my big break. Which might be quite soon,' he said, leaning towards her and lowering his voice. 'I've got this mate who's an estate agent in Inveralan. He's heard a whisper that Skye Friel is thinking of buying a place up here.'

Skye Friel, a Scots model, was, Heather knew, famously looking for a country retreat. The tabloids often compared her with Kate Moss.

'Think who I could interview then. Maybe even the First Minister.'

They again clinked glasses, but Heather couldn't help feeling a slight pang; she hoped he wasn't going to move away just when she'd found him again. Later, they walked along the coast road, talking softly, the now dark water lapping below.

'See you around,' they said in unison as they parted, then they both laughed.

3. *Big Country*

'I've lost Gordon,' said the elderly woman. She looked panic stricken. 'How can I look after him if I've lost him?'

'Gordon's fine, darling,' said Beaulah. 'He was here yesterday, remember?'

'But he's my baby. I need to look after him.'

'He's forty-six, Maisie,' said Beaulah gently. 'I know, why don't we have a nice cup of tea and treat ourselves to a scone?'

Heather watched, deeply moved and upset, as the care assistant slipped her arm round Maisie's stooped frame and helped her to a sofa by the window.

In Treeny's room, Mrs Gillies was carefully wrapping and packing the ornaments and family photos Treeny had brought with her to make the place more homely. Treeny herself was supervising the folding of her clothes, many of them perfectly preserved from the 1950s, her favourite fashion era. She'd told Heather about her aunt who worked as a fashion buyer in a department store in Edinburgh, and, twice a year, she would make the trip south, returning with the pick of the season's styles. According to Mrs Peden, she'd been the Anna Wintour of her day, standing out in Kirklochy, where cable-knit sweaters, jeans and wellie boots were perennially on-trend, like Times Square at night. Heather sunk down on the bed, guiltily relieved that her great-aunt's mind had so far been spared the ravages of dementia.

'Don't just sit around, girl,' said Mrs Gillies. 'Get packing those books.'

Heather began piling Treeny's P.D. James, Caro Ramsay and Ruth Rendell books, which she read over and over, into a box.

'I'll miss some of the people,' mused Treeny, 'but it'll be so good to get home.'

'No wonder you want to go home, Aunt Catriona. You're a geriatric delinquent. The unit manager's out to get you,' Heather teased.

'Greta McEwan turned me in,' sniffed Treeny. 'Wee Free,' she added, lowering her voice.

'You were running a poker school from your bedroom, Treeny.' Heather wanted to giggle. 'That's gambling.'

'We were only betting with pennies,' protested Treeny.

They finished packing and carried Treeny's cases out into the hall, where several care assistants and residents stood, ready to bid her goodbye.

'It won't be the same without you,' said Beaulah.

'Never a dull moment with Miss McAndrew,' added a male nurse.

Heather loaded up the boot of the Morris with Treeny's possessions.

'Don't drive too fast, Chris,' joked Treeny, as Heather helped her into the front seat. 'I don't think my nerves can take it.'

One advantage of Mrs Gillies' excessively careful driving was that it gave plenty of opportunity to admire the scenery. Heather sat in the back seat, sucking barley sugars and listening to the excited chat of the two older women as they headed back towards Kirklochy. She felt a little better for knowing that she wouldn't be alone in the cottage anymore; Treeny would be helping her as much as she was helping Treeny.

'I'm looking forward to having a flatmate,' Treeny said, as if reading her thoughts. 'We'll have plenty of girlie chats.'

༄

The good weather in the village had surprisingly lasted. Heather walked along the main street, feeling the sun on her face and breathing in the fresh, tangy sea air.

'Hi, Heather,' said Duncan, the postman, as he cycled past. Misty waved at her from behind the heavy lace curtains of Maggie's Tearoom. Mrs Peden called out a greeting as she emerged from the chemist's. Down on the beach, a group of women were doing Tai Chi. Walking by the village hall, she could hear someone singing

"Jeannie's Packing Up" none too tunefully – the auditions for Brigadoon must have started.

As she passed the wooden hut which housed the Kirklochy News and Kirklochy FM, she saw Euan standing outside, obviously enjoying the sun.

'Come in for a coffee?' he called.

As she'd left Treeny back at the cottage safely ensconced on the sofa with the *Herald* crossword and a pot of Earl Grey, Heather nodded.

'So this is where it all happens,' she said, as they went inside. 'Wowzer. It's really hi-tech. I feel as if I've suddenly stepped onto the Starship Enterprise.'

Euan looked at her, the corners of his mouth turned down.

'Us teuchters have actually managed to drag ourselves into the twenty-first century, you know,' he said, in pretend annoyance.

'I know, I know. Some of you've even got telly-boxes.'

Broadcasting equipment stood at one end of the room, and a laptop, printer and scanner at the other. She glanced at the computer. Euan was obviously working on the next edition of the paper. **Poacher Poached**, screamed the headline. In the corner was a tray bearing a kettle, two Simpsons mugs and a packet of chocolate Hobnobs. As Euan went to fill the kettle, she grabbed the mouse and began to click down the page. *Women First* caught her eye, as Sarah Michelle Cox had, this week, turned her attention to shampoo for naturally wavy hair. On a bad hair day, Heather looked as if she had a dozen brillo pads stapled to her head, so she began to read with interest.

'Thanks. Does Sarah Michelle live around here?' she asked, as she accepted a mug of Gold Blend. 'I don't think I know her.'

'Er...yes.' Euan looked shifty. 'Listen – and this really mustn't go beyond those four walls - I'm Sarah Michelle Cox.'

'No way,' squealed Heather. 'No wonder you've got such great hair.'

'And Madame Zola,' added Euan.

'You're joking me. You're Madame Zola as well? But what about the horoscopes?'

'Computer generated,' admitted Euan. 'Except, occasionally, I make up a really bad one for Scorpio.'

'Why?' asked Heather, with a grin. She reached for the chocolate Hobnobs, untwisted the wrapping and sank into a chair, biting into the biscuit with enjoyment. She liked hanging out with Euan – it was just like being back in the flat with Ben. She felt brighter than she had since splitting up with Aidan.

'To upset my ex. She really believes in all that stuff.'

'Who is?' Heather sipped her coffee, the sun slanting in the window.

'Rowan Galloway.'

'I think I've seen her around,' said Heather, slightly awkward, now, as she remembered the beautiful, arrogant girl with the flowing copper hair. She'd never met Rowan in all those summers spent in the village as she was the Laird's daughter, and, when she wasn't away at boarding school, lived in a castle surrounded by acres of land. She didn't hang out on Jamie's Cove with the others.

'She's been away at university in Cambridge, but she's back now.'

Euan looked slightly hectic, perturbed, as if he still felt deeply for his ex-girlfriend, as if he were fighting his attraction to her. Perhaps she was his first true love; Heather didn't remember him being particularly serious about any of the other girls he'd dated. Just like her and Aidan. With a spark of pain, she remembered the first time she'd set eyes on him.

↩

She'd been sitting in the office canteen one day with Lucie and Matilda, eating a salad, as both of her friends were perpetually on a diet, when Lucie, who was facing the door, had almost choked on a piece of cucumber.

'What?' Heather had said.

'Don't look round,' Lucie'd whispered, so Heather and Matilda had looked round.

'I said, *don't look round.*'

Heather had caught her breath. Walking between the tables was Dave Sparks, with the most beautiful man she'd ever seen. He was tall, with thick, black hair, piercing blue eyes and a peculiarly sensual way of walking.

'That's Aidan Murphy,' Lucie'd continued, still in a low voice. 'I read all about him in *Campaign*. It said he was a total whizz-kid and Dave's head-hunted him from Saatchi and Saatchi to take over some of the major accounts.'

Heather had also read the piece in the advertising trade magazine and recognised Aidan from his photo, but he was far better looking in the flesh. Actually, all the girls in the canteen seemed to have seen the article and were far better looking than usual as well – with their best clothes on, their nails and make up works of art, their hair shiny and perfumed, in anticipation of him starting. A few had even had a fake bake. It was like being on the set of *Sex and the City*.

'Mike made this big speech about how he's delighted to welcome him to the company,' Matilda, who was Mike Bright's secretary, had said. She giggled as she imitated Mike's plummy, public school tones. 'Not half as delighted as I am, though.'

Heather was as susceptible to Aidan as all the other girls, but she was determined not to fall for him – for a start, he probably really loved himself, and also - look at the competition! Matilda, for example, with her toned body, honey coloured limbs, violet silk dress and dead straight, waist length blonde hair. Being best friends with Tills was very bad for the ego. Then there was Jessica Lomax, the firm's very own J-Lo, and Matilda's great rival. Not the girl to stand next to at a party.

'Anyone want a coffee?' Matilda had asked, rising with self-conscious grace.

'Go on,' Heather had agreed, watching her sashaying up to the counter, giving everyone the benefit of her long golden legs, high heels and short skirt. She noticed several men swivel round in their seats, their eyes following her.

However, although he'd done wonders for the morale within the office – suddenly all the girls were very keen to come to work every morning, and reluctant to leave in the evening – none of them seemed to make any progress with him.

'Maybe he doesn't like to date colleagues,' Lucie had consoled herself, as the three girls sat in The Grapes, sipping red wine and nibbling olives.

'He probably already has a girlfriend,' Heather added.

'Perhaps he's gay,' sniffed Matilda, inspecting her long turquoise nails. But then, she always said that if a man were impervious to her charms.

'Yeah, right.' Heather giggled. 'Exactly what evidence do you have for making that assumption?'

'Well, he really knows how to dress,' Matilda said. 'He's got too much taste to be straight. He always smells delish. He even wears cufflinks. And he's so fresh and clean, as if he'd just stepped out of the shower.'

'That doesn't prove anything,' said Lucie. Heather switched off, lost in imaginings of Aidan emerging from the shower, smelling delish, clad only in a skimpy towel, hair damp, droplets of water clinging to his bare chest.

∽

'Anyway, the word is that Skye Friel's thinking of putting in an offer for Dundrennan Castle,' Euan said, his voice jerking her back to the present. It was evident that he was anxious to move the conversation on from Rowan.

'She's stunning,' Heather sighed. 'Meant to be very clever as well. And she's so cool. There's just such an aura of mystery about her.'

'That's because she hardly ever gives interviews,' Euan said. 'Think what it would mean for my career if I managed to talk to her. It'd be the break I've been waiting for.' His eyes sparkled. 'I just know there's a story there, waiting to be uncovered.'

'It's so exciting,' Heather said, caught up in his enthusiasm.

'Are you still up for the ceilidh next weekend?' asked Euan, as Heather reluctantly got up to leave.

'For sure,' she said. 'I want to get to know some more of the villagers.' She paused. 'Euan, I'm a little bit nervous about the country dancing…reels and the Dashing White Sergeant and Gay Gordons and all that. I don't know any of the steps.'

Euan shrugged.

'It'll be a breeze. You'll pick it up as you go along. I promise we'll have a laugh.'

Heather walked back to the cottage, the sun still shining, much cheered up by the banter.

⤸

'Two pink pills, the big blue one, the jelly bean and the chewy one,' said Heather.

'Check, check, check and check,' said Treeny. Heather watched carefully as her aunt swallowed the pills, and then sluiced them down with water. Treeny was in tearing spirits, overjoyed to be back at Thistle Cottage and among her friends. Last night they'd had a hilarious time as Mrs Gillies, Mrs Peden and Mrs Peden's sixteen year old grandson Craig had attempted to teach Heather the rudiments of the St Bernard's Waltz, Strip the Willow, the Canadian Barn Dance and the Gay Gordons. They'd pushed back all the furniture and Treeny had put a crackly old Jimmy Shand recording on the record player.

'I don't think Bruno Tonioli'll be calling anytime soon,' said Treeny, as they collapsed, flushed and giggling, on the sofa, and Heather poured them each a dram – for medicinal purposes only, as Treeny always claimed. Craig had mooched off to drink cider in the bus shelter, or whatever young people in Kirklochy did those days. Heather found herself humming as she washed and dried the glasses and put the kettle on.

⤸

Treeny leaned heavily on her walking stick while Heather held her free arm, as they made their way down the main street. When she and Aidan had gone on holiday to Dublin, they'd been told that they could visit all the main attractions within half a day. In Kirklochy it was more like half an hour.

As they entered Fratelli's, Rocco, the youngest Fratelli brother, hurried towards them, kissing Treeny on both cheeks, in continental fashion.

'Treeny! Great to see you back. I'll give you my best table.'

'Lovely to be back.'

Rocco's gentle Highland accent was totally at odds with his smouldering looks and eyes as sweet and dark as treacle. He led them to the table at the central window, which commanded a view of the sparkling water. Heather breathed in the delicious aroma of coffee beans, pastries and cinnamon. Someone was feeding coins into the jukebox and a moment later the music of Del Shannon filled the room.

'So – how are you both? How's the family?' Rocco was back, with two frothing cups of cappuccino. He pulled up a chair for a few minutes.

'Great,' said Heather. 'Jamie's qualified as a vet now; he's been working at a small animal practice for a couple of years. He always says it was coming here and hanging about on the farm that made him want to work with animals in the first place.'

'Wow,' said Rocco. 'Respect.' For a moment, he looked wistful. 'When did we all get so serious? I remember Jamie was a wee dare devil, always wanting to go surfing and rock climbing and jumping out of hay lofts.'

'Yeah.' Heather giggled. 'Adrenaline junkie. He's broken quite a few bones over the years.'

'What about Kirsty?' asked Rocco. 'She was right into her clothes, wasn't she?'

Heather laughed.

'Yeah. Some of the outfits she wore were a bit –'

'Mad?' supplied Rocco.

'Original,' Heather said diplomatically. 'She's got big plans as well. She's got a stall at Camden Market selling her own designs, but she wants to open a boutique some day.'

'And you… all you wanted to do was paint and take photos.'

'Still do,' Heather said. 'What about your lot?'

'All still working in the family business, except Paolo. He's just opened a pizzeria in Inveralan.'

'Tempted by the bright lights, eh?' Heather teased.

Rocco nodded with a grin.

'Oh, well, better get back to the grind,' he said, as the door opened and a family of tourists came in, including two squabbling kids. He rose and made for the counter.

Nice arse, Heather caught herself thinking, just as Treeny said, 'A girl can't help but notice his derriere.'

'Shush,' Heather giggled.

⤙

Later, before going to the hairdresser's, they browsed for a while in the chemist's. Heather noted that they didn't stock MAC make up, Urban Decay products or Chanel perfume, but they did do a good line in homemade jam, marmalade and lemon curd. She paused at a stand by the door to look at some hand painted greetings cards – delicate studies of flowers, dogs and local views painted in vibrant watercolour. She lifted one of snowdrops against a blue sky, inspected it and turned it over.

Sean McAllister, Shell Cottage, Kirklochy [she read].

She put it back thoughtfully.

'I'll just pay for those.' Treeny rejoined her, holding a new powder compact and a tube of the pale pink lipstick she'd worn ever since Heather could remember.

⤙

'This place has totally changed,' Heather said, as she pushed open the door of the hairdresser's and stepped into a stylish black, white and silver room, with a chequered black and white floor and mirrors in geometric shapes. The only colour, oriental style, came from a vase of crimson poppies in the window. On a silver table stood an espresso machine and a fan of magazines. She breathed in the fragrance of coffee, shampoo and hairspray.

'Morning, ladies,' said Gregor, sashaying towards them.

'Ladies? Haven't been called that before. You'll definitely be getting a tip, young man,' said Treeny.

'I don't know if I like this place now,' Heather said. 'I think I preferred the nicotine stained walls and the blue photos.'

She groped for the armholes in her robe then selected the latest edition of *OK!* On the front was a ravishing photo of Chloé Marsden in enormous sunglasses and a floaty, floral maxi-dress. *'Split Latest: Chloé in Crisis,'* ran the typescript: "I feel utterly betrayed. I thought

Ryan was the One."

Heather settled in her chair, flicking through the magazine and looking forward to some pampering. If she looked good on the outside, she might start to feel good on the inside. At the next mirror sat a young girl with her hair spiky with foil, who was immersed in a misery lit. book called *Sticks and Stones: a True Story of Stolen Childhood.*

'Gregor,' shouted Sascha, who had begun to unwrap the foils. 'Mix Heather's colour, would you?'

Heather sighed. There were absolutely no secrets in this village.

'Sure,' called Gregor. Snake-hipped with peroxide spikes, thumb rings and wristbands, he was as camp as a sparkly pink feather boa.

While he went through the complicated and scientific process of "enhancing" Heather's bright red hair with streaks of copper and gold, her old friend chattered non-stop, full of gossip and speculation about Skye Friel: an ice-blue Aston Martin had been seen gliding down Kirklochy main street, it was rumoured, and several of his clients reported having seen a very tall, very thin, amazingly beautiful woman with long tawny hair and cheekbones to die for walking along the beach.

Just then Heather caught sight of Sean and Katie passing the window, on what must be their daily walk. Today, Katie looked like a pretty, chubby Little Red Riding Hood in her scarlet coat.

'Greg,' Heather said, managing to interrupt. 'Do you know Sean and Katie McAllister?'

Gregor paused in the act of brushing on the gold colourant and put his hand on his heart.

'So *tragic*,' he declared.

'What happened?'

Gregor hesitated for a moment, part of him, perhaps, relishing the chance to tell a dramatic story.

'Meg – that was Sean's wife – took Katie to Ewensay for the day. There's a really difficult bend on the Ewensay-Inveralan Road. On the way back, she swerved to avoid a cyclist and lost control of her car, crashing into a tree. She was killed and Katie was injured. The cyclist raised the alarm and they managed to get Katie to the hospital at Strathduncan in time. Later, she was flown up to Yorkhill – you know – the children's hospital in Glasgow. She was in there for months. You might have noticed that she walks with a limp.'

Heather shook her head. In fact she hadn't noticed this; she'd been so enchanted by the little girl's dimpled cheeks and big brown eyes.

'How old was she? Meg, I mean.'

'Twenty-seven. Katie was four.'

She'd been so young, thought Heather. Tears were never far away, and she felt her eyes welling up at the thought of this woman she'd never known, who had been only a few years older than herself. And Katie – the poor baby, losing her mum. And Sean...the tears spilled over.

'Sweet-pea, I didn't mean to upset you.'

Gregor's voice seemed to come from far away.

'You didn't,' said Heather. 'I asked you.'

Taking a paper hankie out of her pocket, she wiped her eyes.

'I met Sean the night I got here,' she told Gregor. 'He saw a light on in the cottage, thought I was a burglar and came down to investigate. I heard a twig cracking outside, then saw a shadow at the window, freaked out and thought he'd come to murder me in my bed.'

Gregor laughed, seeming relieved to move the conversation on from Sean's terrible loss.

'Did your life flash before you?'

Heather nodded.

'And I could just see the headlines.'

'Flame haired stunna butchered in death riddle,' said Gregor. 'That was *The Sun*,' he explained. 'Have you ever planned all the details of a totally fabulous funeral?'

'Can't say I have, Greg, and you're meant to be cheering me up.'

She'd certainly planned all the details of a totally fabulous wedding – but it didn't look as if that was going to happen any time soon.

'I have,' said Gregor. 'The floral arrangements, the music, the costumes, the grieving friends, the sobbing exes – or, at least, they'd better be.'

But she couldn't put Sean's tragedy out of her mind for long, and sat quietly as her hair was washed, cut and blown dry, the celebrity magazine lying forgotten on the counter in front of her. Treeny, her snow-white waves cut into a stylish bob which swung at chin length, had decided to hang out and was sipping espresso and catching up with the news of everyone who came in.

'How's that for you?' asked Sascha, holding the mirror behind and to the sides of her head, showing her her cut from all angles.

'Wow. Hats off to you. You really know how to cut curly hair,' Heather said. She estimated that, for the prices her London hairdresser, Michel of Bond Street, charged, Sascha would probably throw in a boob job and full face lift as well. Plus, it was *de rigueur* for Michel to throw a tantrum and sack at least one stylist each time she visited, which didn't make for a relaxing experience.

'Gorgeous,' said Treeny. 'I always said you should make the most of your curls.'

'Thanks, you look pretty good yourself,' said Heather. She took Treeny's arm as they made their way slowly back to the cottage.

4. *The Past is Another Country*

Much later, Heather stood at the mirror in her bedroom, still delighted with her new hair-do, which hung in smooth curls around her shoulders and down her back. Apart from some lipgloss and mascara and a little shadow around her eyes, which were a pale peridot green, she didn't bother with make-up – her face was clear, glowing and sprinkled with freckles due to the sun and the sea air in Kirklochy.

Now – clothes. She had no idea what was suitable for a ceilidh. Finally, she put on a white ruffled shirt Matilda had given her for her birthday, and a short, full tartan skirt which had been all the rage at Camden Lock that spring.

In the living room, Treeny, Mrs Gillies, Mrs Peden and the postmistress were sitting round the table, starting a game of bridge. Heather watched as Treeny expertly cut the pack, shuffled and began to deal. Scottish country-dance music blared out of the radio.

'...and that was Accordion to Angus with *Lament for Big Hamish*, written on the death of a favourite horse,' said the presenter, in the now familiar sing-song Highland accent.

'How do I look?' asked Heather.

'Ridiculous,' said Mrs Gillies.

'Sorry, darling, but if it wasn't for my hip, I'd break into a Highland fling,' Treeny added.

'You look like you're auditioning for a Fran and Anna tribute act,' scoffed Mrs Gillies.

'I've no idea what you mean, Chrissie,' sniffed Heather.

'Just wear something you feel comfortable in,' advised Treeny.

A few minutes later, Heather returned in her old, faded jeans and a leaf green tee-shirt which set off her hair and eyes.

'Much better,' said Mrs Gillies. 'Now, I hear you've been seeing a lot of Ruairi Buchanan's lad.'

'Chrissie, I have not been seeing...honestly, this place! Euan's a great guy and I like him, but we're just friends. I'd rather be chained up, naked, outside Finsbury Town Hall than try to get romantically involved with a man.'

Even so, she felt a spark of happiness deep inside as she thought about how much she'd enjoyed Euan's company the other morning.

'So you say,' said Mrs Gillies, pursing her lips.

〜

She was probably marginally more nervous about this night out than she had been as she prepared for the one where she and Aidan had finally got together. The agency had just won another prestigious pitch for the launch of a new white chocolate bar, a competitor for *Milky Bar*. The advert was expected to make a star of Chloé Marsden, who was featured, writhing on the bonnet of a white Rolls Royce, sensuously eating the chocolate. As from the next day, she'd be lying languorously across billboards up and down the country, desired by men from Aberystwyth to Aberdeen. Dave Sparks, the original party animal, aided by the flashest party planners in town, was to throw a huge bash in celebration.

The venue was a barge moored on the Thames. As Heather climbed out of her taxi, she gasped at the sight of all the fairy lights strung across the deck, and reflected in trembling kaleidoscopes of colour on the dark water below. She walked across the gangway onto the boat and there they all were – the Bright Sparks staff. Chloé Marsden, in all her seventeen-year-old loveliness, was the guest of honour. She had long, platinum blonde hair, and wore white frosted lipstick, nail polish and eyelashes and a white maxi-dress of diaphanous layers. On her dainty feet were slippers covered in iridescent white sequins. Standing nearby, sipping a White Lady, was Matilda, in a white dress approximately the size of two dusters. Scary Alex Day, one of the account executives, marched past in one of her trademark tailored trouser suits in ivory, not even deigning to acknowledge the two girls.

'Heather,' Matilda was saying, hurrying towards her, as fast as anyone could, while wearing white five-inch stilettos and a skin tight skirt.

'It wouldn't hurt her to crack a smile,' Heather said, glaring at Alex's departing back.

'It probably would, actually,' said Matilda. She lowered her voice. 'Botox,' she explained, as a ghostly apparition drifted by, again in a white dress. Heather clamped a hand over her mouth. She'd completely forgotten that everyone was supposed to be wearing white this evening – that was the theme of the party, in honour of the chocolate. With everyone else dressed accordingly, including Dave Sparks, who looked like John Travolta forty years out of date in a white suit, and the tables covered in sparkling white damask, white tea lights and bowls of fresh white lilies, the venue looked like some Hollywood director's vision of Heaven. In her simple cornflower blue dress, which was usually so understated, Heather felt everyone was looking at her. Also, it had been raining earlier and her hair had managed to break out of its sleek curtain into its natural wild curls.

'I need to go home and change,' she bleated. 'Although, Ben says my white dress makes me look like a dental nurse. My flatmate really knows how to boost a girl's ego,' she added gloomily.

'Don't worry about it,' Matilda said. 'No one will notice. Or, at least, after a few drinks they won't care. White wine or White Lady?'

'Er, white wine, thanks,' Heather said, raising her voice over the music, *A Whiter Shade of Pale*. 'Who on earth dreamed up this white theme?' she wondered aloud. 'I think they've gone a bit over the top.'

'It was me, actually.'

Heather held her head.

'Sorry, Tills. It just isn't my evening.'

Sipping her wine, she decided to stay just a little longer, be seen to have done her duty – not hard, since she stood out like a Christmas tree in mid-July, then slip away. Film 4 was showing a Woody Allen tonight. She'd set it to record, but she'd prefer to watch it live and she longed to be curled up on her sofa in front of the TV, eating Chunky Monkey ice-cream. Ben was on night shift at the hospital, so she'd have the place to herself: she'd put on her old comfy PJs, bed socks and hand knitted cardigan and scoop the ice cream –

cunningly hidden from her flatmate under an ancient bag of frozen broccoli – straight out of the tub. Surreptitiously, she glanced at her watch. She'd stay just an hour.

The music was deafening, and people were yelling at each other, trying to be heard above it; any minute, they'd have to resort to texting each other. The soundtrack had now changed to the Beatles' *White Album*. Everyone looked incredibly glamorous. Heather escaped out onto the deck, enjoying the cool air, and looking out at the Embankment, the lights like sequins on black silk moiré, the music now muffled.

Some minutes went by before she realised she wasn't alone. Aidan was standing a few feet away, staring broodingly ahead. For a moment she was paralysed with indecision. He likely didn't want her to speak to him. She bet he'd come out on deck to avoid the attentions of Matilda and co. He'd probably suspect her of fancying him... but if she didn't, he might think she was being rude and standoffish...mentally, she gave herself a slap – just do it, Heather.

'Hi, Aidan.'

'Hi, Heather.'

Aidan turned to her with a smile, and she found herself melting. She didn't think he'd even know her name, although everyone knew who *he* was. She'd thought he'd be all moody and distant, but his smile was warm.

'So, having a nice time?' she managed to say, after searching her mind unsuccessfully for a witty comment. If ever a girl needed Woody Allen, it was now.

'Swinging,' Aidan said.

'Oh... I thought you'd like parties,' said Heather. She couldn't imagine him having that sweaty-palmed-bad-hair-day-totally-wrong-outfit-standing-in-the-corner sort of feeling she often got as she looked after Matilda and Lucie's handbags. Not looking the way he did. In his white shirt and ivory trousers, he could have been cast as the Angel Gabriel.

'Not a lot,' said Aidan. As well as having all the right credentials – dark hair with a slight wave, blue eyes and a husky voice, he had to have a killer Newcastle accent as well. Not fair.

'... anyway, there's a Woody Allen on tonight,' Aidan went on.

'I know,' Heather agreed, longingly.

'*Play it Again, Sam*, my favourite,' they both said, in unison, then burst out laughing.

'Beating *Annie Hall* by a whisker,' said Aidan.

Soon, they were deep in conversation about their favourite films by Woody, which led onto their mutual love of American sitcoms.

'I love *Friends, Cheers, Big Bang Theory* and *Frasier*,' said Heather. 'But *Spin City*'s my favourite.'

Aidan high-fived her.

'Shut up! Mine, too.'

'I was just going to stay an hour, then sneak away home to watch Woody,' Heather said, realising that the hour had now whizzed by.

'Shall we go?' Aidan asked.

Heather slipped back into the party to fetch her coat. Matilda and Lucie, strutting their stuff on the dance floor with two of the creatives, didn't even notice her creep past, grabbing a bottle of Pinot Grigio on the way.

⌐

The village hall was crowded. A couple of hay bales stood at the back, and there were chairs all round the walls. Two trestle tables were set out with cans of beer piled high. Long tables ringed the dance floor and the seating was more hay bales covered in white cloth.

'Hi, Heather,' called Euan. He was standing with his brother, who looked just like him.

'You remember my older, not so good looking, brother, Callum?' he asked.

'Of course,' Heather said. 'Hi, Cal.'

She and Callum grinned at each other and she threw her arms round him and hugged him – then wondered if it was the done thing in this part of the world. They chatted and sipped beer as the all-women ceilidh band – the Drystane Dykes – cranked up their bagpipes. They had cropped hair and wore big earrings, white tee-shirts, red braces, short kilts, pink fluffy sporrans and red Dr Marten boots.

'They're awesome,' Euan said. 'Like a female version of the Red Hot Chilli Pipers on speed. Might use that in an article, actually,' he mused, pulling his iPhone out of his pocket.

Heather laughed.

'Hi, guys.' Misty was approaching, hand in hand with Duncan the postman.

'Hi, Misty, Hi, Duncan,' said Heather, managing a big smile, although she'd been overcome by a wave of loneliness on seeing how loved-up they were.

As the evening wore on, she realised that she was actually enjoying herself – a combination of the atmosphere, the alcohol and being with friends who really cared about her. She still hadn't quite got the hang of the dances, though. During Strip the Willow, Euan had lost his grip on her hands and she'd lost her balance and cannoned into Cal, nearly knocking him to the floor. Eventually she and Misty found themselves separated from the rest of their six in the Dashing White Sergeant and they stood by the wall, helpless with laughter as the four men cavorted around without them.

At the interval, bacon rolls were served.

'Having a good time?' asked Euan.

'Surprisingly, yes,' said Heather.

Just then, the volume in the room seemed to drop a level, and the sound of high heels clattering on the floorboards could be heard. The crowds parted so that Rowan Galloway could make her way through. Heather looked at her as she approached. Rowan was even taller than she'd realised whilst the girl was on horseback – a good five feet nine or ten. She was simply dressed in a denim skirt and a white vest, but she radiated sex appeal. Her shimmering, amber coloured hair hung down to her waist and she had large eyes of a stormy grey-green. Everyone seemed to have stopped talking, now, as they turned to look at her.

'Out of my way, Ms Bright Lights,' she said, in a ringing cut glass English accent.

'Excuse me,' Heather fumed. 'Don't you dare speak to me like that. Who do you think you are?'

'I'm Euan's girlfriend, I think you'll find,' Rowan said, her gaze haughty and cool. 'You would do well to remember that. I do hope we're clear.'

'Rowan –' Euan began to protest, but Rowan pushed past Heather, threw her arms around his neck and began to kiss him passionately. Heather hurried away, humiliated, as they went on kissing, seemingly now oblivious to the crowds, in an erotic tango.

Outside in the still warm air, she sat down on the seawall and felt a light wind ruffle her hair. Rowan had obviously thought that she'd been trying to make a move on Euan and had decided to stake her claim. She closed her eyes: there was an echo of Aidan and Savannah which hurt her heart and, despite her tranquil surroundings, she was back in the Bright Sparks canteen, surrounded by the buzz of conversation, the scraping of cutlery on plates and the clink of glasses.

'Guess what?' J-Lo plonked her lunch tray – salad and sparkling water as usual – down on the table, and slipped into her seat. 'Aidan's got a girlfriend.'

Heather and Matilda exchanged puzzled glances. For a moment, she wondered if J-Lo meant herself, despite her rather odd phrasing, and despite the fact that no one in the office except close friends knew she and Aidan were together – because Aidan was so much fancied by the girls, speculation was intense about his romantic status and Heather didn't think she could take the pressure.

'Er, does he?' Matilda said, carefully, still looking perplexed.

'Yeah.' J-Lo smirked, enjoying having everyone's undivided attention: Heather, Matilda and Lucie's eyes were all fixed on her. 'Justin and I went to NoHo for dinner on Friday night –' NoHo was a currently hip restaurant near the office and J-Lo could never resist name dropping. 'He was in the bar with a girl. Quite nice looking.'

This was high praise, coming from J-Lo, who saw every woman she ever met as competition – Aidan's drinking companion probably made Keira Knightley look like a troll.

'What did she look like?' Heather managed to ask, through frozen lips.

'Tall, slim, long dark hair, right down her back. Fabulous leather jacket – I think it was DKNY –'

Heather's ears buzzed with shock and pain, so that she could no longer hear the background chat and laughter in the canteen. That evening had been the first Friday she and Aidan had spent apart since they met – he'd neglected to say that the "old friend from university" he'd arranged to meet was a woman.

'Who says she's his girlfriend?' said Matilda loyally. 'She could just have been a mate.'

'Er, I don't think so,' protested J-Lo. 'Not unless he's in the habit of sticking his tongue down the throats of his mates. You had to be there. They looked all serious and lovey-dovey –'

'Excuse me,' Heather said, desperately, jumping to her feet. 'I feel sick.'

She hurried across the canteen towards the ladies' room. It seemed much further away than she'd remembered. Once inside, she looked at her face in the mirror. It was ashen, while her neck was mottled red with shock. Suddenly, she realised that she did feel sick, and she hurried to the toilet, only just making it in time.

'Heather,' came Matilda's voice from the door, and she heard her friend's shoes tapping across the floor towards her. Next moment, Matilda was kneeling beside her.

'Drink,' she said, passing her a glass of water from the cooler outside. Heather sipped obediently, trying to get rid of the sharp acid taste in her mouth. Matilda produced some wipes from the capacious portable chemist which was her handbag and gently began to wash Heather's face, stroking off the tears and make-up.

'Is she all right?' came another voice. It was J-Lo, and Heather could hear her distaste.

'She'll be fine, Jess. Finish your lunch.'

The door closed again.

'It's okay, baby.' Matilda put her arms round Heather as they crouched on the floor, rocking her gently, kissing her forehead. 'We'll go home and we'll talk.'

'Okay,' said Heather, in a high voice. She felt like a child again, and was grateful for Matilda's strong, capable presence.

'Is there anything I can do?' Lucie was standing beside them. Heather hadn't even heard her come in.

'Yes. Tell Mike and Suzie that Heather's ill and I'm taking her home.'

The next half hour or so, as she and Matilda left Bright Sparks House, got into a taxi and climbed the stairs to Heather's flat, passed in a blur of tears and pain.

Once inside the flat, Heather went into her lilac bedroom and lay face down on her bed, crying until her pillows were soaked, while Matilda stroked her back and hair. Eventually, when she could cry no more, she sat up, the tears giving way to long, shuddering gasps.

'Where is he?' demanded Matilda, passing her a cup of hot, sweet tea.

'Dorset,' whispered Heather. 'Shooting a shampoo commercial.'

By the bed were a bunch of freesias and two melted vanilla scented candles. On Saturday night, she and Aidan had slowly made love as the fragrances sweetly mingled, his face serious in the moonlight. Afterwards, they'd lain in each other's arms, kissing and talking softly for a long time, and she'd thought this meant that he really cared about her. How stupid was she? And how could he, when he'd been with *her* only the previous night? Again, she thought that maybe Aidan had been cheating on her all this time they'd been together, that she'd only been filling in.

'Matilda, you'll stay with me, won't you?'

''Course I will,' said Matilda.

'Thanks,' murmured Heather, sipping her tea. Without Aidan, she was absolutely desolate. She had no idea how she was going to make it through the afternoon, let alone the rest of her life. She and Matilda talked for a long time, then Matilda fed her scrambled eggs on toast. Later, they got into bed, and, although she couldn't sleep, she was comforted by the warmth of her best friend's back against hers.

⤳

She was jolted back to Kirklochy as she felt a cold nose press against her arm, and opened her eyes to see the black and white face of a border collie.

'Are you all right?' came a voice. Sean was standing behind his dog, but he stepped forward to help her to her feet, his hand on hers feeling cool and dry.

'I'm fine,' said Heather. 'It's just... there was a bit of a floorshow in there.' There was a strength and stillness about Sean that invited confidences. She was so glad he hadn't been there to witness her humiliation. Inwardly, she cringed. Time after time, she vowed to control her temper, to remain calm, cool and sophisticated. And then the red mist would come down again.

'Euan invited me to the ceilidh and I really was enjoying it – it was great to see everyone again. But then Rowan came in,' she told him.

Sean said nothing, waiting for her to carry on.

'I've been hanging out with Euan a lot – he's an old mate, but Rowan must have thought I was coming onto him and decided to mark her territory. She wasn't even with him. They were on a break –'

'Another one?' said Sean.

'Looks like they're back together again, as of about fifteen minutes ago,' said Heather. She kicked a stone at her feet. 'I don't even want a boyfriend,' she added. 'Least of all someone else's.'

Sean laughed, and from somewhere she felt a spark of happiness that she'd made him do so.

'I wouldn't worry about it,' he said. 'Rowan always likes to put on a show. She's unbelievably high maintenance.'

But I bet you fancy her, anyway, Heather caught herself thinking. She imagined all the men would.

One of the best things about Kirklochy was the starscape: like huge, glittery snowflakes against the dark sky. Heather contemplated those for a few moments.

'They just don't make stars like this in London,' she said.

'I'll walk home with you,' offered Sean, calling to his dog, who trotted along behind them as they walked the two hundred or so yards to Thistle Cottage.

'See you around?' ventured Heather, when they reached Treeny's gate, and she hoped she would.

5. *Sex and the Village*

'Back so soon?' called Treeny, as Heather let herself into the cottage. In the living room, in flannelette PJs and a fluffy dressing gown, she was engrossed in an Alex Gray novel. The Golden Girls, as Dad called Treeny's posse, must have left quite early.

'Er, yes. Aunt Treeny, I think I'll just go to bed –'

Treeny peered at her over her reading glasses.

'No. Come and talk to me for a wee bit.' She laid her book on the coffee table and patted the sofa beside her. Heather sat down, breathing in the comforting smell of Treeny's Tweed perfume, faded now in the late evening. Treeny got up slowly, and, leaning on her stick, went into the kitchen and returned a few minutes later with two mugs of hot chocolate with marshmallows floating on the top, a treat Heather used to enjoy as a child. She sipped hers. There was a slight alcoholic bite, showing that Treeny had added another ingredient not present in childhood – a dash of brandy.

'All right, what's wrong? I know something is.'

Heather explained about the events of the evening, how Rowan Galloway had warned her off Euan in front of most of the village.

'It must have looked to everyone as if I'd tried to steal her boyfriend,' she finished. 'Which I'd never do.'

'I know you wouldn't, dear,' said Treeny, gently stroking Heather's wrist. She paused and sipped from her mug. 'Attention seeking,' she pronounced. 'Young Rowan hasn't had the easiest of lives,' she went on. 'Only child, plenty of money, lots of spoiling, but not much love.'

Treeny stared at the fire for a moment, a Catherine Cookson moment coming on.

'Ranald, her father –'

'*Ranald*,' interrupted Heather. Treeny frowned.

'Very dashing, very charming. A touch of James Bond. It's well known he has affairs. Her mother's Miranda Wood.'

'The actress?'

Treeny nodded.

'She's away a lot, of course, and Ranald never had much time for the girl.'

'Good judge of character, was he?' Heather asked.

'Heather, really –'

'Sorry. Go on.'

'Hired a nanny when she was a baby, packed her off to boarding school as soon as he could. She's a good deal closer to her old nanny than she ever was to either of her parents.'

'I see,' said Heather, some of the hurt of the evening melting away. She drank again from her mug, savouring the delicious sweetness. She thought about her own dad, a gruff, quiet Scotsman who would do anything for his family.

'Heather –' Treeny seemed hesitant now. 'We never did talk about your young man. Aidan, wasn't it?'

'I know, and we will, Aunt Treeny. I just don't feel strong enough right now.'

Something in Heather's voice must have got through to her aunt:

'Did you hear how Kirklochy Thistle got on this afternoon?' she asked.

'Er…no?'

'They thrashed Inveralan Town 12-3.'

'Good for them. Go the Thistle.' In spite of herself, Heather giggled, punching the air.

'There were 56 people there,' Treeny went on. 'Nearly a capacity crowd. But it'll be the last home game for a while: some cows from Galbraith's farm invaded the pitch.'

Heather giggled again: Stamford Bridge it wasn't.

⤿

Later, as she lay in bed, drowsy from brandy and the emotion of the evening, she thought about her and Aidan's accidental first date. Treeny's mentioning him had once again brought him back to the forefront of her mind. After they'd absconded from the launch party, he'd hailed a taxi. As it threaded its way to Heather's Bayswater flat, they hadn't talked much, just making the occasional remark, but the atmosphere between them was comfortable rather than awkward. Heather watched the young people in their Saturday night clothes, calling out to each other, and the lights, splashed against a dark sky, slide past the window.

'Nice gaff,' Aidan said, as they entered the flat. Thank goodness Ben's parents had come round for dinner a couple of nights before, prompting a massive clean-up operation, and the flat had not yet reverted to its usual chaotic state. Nipping quickly into the bathroom, she hid her corn plasters in the medicine cabinet and an ancient, greying bra under a pile of fresh towels and looked in the mirror. Not too bad. Her cheeks were rosy and her eyes bright with the cold. Her hair looked wavy, short damp tendrils framing her face.

She and Aidan sat on the sofa and she switched on the television. Ben's most treasured possession, it dominated the room. It had cost marginally more than a fitted kitchen and was approximately the size of a double decker bus. Consequently, the living room was often full of West Ham supporters watching the football – clapping, cheering, swigging lager straight from the can, munching crisps. Sometimes, on such nights, Matilda would happen to be passing by and would drop in for a few hours.

Their feet up on the table, they watched Woody Allen, sharing the ice cream. On the stroke of midnight, they kissed, seeming to fit perfectly, and, from that night on, they were inseparable.

Matilda was gracious in defeat.

'J-Lo thought she was in with a chance,' she had crowed. 'There is some justice in the world.'

'Thanks, Tills, that's very sweet of you.'

∽

'God, it's freezing,' Heather said, some days later. She'd put on a long-sleeved tee-shirt, jeans, thick socks, Ugg boots and a thick Aran sweater. 'The weather's well and truly broken.'

She stood at the window, watching the waves crashing onto the beach and, sometimes, splashing onto the main street.

'It's spectacular to watch, but I guess it's dangerous, too. Is it true that a young boy was once swept away and never seen again?'

Treeny nodded, her expression sombre.

'Brrr.' Heather pulled down the sleeves of her sweater to cover her hands.

'The heating in the Free Church hall's been turned up full blast – all three bars,' Treeny said, with a wicked smile.

Heather had finally got her broadband connection installed, and, since then, had been cooped up in her new office, Jamie's old bedroom, working on a campaign. The brief was to make a well known brand of medicated soap "sexy".

'Will you be okay if I go out for a bit, Treeny?' she asked. 'I really need to stretch my legs and get some fresh air.' Her aunt nodded. She put on Treeny's sou'wester.

She almost forgot her vow of chastity as she strode along the front in the bracing wind, for, approaching her, was a beautiful man, with a striking resemblance to Orlando Bloom. Although it was late morning, he wore a dinner suit, with a black bow tie flapping loosely at his neck. Behind him, and hurrying to keep up, was a girl in a pink satin dress. She had thick shining blonde hair, pure to the roots and precision cut, and was carrying a bottle of Laurent Perrier.

'So this is Kirklochy on a Saturday,' she boomed, in a voice straight out of *Brief Encounter*. She swigged champagne straight from the bottle. 'Rock and Roll.'

Kirklochy had its golden youth, the landed gentry, people who lived in large country piles, of whom one was Rowan Galloway, of course. There were rumours – always rumours in Kirklochy – about the parties, with university friends who flew up from Cambridge, London and Bath, where the champagne flowed freely and, it was muttered darkly, cocaine was readily available.

Orlando Bloom and the blonde girl ignored Heather. They were followed by half a dozen more partied out, but still glamorous, young people. Rowan, who had evidently been contemplating the waves, lagged behind them. She was wearing a cream silk dress, trainers and a Crombie.

'Hey, Essex Girl,' she called. Heather walked towards her, her heart thumping. As she drew near, she noticed that, whereas J-Lo was worked out, buffed, styled and made up to within an inch of her life, Rowan had a wild, untamed, natural beauty like that of her native country. Her amber coloured hair hung down her back in pre-Raphaelite ringlets, her eyes, fringed with thick, dark lashes, were the colour of stormy winter seas and her skin was pale and smooth like pearl. On the other hand, in her old jeans and yellow oilskin, hair scraped back and no make-up, Heather was not looking her best. While Rowan's hair glowed like polished copper, Heather's bright red curls were wilder than ever and tangled by the brisk sea breeze.

'Keep out of my face, keep away from my man, and we'll get on fine.'

'Wrong on all counts,' said Heather, clasping up her hands into fists. 'Euan was never anything more than a friend, I don't come from Essex and we will *not* get on fine.'

To her own ears, her voice came out sounding very "Saff Larndon" in comparison with the cultured tones of the other girl, but she was proud that, for once, she hadn't flared up.

'Oh, come *on*, Rowan,' called the blonde girl, who was shivering dramatically and hugging herself, her hair kiting around her head. The group was obviously bound for Fratelli's for hangover cures – a fry-up followed by black coffee and coke floats in rotation was the favourite. The invigorating walk along the promenade to the café, with a brisk, salty sea wind, also played a major part in rehabilitation.

Just then, the café door opened and Euan, obviously having heard the raised voices, came out.

'Shut up, Rowan,' he said. 'Heather's an old friend; leave her alone. I'll phone you later, Heather,' he added, in defiance of Rowan's killer stare.

'Who do you think you are?' he asked Rowan, but his voice was gentle, now, and he slipped his arm round her waist as they went inside.

Rowan's friends grabbed all the available tables, sitting around indolently like something out of a Scott Fitzgerald novel. Heather slipped into the tearoom next door. Maggie's tended to be patronised by the older people in the village, and, as Sascha did a half price pensioners' special on a Friday morning, the room was awash with neat fringed bobs in subtle blonde shades.

'I'll be with you in a minute,' said Misty, passing by Heather's window table with a large plate of homemade cakes in each hand.

'Just a black coffee, please,' said Heather, when Misty was ready. 'If I give into the temptation of all those gorgeous cakes, you soon won't know whether to serve me or harpoon me.'

'Do you want the coffee intravenously?' asked Misty.

'Yes, please.'

'Are you all right?' Heather asked, when Misty returned with the coffee in a blue and white Spode cup. Her friend looked tired and careworn.

'Just knackered from working here *and* at the B&B,' said Misty. 'No rest for the wicked. We're fully booked so I haven't had a night off all week. Why don't you come over for a drink tonight? Say about 7.30? We'll have a catch-up. And we'll need to find you a suitable man.'

'You certainly will, dearie.' A voice floated over from four tables away. 'She's been mooching about like a poor wee lost soul since she got here, hasn't she, Mrs Crombie?'

'That she has, Muriel,' said a woman with a sour face under a hat like a tea cosy.

'And you're so gorgeous,' said Misty. 'You look like Merida out of *Brave*.'

'Hum,' said Heather. She supposed this, too, was a step-up from Sideshow Bob.

'Aye, she's a bonnie wee lassie, right enough,' said a woman sitting in the corner, to murmurs of agreement which spread across the room.

'Anyway, I'll see you later,' murmured Misty.

Heather nodded. As she left, she could see that the beautiful people were still hunched over their breakfast next door.

⌒

The décor of the foyer in the B&B, where Misty lived, was an anthem to Scottish kitsch. There was a tartan carpet, a Wallace clan coat-of-arms on the wall, and a china model of the Loch Ness monster in a virulent green on the windowsill, beside two fluffy white Scottie dogs and a plastic set of bagpipes. Nothing, though, could have impressed the tourists more than the view: Ben Lochy was framed in the large window, its peak snow covered against the bright blue sky.

There was a rack of maps and postcards of local views: hills, lochs and the beach, and leaflets advertising local attractions: the bird sanctuary at Ewensay, where a pair of peregrine falcons had recently been sighted, the perfume factory at Inveralan, and a whisky bond at Strathduncan. A poster, hand painted in lurid colours, proclaimed that pipe band The Reel Thang would be in concert the following weekend.

Heather pressed the bell, which chimed out a couple of bars of *Scotland the Brave*. Misty appeared through a tartan door.

'Hi, Misty.' Heather smiled.

'Hi,' said Misty. 'It's a bit quieter tonight,' she added. Heather followed her down the corridor, past a comfortable sitting room where guests were relaxing over coffee and whisky. Two hill walkers sat in deep armchairs, boasting about the number of Munros they'd each completed.

Misty's bedroom was obviously her sanctuary away from the bustle of the rest of the house. It was small and decorated in neutral colours – cream, beige and terracotta, the only bright colour coming from the spines of the books and CDs. There was a small television on a shelf, and Heather guessed that Misty treasured the short periods of privacy the room afforded.

While Misty went to fetch the coffees, Heather looked out of the window at the view of the loch, smooth and azure. She was totally lost in it when Misty returned, pushing the door open with her hip as she carried through a tray bearing two mugs of coffee and a plate of marble cake.

'One of the perks of working for Auntie Maggie,' she said, and the two girls sat down on the bed for a good gossip.

'This reminds me of sitting on Kirsty's bed back home, talking about the other kids at school, who was going out with who, our crushes, what we were going to wear on Saturday night… happy days,' Heather said.

'I heard Rowan Galloway having a go at you earlier,' said Misty. She balled her hands into fists. 'I can't stand that girl. Are you all right?'

'Oh, I'm fine,' said Heather. 'Aunt Treeny told me a bit about her. She says she had a terrible childhood.'

'Huh. I didn't know Treeny was into all that touchy-feely stuff,' said Misty. 'And I can't believe Euan's let her get her claws into him again. But it won't last. She just thinks it's fun to slum it. She'll mess him about for a while, then ditch him for some up-himself posh twit. She always does. It's been going on for years. She doesn't even care about him, but she doesn't want anyone else to have him.'

'What's she got that we haven't?'

Misty considered.

'Well, apart from modelesque looks, the body of Lara Croft, legs that go on forever, a degree from Cambridge University and her very own castle, not a lot.'

Heather giggled. Misty didn't, but instead gazed out of the window, forehead furrowed into a frown.

'I just can't believe Euan, though,' she said. 'I know I'm biased, 'cos he's my big cousin, but he's funny, he's intelligent – he could have anyone. Well, usually he's intelligent, just not when it comes to horrible Rowan. He's not bad looking, either, when he makes an effort.'

'You guys are super-close, aren't you?' said Heather. Now that she came to think of it, Euan and Callum had always been protective of their little cousin: made sure she was by their side in the café, at the cove or on their gang's long summer walks. The three of them had always been talking and laughing together at some in-joke.

Misty smiled.

'Yes,' she said. 'He's brand new. He's always been really sweet to me. I don't suppose you'd consider taking him off my hands?'

'He's lovely – I mean, he's one of my best mates, but I've put men on hold for now. And I'm sure he'll come to his senses soon,' Heather said. 'And he and Rowan will never last. It's a grand passion and it'll burn out.'

'Heather.' Misty's voice was hesitant. 'Do you want to talk to me about your ex? Aidan, wasn't it?'

Heather nodded, letting her hair fall forward to cover her face.

'I guess. It's easier to talk here. London feels so far away.'

Misty said nothing, but waited for her to speak.

'I couldn't believe it when Aid asked me out – he could've had anyone at work, like my mate Matilda or Jessica Lomax who we all call J-Lo because she's so stunning. We got on great. I'd even met his family.'

Heather swallowed as she remembered the Murphys' warm, crowded, noisy home, the rowdy dinners, how welcoming they'd all been.

'I knew he'd just come out of a long-term relationship before I met him, but Savannah, his ex, was living in Singapore and had a new man. It was such a shock when he ended it with me, but he told me there was no one else, he just wasn't ready to commit –'

Misty nodded, taking Heather's hand.

'I felt such a fool when I found out that Savannah was home and he'd got back with her. To make it even worse, he didn't tell me himself: I found out from J-Lo. He said he'd thought he was saving my feelings by telling me there was no one else.'

'Men.' Misty shook her head. 'They *always* say there isn't anyone else when there is.'

'They do. Thanks, Mist,' Heather breathed.

After this, they changed the subject, Misty wanting to know all about the London she'd read about in her magazines: The Ivy, Primrose Hill, the Ministry of Sound, Notting Hill, Camden Lock, Oxford Street, light years away from the tranquil twilight scene outside the window.

⌒

The next morning, Heather met Sean and Katie outside the post office.

'Thanks for... the other night,' she said, a little embarrassed and finding it hard to meet his eye.

'No problem. I know what Rowan's like, but you shouldn't let her get to you.'

'No.' Shyly, Heather looked up at him. Close to, she again took in the beauty of his silvery eyes. His skin was pale and his hair dark – what she had begun to think of as traditionally Celtic looks.

'This is Katie, by the way.' He placed his hand on his daughter's curly head. Heather knelt down so that she was on a level with the child. She was gorgeous, her eyes round and brown, her creamy skin scattered with freckles.

'Hi, Katie. My name's Heather.'

'Hello, Heather,' Katie said, in the lilting Highland accent that was now familiar. Heather had expected her to be shy and withdrawn, but she seemed bright and confident.

'I love your coat.' Heather touched one of the toggles on it. It was bright red, with a hood trimmed with scarlet fake fur. 'I wish they made those in my size.'

'It would match your hair,' Katie said.

She bumped into Sean and Katie again a few days later and had another chat with the little girl, discovering common interests in drawing and painting, and in ice cream, and they discussed Angry Birds, the *Little Mermaid,* Katie's favourite film and her favourite author, Lynley Dodd. Heather wasn't familiar with her oeuvre but Katie brought her up to speed on Hairy MacClary, Slinky Malinki and Zachary Quack.

'Eilidh likes Katie Morag better,' she explained.

'Who's that?'

'Eilidh MacDonald. My best friend.' Katie rolled her eyes and sighed at Heather's ignorance, like Jeremy Paxman on *University Challenge.* Heather giggled and she and Sean led the child into Fratelli's for a Knickerbocker Glory.

⌐

Heather rose early. Sun poured in her bedroom window, casting pools of light on the polished wooden floors. The windows no longer rattled in the breeze and the swell of the sea had dropped. She pulled on old jeans and a hand knitted sweater and gulped tea while running around the cottage packing up her sketch pad, pencils and paints.

The ground was springy and mossy under her trainers as she strolled along. She paused, catching her breath in awe, as a stag with huge antlers crossed a burn just a few yards away. After a short while she put her padded jacket down on a rock and sat on it. Looking intently at the scenery, she began to sketch.

She didn't know how long she had been sitting there, she was so absorbed. Probably hours had passed, as she forgot everything except the shape of the hills, the depth of the water, mixing just the right colour for the bracken. Painting was what she loved most and she'd drifted off into her own private world, untroubled by any of the cares of past or future, freed from the pain of missing Aidan.

'Hello, Heather.' A loud voice brought her back to reality. She looked up to see Katie scampering across the grass towards her, hampered only slightly by her limp.

'Hi, Katie-bubble,' said Heather, patting the grass beside her. Copying her, Katie took off her pink anorak and sat on it.

'You're good. Very good,' said Sean, running an expert eye over the watercolour.

'The quality of light here's so fantastic,' said Heather. 'I'd paint more if it wasn't for the tedious necessity to work.'

She moved and sat on the grass. Her buttocks had begun to seize up from perching on the rock for so long. Katie lifted a sketch pad and began to draw, making Heather smile with her intent glances and her pink tongue jutting out in concentration. Sean sat beside them and Heather closed her eyes, feeling the warmth of the sun on her face. Knowing his story, she still felt awkward.

'So – how are you settling in now?' he asked.

Heather shrugged.

'Good. I like it.'

'It's just... sometimes you look a bit lost.'

'I'm... it's just culture shock.'

She didn't want to mention Aidan. He might not be the person she once thought he was, but he was alive and well, whereas Meg was lost forever.

Katie launched into her own version of Amy Winehouse's *Rehab*, her head still bent over the sketch pad. Heather grinned, then, catching Sean's eye. He was also smiling and it broke the ice somewhat.

'There are some advantages, though,' she said, taking a deep breath of the pure air. 'I mean, in London, although we're neighbours, it would be about seven years before we'd nod to each other and about another three before we'd speak.'

She paused, then, feeling a pang of homesickness for London – the buzz, the excitement, the privacy, Fulham Road. Sean said nothing, but the silence was relaxed and she liked that he didn't seem to feel intimidated by it.

'I'd like to paint you,' he ventured, at length. 'Your hair and your eyes are amazing, and you've got such great bone structure.'

'You would?' Her mouth was dry.

'Yeah – wearing that jumper.'

'This old thing?'

'Yup. The colour's perfect.'

Their eyes met in a long, charged look.

'Yeah,' cried Katie. Heather had almost forgotten the child was there. 'And, after, we can eat ice cream and watch my Little Mermaid DVD. You said it was your favourite.'

'I did. Deal.'

⤶

As Heather passed the village hall a few days later, someone was singing "Almost Like Being in Love" in a sweet, clear soprano. Local gossip had it that Rowan Galloway had turned up for the auditions drunk, wearing just Ugg boots and one of Euan's checked shirts, but had wiped the floor with everyone else, so that they had had to give her the lead part. Damn, she was good, pure as a bell, effortlessly hitting even the highest notes. Even Simon Cowell and David Walliams would have to admit it. As stunning as Rowan's voice was, she couldn't linger, as she was on her way to Shell Cottage with two different flavours of Fratelli's ice cream.

Minutes later, she was knocking on Sean and Katie's door. Frantic barking came from within.

'Trudie.' She could hear a female voice. The door swung open and the dog shot out, jumping up on her and nearly knocking her over.

'Trudie! Bad girl.' Heather looked up from fondling the collie's ears, coming face to face with a woman of about her own age. Her face was bright and alert, and her warm brown eyes peered out from under a thick fringe. She smelled of a rich, fruity perfume.

'Hi, I'm Cara.'

'Heather.' They smiled at each other.

'This way,' said Cara. 'We tend to hang out in the kitchen diner. It's cosy in there.'

Heather followed Cara down the hall, her eyes on her glossy, dark sweep of hair. The kitchen was, indeed, warm and welcoming, painted in terracotta and with several of Katie's drawings on the wall. On a pine shelving unit was a photo of Katie when she was younger and one of Sean and Cara, arms round each other, sitting on a bench in the garden, Cara's long hair blown across her face.

‿

After tea and some of Cara's homemade biscuits, Sean took her into his studio, bright and airy from the skylight windows. Outside, she could hear birdsong and the constant rush of the tides. There was a strong smell of white spirit. Several canvases leaned against the duck egg blue walls.

She sat on a chaise longue, wearing her rust coloured sweater as Sean had requested, and loosened her hair from its top-knot so that it fell in a mass of curls around her shoulders.

As Sean alternately gazed intently at her and sketched, she felt a slight pang, and tried to work out why. She wasn't interested in romance; it was just good to have a new friend who shared her passion for art. And, as pretty and sweet as Cara was, she'd always known Sean must have a partner. In the end, she decided that it was seeing such a warm little family unit that was making her feel low – it was what she'd hoped the future with Aidan would hold.

‿

'Let's see, let's see.' Cara and Katie, back from spending the afternoon with Eilidh and her mum, burst into the room. Heather rose from the chaise longue, stretching her aching limbs, and they all crowded round Sean. She'd have to sit for him a few more times, but, for now, she looked at the sketch of herself, her pensive expression, her mass of tousled curls, the line of her jaw. It was just like the Pre-Raphaelite paintings she loved so much.

'Wow. This is lovely. Very enigmatic,' said Cara.

'What does that mean?' piped up Katie, pulling at Cara's hand.

'Mysterious.'

∽

Later, they watched the DVD as promised. Katie climbed onto Cara's lap. Heather found it hard to concentrate, buzzing from the afternoon with the family, with the beauty of Sean's work.

∽

She emerged from the shower, wrapped herself in a soft, faded old towel and began to squeeze the water from her hair. She found herself humming, looking forward to the evening ahead: Euan, as promised earlier in the week, was picking her up and they were driving up to Inveralan to a gig he was covering – Irish jazz/blues singer Dolores Furey.

Some time later, in her oldest, most faded and comfy skinnies, pumas and a purple tee-shirt Kirsty had made her, she stood in front of the mirror. She didn't bother with make-up other than a little mascara and nude lipstick – her skin had a healthy, golden glow. She didn't have the flutter of butterflies inside that would have been present had this been a date. Euan had already seen her in the raw: running out of the freezing cold sea, whooping, shivering and with a lump of seaweed on her head; with mascara lanes and foundation trickling down her face when they'd been caught in an unexpected downpour; wearing an avocado face pack and, last but not least, badly sunburned after a day at the beach. Her brick red skin had clashed with her hair and Jamie had made matters worse by yelling, "You look like a stick of rhubarb". Only Kirsty, out of sisterly loyalty, had managed to keep a straight face at that. It was at least ten years too late to try to convince Euan that she was a sophisticate.

～

As she watched for Euan's car, she remembered her first date with Aidan. She should have felt nervous. She should have got up at the crack of dawn and spent hours trying on, and discarding, every outfit in her wardrobe, before leaving her room looking like the first day of the January sales and rushing into town for something new which would turn her into the glamorous woman she longed to be.

But she already felt comfortable with him. After dressing simply in jeans, trainers and a tee-shirt, with a sweater tied round her waist, she walked through Hyde Park to the Serpentine, keyed up, excited, but not nervous.

He was waiting for her when she got there, looking even more gorgeous in faded Levis and a grey sweater than he had at the party. Her stomach twisted with desire.

'Hi.' He bent to kiss her, even the touch of his lips on her cheek making her quiver.

'Hi, Aidan.'

She was filled with a sense of happiness and well being – there was no place she'd rather be than the slightly chilly Hyde Park, and no one she'd rather be with. She could barely even call to mind what Orlando Bloom looked like. She smiled as they passed several geese and a swan which was walking clumsily on big, grey feet.

Aidan had decided they should hire a boat, and they clambered aboard and sat down carefully.

'Thought it would be different,' he said, and he looked slightly shy, as if he'd spent some time planning their date. She was touched. Watching the ripple of his shoulders as he rowed, her stomach twisted even more.

'Can I try?' she asked. She took the oars, feeling the old skill coming instinctively back to her.

'You're good,' Aidan said.

'Lots of practice,' admitted Heather. 'My dad comes from a village in the Highlands, and we would go there every summer on holiday, and stay for weeks. We love it. We'd go walking, sailing, fishing. We had our very own private beach: Jamie's Cove. Only our friends ever went there.'

She told him how, on rainy days, they would sit in Fratelli's Ice Cream Parlour, as close to the jukebox as possible, sipping cappuccinos, which they considered at that time to be the last word in sophistication, but, any time the weather was halfway decent, they'd all be hanging out, partying and singing round the fire on the little stretch of beach. The fact that her brother had discovered the cove had instantly made her, Jamie and Kirsty feel more accepted by the village youth.

'Sounds great.'

'It was. It wasn't so much sleepy as unconscious. So peaceful. I used to paint all the time.'

Kirklochy had been as wonderful for that moody teenage phase as it had been when she was a child, with miles and miles of stormy, windswept beaches which she'd mooch along, the soundtrack on her iPod dark, angsty music, pausing now and again to gaze broodingly at the horizon.

'Is that what you want to do, paint?'

Heather nodded. Already, the conversation was intimate and she felt relaxed, yet excited at the same time.

'If you weren't in advertising, what would you do?'

'Be in a band,' said Aidan. He went on to explain about his song writing and how he played guitar. They talked about music, then, Aidan's knowledge being encyclopaedic, and managed to find much common ground in Paul Weller, Noel Gallagher and Dermot O'Leary's Saturday sessions.

Later, they walked in Hyde Park, and, not wanting to part, ended up in a Spanish restaurant near her flat, eating tapas from square white plates.

'Apart from everything by Woody, what's your favourite film?' Aidan asked, as Heather tucked into spicy potatoes, creamed garlic mushrooms and deep fried cheese in citrus sauce, her appetite mercifully unaffected.

'Anything directed by Greenaway,' she said. Then she burst out laughing. 'Actually, it's *Dirty Dancing*.'

Much later, after they'd had a few glasses of wine, Aidan spoke about his childhood, his upbringing on a tough council estate in Newcastle. They talked more about their lives and what they hoped for from the future. He was so easy to be with. Heather held his hand under the table and she was happy.

They'd held hands still as they walked home, blossom falling softly from the trees making a pale, sweet confetti.

⌐

Hearing a horn sounding out in the street, she grabbed a sweater in case the temperature dropped later and picked up her bag.

'Bye, Treeny, bye, Chrissie,' she called as she hurried out the door. It was a bright evening and she settled comfortably into the front seat beside Euan and put on her seatbelt. Euan turned towards her with a whiff of minty fresh toothpaste and a waft of musky aftershave.

'Hi.' She grinned at him.

'Hi, Heather, you look great. I just love your hair.' He reached out and touched a long tendril. She just left it to dry naturally these days, and it had sprung up into a riot of curls.

'Thanks, you look great, too,' Heather said. Euan, also, had an outdoorsy tan. It was weird, relating to him as a grown man – and a very attractive one – when they'd spent so many years larking about and teasing each other as teenagers, as if they had to get used to their current selves.

'So, she's really good, this woman?' she asked.

'Brilliant. She's got an amazing voice, really raw and bluesy. I think she's been round the block a time or two: three ex-husbands, six kids, several addictions. Hold on –' Pulling into a lay-by, he slid a CD into its slot. He drove off again and Heather leaned back in her seat, listening to a voice both husky and sweet singing a traditional song of love and loss. She looked out of the window at the countryside sliding past: the blurred pink and yellow of wildflowers, the silver of a burn rushing down the mountainside, the variegated green of trees; the deep blue of a loch.

'Does she write her own material, too?' Heather asked, not recognising the next track.

'Yeah. She does a mixture of original material and traditional ballads.'

She was almost disappointed when Euan parked on the promenade in Inveralan, just a stone's throw from the arts centre; she'd been enjoying their conversation so much. She'd decided that men were acceptable in certain circumstances – as long as you never contemplated romance. Opening the door, she got out, immediately feeling the brisk sea breeze whipping her hair back. She listened to the squall of seabirds and breathed in the salty tang of the surf.

'So relaxing not to have to drive around for hours looking for a parking space, then end up having to walk miles to the venue,' she told Euan, as they strolled along in the seaspray.

The room in the arts centre was small, intimate and lit by flickering tea lights. As they took their seats, Heather could feel the buzz of anticipation among the audience. Soon, the band was walking onto the makeshift stage. Dolores Furey was barefoot in a black maxi dress. She couldn't be young, but, in the subdued lighting, with her long, wild tawny hair, she looked it. The men assembled behind her, including two fiddlers.

Heather closed her eyes, moved almost to tears by the singer's mesmerising voice, the beauty of the melodies and the plaintive sound of the violin. But, soon, she was laughing also – Dolores Furey was extremely rude, achingly honest and very funny.

'Thanks so much for bringing me here. I've had a lovely evening,' she said, much later, when, after three encores, Dolores and her band had finally left the stage and she and Euan were shuffling out of the hall amid numerous appreciative remarks from the audience. Euan grinned down at her.

'Glad you had a good time.'

She'd been so engrossed in the music that she was taken aback that it was still broad daylight outside.

'It was amazing.'

'I like hanging out with you,' Euan said. 'You're so passionate about the stuff you love.'

'Awww. I like hanging out with you too.'

For a moment, she felt terribly sad – Aidan always used to say that he loved her passion and zest for life also.

'Are you hungry?' Euan went on, breaking the spell. 'I could murder a fish supper. This is the best chippy in Scotland. No question.'

He'd stopped walking outside a shop with a dark blue awning and a white tiled frontage decorated by fish shapes in various bright blues and turquoises.

Heather nodded. It was a very long time since a chip had passed her lips. Probably it was the sea air but she felt ravenous. She and Euan joined the queue and were soon leaving the shop with a warm, newspaper wrapped package each. They sat down on the seawall.

'This is the Kirklochy News,' cried Euan, recognising his own publication wrapping the chips and a little damp with vinegar. 'How dare they?'

Heather couldn't help giggling at his outraged voice as she unwrapped hers. She bit into a chip, sighing in ecstasy, as it was crisp on the outside and fluffy on the inside.

'Yum!' she said, as she broke off a piece of batter-covered fish, dripping in lashings of vinegar. 'You win: this is the best fish and chips I've ever tasted. I don't know if it's the actual fish or the fact that we're eating it in the sea air.'

If she'd been out for dinner with Aidan, she wouldn't have dreamed of tucking in with such relish, licking the vinegar from her fingers or, especially, crunching into a pickled onion. Sitting on a wall eating out of damp newspaper didn't really compare with the super-posh oyster and champagne bar Aidan had booked for her last birthday – but it was the most fun she'd had in ages.

6. *Brigadoon*

'Mmm.' Treeny sniffed the air. 'That smells wonderful.'

'Just some artisan tomato bread which I threw together,' Heather said.

'With a lot of help from me.'

'I could charge a fortune for this in Islington Green, you know.'

Although it was a summer evening, it was chilly, so Heather had lit a small fire in the hearth. She sat in an ancient brown moquette armchair, lace antimacassars on the arms, her BlackBerry – or Blueberry, as Treeny called it – on her lap, catching up on her emails. The latest one from Matilda brought her up to date with Bright Sparks gossip: who was romancing whom, who had been sacked, who had been promoted. She concluded gleefully that something had gone wrong with Alex Day's latest botox treatment, so that her right eye was frozen at a peculiar angle and would remain so for several weeks, until the injection wore off. Heather reached for her mug. The desire to look perfect all the time didn't seem to matter much here. She hadn't eaten so well for years: porridge oats, organic vegetables grown in Treeny's kitchen garden, fresh eggs and milk from Galbraith's farm. She knew she'd put on some weight but it suited her. Her hair gleamed and her skin glowed with fresh air and exercise. She hardly bothered with make-up and lived in comfortable old jeans and sweaters.

There was a knock at the door, and Treeny went to answer it, wiping her hands on her apron.

'Treeny, where's your stick? You're trying to do too much.'

Heather heard the two voices in the hall: Treeny's soft Highland lilt and a cultured English accent. After a moment, her aunt returned, followed by a woman who could only be Valissa Lavender.

Heather had heard a great deal about Valissa; her reputation had gone before her. However, no one in the village had any idea how old she was or where she'd come from, just that she'd moved to Kirklochy to "opt out of the rat race and enjoy a better quality of life". Now, Heather looked at her with interest. She was the epitome of boho chic, wearing a purple vintage dress, Ugg boots, a fur shrug, a sequinned headband and dangling earrings. Her unnaturally black hair was cut in a sharp bob, like that of Louise Brooks, whom she was obviously trying to emulate. She looked as out of place in Treeny's cottage as a flamingo among pigeons.

'Someone to see you, Heather.'

Heather switched off her BlackBerry and got to her feet.

'Valissa Lavender,' said Valissa. She spoke in a rich contralto voice. A likely story, thought Heather; that surely wasn't the name she was born with. She held out her hand to shake. Valissa's bangles jangled as she took it.

'Nice to meet you, Valissa. I'm Heather.'

'I need people to paint the scenery for *Brigadoon*, and I've heard you're an artist.'

'Well, a graphic designer, really.'

'No matter. I'm sure you'd do a splendid job.'

'Well, I don't know –'

With Italianate hand gestures, Valissa waved away Heather's feeble protest:

'I have big plans for this show, dahling. Enormous. I've asked Rob Kingsley to direct. Marvellous actor, you know: his Lear is legendary. He's played all the great male leads – Hamlet, MacBeth, Romeo –'

'Widow Twankey,' put in Treeny.

'That was later in life, and in pantomime,' boomed Valissa, a touch of Birkenhead showing through her cultured tones.

'Of course.'

'Entre nous,' went on Valissa, 'I'm planning to take the show to the Edinburgh Festival Fringe next year.'

'In that case, how can I refuse?' Heather said, excited despite herself at the chance to do some more painting, to help to transform the stage into the mythical, magical Scottish village.

'Can I offer you a piece of homemade shortbread, Miss Lavender?' asked Treeny.

'Oh, no, thank you, dahling. I'm sure it's delicious, but simply loaded with calories.'

'A peppermint tea, then?'

'That would be divine.' As Treeny shuffled towards the kitchen, Valissa went on: 'We're very lucky to have Rowan Galloway in the female lead. Quite wonderful. Take it from me: that girl will go far.'

But not far enough, Heather caught herself thinking, but didn't say out loud. If she only had to see Rowan for one day every hundred years, that would suit her just fine.

'Gregor's going to be amazing too,' she said instead. 'He's got a brilliant voice, and his dancing could put Justin Timberlake to shame.'

She hid a grin: Gregor had been cast as Rowan's lover, but was possibly the one man in Kirklochy who would actually have to act as if he fancied her.

'Quite.'

⌒

'I'll phone you on Wednesday,' Euan said.

Heather thought for a moment: 'I'll phone you sometime in the next few weeks, when I can fit it in between footie and the lads,' she said at last.

'Good call,' Euan said, typing swiftly.

'It's not you, it's me?' he went on.

'It's definitely you.'

'You've got a brilliant personality.'

'I don't remotely fancy you,' Heather said.

They high-fived, then Euan again typed speedily.

'There's no one else: I'm just not ready to commit.'

'I'm in love with another woman,' Heather said, almost to herself. She was struck by such a surge of pain that it nearly winded her.

'Heather? Are you all right?'

'Yeah, I –' She turned her head to the side slightly, so that he wouldn't see her expression. Euan put his arm round her shoulders.

'You're not.'

She shook her head, a tear creeping over the edge of her eye.

'My… my boyfriend dumped me not long before I came here. He swore there was no one else, then I found out that he'd been seeing his ex.'

Euan put his arms round her and began to stroke her back.

'It's okay. I've got you.'

She cried for a few moments in his embrace, then felt immensely better for it.

'Why don't we go out for lunch?' Euan asked. 'Will Treeny be okay for a bit longer?'

Heather nodded, sniffing.

'She's got Chrissie and Grace coming round for a game of Scrabble.'

'Let's go, then.'

They walked along the coast road towards the Claymore Inn. It was a beautiful day and a light breeze ruffled her hair as the delicate yellow flowers by the roadside swayed. Beyond the golden sand, the sea sparkled. The sky was clear and blue and she could see right across to the group of white cottages perched on the Tara Isles.

'Will we sit outside?' Euan asked.

While he went inside to order at the bar, Heather took a seat at a small wooden table in the shade. After her short burst of weeping, she felt happier and even more so as they chatted easily and ate a delicious fish pie topped with fluffy mash and a thick coating of grated cheese, followed by sticky toffee pudding, which was the speciality of the house.

'Thanks, mate.' She polished off the last of the pudding, which was drenched in thick, fresh cream. 'You've really cheered me up.'

'Any time. I hate to see you so down. You really liked this guy?'

'Yeah.' She tried a casual laugh, but it came out sounding strained. 'He was everything to me… you know, at the time. But it's over and I need to accept that.'

'Easier said than done,' Euan said, his eyes, warm and chocolate brown, on her. She supposed he'd been there quite a few times, on the emotional rollercoaster that was his relationship with Rowan.

'Mmm. I'll go and get us some coffees.'

⤶

Later, after making sure that Treeny was comfortably settled in front of the television, she walked down the hill to Kirklochy Village Hall. With its scuffed floorboards, plastic chairs and hand-written posters advertising the church fayre, the cleaning rota and meetings of the Rural and local Boys' Brigade (although "brigade" was stretching it somewhat), she couldn't help thinking it was a shade off being Convent Garden. Valissa, a vision in violet silk, was standing at the door.

'Heather, this is Robert Kingsley,' she said. The man standing beside her had smooth white hair and a neat moustache, and sported a Paisley patterned cravat and a maroon velvet jacket that even Austin Powers would baulk at. He gave a slight, formal bow.

'Rob's going to be producing the show,' Valissa went on. 'Rob, this is Heather McAndrew.'

'Any relation of Catriona McAndrew?' boomed Robert Kingsley, in a deep, ringing actor's voice. Heather felt a light breeze on her cheek. "Dram" seemed to be the operative word in his case: he had the florid complexion of a heavy drinker.

'Great-niece.'

'Damn fine looking woman, Catriona,' remarked Robert, telling everyone in the room. Heather nodded. In her late seventies, Treeny, with her stature, her style, her thick, snow white waves, large green eyes and elegant bone structure, was a handsome woman still. As Heather knew from her perusal of the family photos, she'd been a beautiful girl with long, thick dark curls, a figure to die for and look of mysterious self possession, all this enhanced by their being black and white. Heather wondered, as she often had before, why Treeny had never married, why there had never been any suggestion of romance during all those summers she used to spend here.

Rowan Galloway was sitting on the edge of the stage, swinging her legs and eating a Bombay Bad Boy with the air of someone eating fresh oysters prepared by Nick Nairn. Everyone agreed that Rowan was a liability, a loose cannon – unpredictable, but too talented to lose. Flora Munro, Treeny's friend from the post office, had turned out to be a wonderful pianist, and she was currently sitting at the old upright piano, with its stained ivory keys, playing the overture.

As the evenings passed, Heather enjoyed being involved in the rehearsals. It was more satisfying than she had imagined to watch the show slowly come together, to get to know the music. The orchestra was a motley crew, including Craig, Mrs Peden's grandson, who played violin and mooched around in a beanie hat, headphones permanently glued to his ears. Whatever the weather, he wore jeans low across his stomach and revealing his boxer shorts. Mrs Niven, the double bassist, was ninety if a day and had more of a beard than Craig could muster. They played well, though, getting even better as time went on. Heather caught herself humming the big numbers as she worked at her Apple Mac during the day.

Tonight, while Katie sat on a beanbag cutting out leaf shapes from green sugar paper, and Heather and Sean painted layer after layer of delicate blue to depict the loch, Rowan was singing, her pure, clear soprano accompanied by an intense young woman who played the clarsach, a Gaelic harp. Valissa was clasping her hands together in delight. Despite Rowan's insouciance, couldn't care less attitude and persistent late coming, Heather felt that, deep down, she really cared about the show, and was determined to make it a success. She supposed that Rowan simply didn't do failure.

At eight o'clock, Cara breezed in to collect Katie. The child enjoyed helping out and being part of the adult world of the show, and complained for a few minutes, protesting loudly that she wasn't tired, but then allowed herself to be scooped up and carried the couple of hundred yards home.

After rehearsals, it was customary for everyone to go to the Claymore for a drink, hurrying to avoid the midges. They packed up for the night and Rowan pulled on a faded and frayed denim jacket and then shook out her glorious titian hair, so that it caught the light, shimmering down her back. Heather shrank inside as the girl approached her.

'Clover,' she said, 'just to let you know that Euan isn't asking for you.'

'He doesn't need to,' said Heather. 'I had lunch with him today.'

Up until her teary episode, the day had been great fun, as they'd worked on Sarah Michelle Cox's column, *"What he Says... What he Means"* for that week's issue of the paper. Heather had thought this was a good answer, but Rowan looked unfazed.

'He didn't mention that when I saw him this afternoon,' she said. 'In my bed.'

'Rowan,' cut in Sean, his voice cool, 'it might surprise you to know that no one's interested in what you get up to in the bedroom.'

'Really, Sean?' said Rowan. She raised one eyebrow, slowly looked him up and down, then turned away to pick up her bag.

'Come on,' said Sean. Gently, he placed his hand on Heather's back and guided her out of the hall.

'Can't believe how light it still is,' she said.

'That's because we're so far north.'

Rowan climbed into a shiny, black four-by-four, and roared off down the coast road.

The Claymore was busy tonight. Two American tourists were talking to Murdo, the landlord, about their Scottish ancestors, several farmers were occupying one corner of the room, loudly discussing their crops, Bruno Fratelli, the owner of the Italian café, affectionately known as the Godfather, was playing darts with three of his sons, and a bunch of older people were sipping stout and playing dominoes. Heather raised her hand in greeting to Alfie Bolt, a fellow Londoner she'd befriended, who was propping up the bar.

'Hey, Alfie,' she called, strolling over for a chat. She could smell his leather jacket from here.

''Allo, darling.'

'Have you just been elected Lord Mayor of London?' she asked, indicating the thick, heavy gold chain round his neck.

'Not yet, my laaarve, but it's on the cards for next year.'

'I'll have to keep in with you.'

'Plus, you'll be glad to know I've asked Sandy at the village store to order in jellied eels and potted shrimps.'

Heather giggled.

'That's the best news I've had all year.'

The Brigadoon cast took possession of all the available chairs, Heather managing to grab one by the window, so that she could look out at the view, and far enough away from the roaring fire that she would be warm, but her face wouldn't go as red as her hair. A glassy-eyed stag stared down at her.

Sean, returning from the bar, gave a sweet sherry to Flora Munro and a pint of Old Sheepshagger to Heather. She had developed quite a taste for the rich, peaty local beer.

'You've been doing a lot of painting since you've been here, haven't you?' said Sean.

Heather nodded.

'It's this place. It's so inspiring. I've got quite a few paintings piled up in my bedroom: the mountains; the forest; some fishing boats in the harbour; the beach, the view over to Keel Island; some old crofts and the sun setting over the loch.'

'There's an arts centre in Inveralan where they exhibit local artists,' explained Sean. 'I think you could sell some there, if you're serious about making a living out of it.'

'Oh, I am,' sighed Heather. 'It's always been my dream.'

'Well, we could go down to Inveralan on Saturday to have a look around.'

'Fantastic,' said Heather, in excitement. The warmth of the fire and of the alcohol spreading inside her made her feel relaxed. 'But won't Cara mind?' she heard herself ask.

'She'll be fine. She's taking Katie to Glenstruan for the day to get some new clothes.'

'Primrose Hill-On-Sea,' Heather remarked.

Sean smiled. His silver-grey eyes looked luminous in the evening light. She'd like to know him better, to break through his reserve. He'd nearly finished her portrait, but they didn't get the chance to talk much during those sessions, and afterwards, Katie always mono-polised her, begging for a story, a game, or for Heather to watch one of her Disney DVDs with her.

'I'll get another round in,' Sean said, breaking into her thoughts. 'Same again?'

'No, let me,' said Heather. Getting out her purse, she stood up and walked towards the bar.

'My great-great grandmother on my father's side was a McCor-mack,' one of the Americans was saying.

'Heather,' said Murdo, at last making his way along the bar towards her.

'A sweet sherry and two pints of Old Sheepshagger, please, Murdo,' said Heather. It was impossible to speak those words and not smile.

'So,' she said, sliding a glass across the table towards Sean. She sat down. 'Katie's absolutely adorable. You must be so proud of her.'

He did become more open then, and, while they finished their drinks, he talked about how much the child had blossomed lately, how much more confident and outgoing she was. Sitting so close to him, seeing him, for once, bright and animated, she was struck again by what an attractive man he was – long lashes framing those stunning eyes, faint stubble on his lean jawline, his black hair curling slightly against his collar. She could smell the familiar combination of lemon soap and white spirit, and she liked it: it made her feel at home.

Sean glanced at his watch.

'We should go. Cara must be wondering where I am.'

They walked slowly along the coast road, Heather averting her eyes from the nauseatingly Mills and Boon scene of Euan and Rowan locked in a passionate embrace against a backdrop of the setting sun, a fiery golden ball sliding down the red-streaked sky.

'I'll see you on Saturday, then?' said Sean, as they walked up the hill to Thistle Cottage.

'Yes, and thanks,' said Heather, as they reached Treeny's gate. She felt a spark of excitement deep inside at the thought of her own paintings on display, maybe even selling some.

⌒

The next day, after nine solid hours working at her Apple Mac, Heather decided to walk into the village for a coffee. A cool breeze blew back her hair as she breathed in the scent of the sea and watched the movement of the boats as the water lapped around them. A bird was singing, and the path was bordered with heather in the deepest, richest wine, interspersed with a delicate yellow flower whose name she didn't know.

'Heather,' shouted a voice from behind her. She stopped walking;

she'd never get used to the way everyone knew each other here. Cara, slightly breathless from hurrying to catch up with her, drew level.

'Are you walking into the village?' she asked.

'Yeah. I've been working since seven. I need a caffeine fix.'

'What is it that you do?'

'I work for Bright Sparks. It's an advertising agency.'

Just for a moment, Heather wished she were back there, sitting gossiping over a salad in the canteen with Matilda and Lucie. She even missed J-Lo.

'I've heard of it. It's as big as Saatchi and Saatchi, isn't it?'

'I guess,' said Heather despondently. 'What is it you do?'

'I'm a nurse at the cottage hospital in Inveralan.'

They walked on, chatting about work, until they reached Fratelli's. Inside, Tino, the oldest brother, was wiping down tables, but he stopped at once to give them a big Italian welcome.

'It's good to meet another townie,' said Cara, as they sipped frothy cappuccinos. 'You're from London, aren't you?'

'That obvious, is it?'

'A bit. You sound just like Danny Dyer.'

Heather giggled.

'Thanks.'

'I'm from Glasgow myself,' said Cara, a faraway look crossing her face. 'Sometimes I wish I was back there. Sauchiehall Street, Byres Road, Buchanan Galleries, Princes Square, Merchant City –' She grabbed Heather's wrist. 'We should get together Gregor and a bunch of girls and go. We'll shop till we drop then club all night –'

'I'd love to go to Glasgow,' said Heather, in excitement. 'Style Mile, this isn't,' she reflected. 'There are some advantages, though.'

'A few,' agreed Cara, her bright face breaking into a grin, her cheeks slightly pink.

'He is lovely,' Heather found herself saying. 'And good looking with it.'

'Isn't he?' Cara's smile stretched wider.

'And there's Katie too.'

'Oh, I know. I love that wee girl as if she was my own. Which she nearly is.'

An elderly man shuffled over to the jukebox and fed some coins in. *Hats off to Larry* blared across the café.

'Heather, I know you're really fond of your Aunt Catriona, but there's got to be a man at the bottom of this somewhere.'

'Wrong. I just wanted to opt out of the rat race and enjoy a better quality of life.'

'Aye, right,' said Cara.

7. *Little Lies*

After breakfasting on toast and Mrs Gillies' home-made plum jam, Heather went into her bedroom to get dressed. She pulled on her comfy old faded jeans and a pair of trainers, then reached into the top drawer of her dressing table and pulled out her favourite sweater. It had been a Christmas present from her sister, hand knitted in the softest angora, in what Kirsty said was heather-colour, of amethyst purple. She slipped it on. It had a wide boat neck, and a cropped hem which just hugged her waist. It clung to every curve. She picked up a portfolio case, into which she'd zipped her best paintings the previous evening.

'Aunt Treeny, will you be all right?' she asked. 'You've got your mobile phone?'

Treeny was much improved as her hip had healed somewhat, but her old bones would never be the same again. She cast a suspicious glance at the phone, which was sitting on the coffee table beside her crossword dictionary. On speed-dial, Heather had programmed her own number, as well as the numbers of Mrs Gillies, Mrs Peden and Doctor McLuskie. Treeny mistrusted the phone, deeming it a "new fangled" invention.

'I'm perfectly fine, lassie,' she said. 'Off you go.'

Outside it was dull, but the sun was bravely trying to break out from behind a cloud. At Shell Cottage, her knock was answered by Katie.

'Hello, Heather,' she said, twirling round. 'Is this a good look?'

She was wearing a white tee-shirt and apple-green trousers printed with white daisies.

'She's having a clothes crisis,' said Cara, from the hall behind her.

She looked as cute as ever, with her round brown eyes and her hair tied up on top of her head with Katie's red bobbles.

'It's a great look,' said Heather. Katie also looked totally edible.

'Okay, baby, teeth,' said Cara, putting her hand on Katie's shoulder and guiding her into the bathroom.

Heather went into the kitchen, again thinking how cosy and homely it was. The smell of roast coffee beans drifted over from a pot on the counter.

'I'll be just a couple of minutes, Heather,' called Sean, from the hall.

Katie's head, haloed in curls, appeared round the door.

'Bye, bye,' she said.

'Bye, Katie, have a nice day.'

She looked out of the window as the child walked down the grassy slope towards the gate. Then Sean knelt down in front of her and spoke quietly to her. After a couple of minutes they walked over to the car and he strapped her in and closed the door gently. He watched as Cara drove slowly down the hill towards the promenade.

'She's still nervous about getting in the car?' Heather suggested, when Sean returned.

'Yes,' he said. 'Or maybe that's just me.'

There was silence in the room; Heather could hear the swell of the sea outside.

'Will we go?' said Sean. His face cleared and he smiled, looking much younger and even more attractive, his eyes the same pewter colour as the water. Heather nodded and they began the short walk to the station. The sun had broken through and there were patches of blue sky among the grey. They walked down the hill and along the promenade. They'd decided to take the train, as Treeny had said that the journey, along the coast, boasted spectacular scenery. The train, which had come all the way from Edinburgh, chugged into the station. They boarded and sat down, the gentle rocking evoking a memory of Aidan:

The train sped north, fields and towns, becoming steadily more grey and industrial, flashing past the window. Aidan was briefly explaining about his family.

'There's Mum, Dad and Gran, who lives with us. Michael and Dana'll be there with their kids. Then there's Ciaran and Sinead, and probably a few cousins as well.'

Aidan was the middle child of five.

Heather put down the copy of Marie Claire she'd been reading.

'No pressure, then?' she grinned.

'You'll be fine.'

She was excited about meeting his family, but also, over a long brunch in Caffe Lucia, Matilda and Lucie had said it was a breakthrough in the relationship, showing that Aidan was serious (which always made Heather think of a disease).

At the station at Newcastle, they hailed a taxi and were soon knocking on the door of Aidan's family home. The street he'd grown up in was a red brick terrace, similar to Coronation Street.

The door was opened by a plump, cuddly woman. After greeting Aidan warmly, she turned to Heather.

'You must be Heather. Come in, pet.'

'Hello, Mrs Murphy.'

'Call me Trish,' invited Mrs Murphy. She was wearing an apron and smelled of freshly ironed cotton and home baking, just as a mum should, as comforting as stepping into a hot bubble bath. The hall was tiny and papered in mushroom coloured woodchip.

In the living room, Heather's senses were assaulted by a television turned up loud, in front of which Aidan's Granny Rose was sitting, cartoons on the computer which two of the nephews were watching, while two other children were curled up on the sofa playing 3DS games.

Heather could see why Aidan was so modest about his extreme good looks – his brothers and sisters were equally as good looking as he was. Take Sinead, for instance, who was just seventeen and still at school. With her glossy black hair, wide blue eyes, rosebud mouth and milky complexion, she looked just like a Disney princess, albeit in a cropped top and glittery denim mini skirt.

Before dinner, she and Aidan went out, holding hands as they walked down the street. Aidan showed her his old school, the playground where he used to skateboard, his old youth club. She was fascinated by every aspect of his life, past and present.

Later, they sat down to a big, shouty, boisterous meal. Afterwards, Heather collapsed on the sofa beside Sinead, who was painting her nails purple, and watched as Aidan crawled around the floor, two of his nieces riding on his back. She wondered what their colleagues would think if they could see him now.

Later still, lying in the top bunk in Sinead's room, which was lit only by the orange sodium glow of a streetlight, Heather thought that, having seen Aidan with his family and in his home town, she loved him more than ever, if that was possible.

∽

The carriage was empty apart from an elderly woman in a tweed hat, who was engrossed in a novel. Most of the remaining passengers would have got off at Inverness. Heather relaxed as she slipped off her jacket, shaking off thoughts of Aidan. It was good to get some privacy. She hadn't fully realised until now how oppressive the gold-fish bowl atmosphere in Kirklochy could be. The buffet car was still open and Sean fetched two coffees in plastic cups. The train was clanking through wild, open country now. Hedges starred with yellow flowers, mountains stained with bracken and tall, dark Scots pines flashed past the window.

She was glad this wasn't a date. If it had been a date, she would have had to pretend to be cool and sophisticated while wondering if she passed and he would want to see her again. She wouldn't have been able to dunk KitKats in her coffee, or put her feet up on the seat opposite and sit in relaxed silence and look out at the magnificent scenery – miles of golden beach curling round the now blue sea.

'I thought Kirklochy was a quiet place,' she said, as she ate the last piece of KitKat and licked chocolate from her fingers. 'But it's a hotbed of gossip and scandal.'

'Wait until the Lammas Festival,' said Sean.

'What's that?'

'It's this big pagan festival in August: witchcraft, voodoo, shaman stones, incense –'

'Rituals, spells and cauldrons?' asked Heather. 'Book of Shadows?'

Sean nodded.

'Where am I meant to get a cauldron?' wondered Heather. 'Or a Book of Shadows?'

'On eBay,' explained Sean. '£12.99.'

'Doesn't seem right,' mused Heather. 'You should only be able to get them from a dark poky shop up a narrow alley, and then only when there's a full moon. There'd be wind chimes in the doorway and the smell of incense.'

For a moment she entertained a pleasant fantasy of casting a spell on Rowan so that her whole body would be covered in cellulite.

'You're joking, though, right?'

'Yeah, but there is a Harvest Festival on the first of August, if you'll still be here.'

'I will be,' said Heather, and smiled.

The train journey was over all too quickly. Inveralan was bigger than Kirklochy, big enough to be considered a small town – a very small town. The main street, edged by low whitewashed houses, led to the Wallace Arms Hotel at the foot of a mountain range. Four hill walkers, in gaiters and with rucksacks the size of Millport, walked towards it.

'Ooh – Paolo's Pizzeria. Yum. I can smell the garlic from here,' Heather said, glancing through the windows at the intimate restaurant with its subdued lighting, red and white checked table covers and gently flickering candles stuck into Chianti bottles.

'Yeah,' agreed Sean. 'Cara and I take Katie there quite often. His four seasons pizza's amazing. Plus, we always get the best table, because he's biased.'

The arts centre was in a converted church, the focal point a huge arch shaped stained glass window which had been carefully restored. To the back there was a theatre little larger than Treeny's bedroom. Heather paused for a moment to glance at the posters which were wall to wall in the foyer, advertising various cultural events.

'I must go to see the *Slab Boys*,' she said. 'It's a classic, isn't it? Ooh, didn't know you taught art here.'

'Yup, still life and watercolour. I need to earn enough money to keep my wee princess somehow.'

In another room, the faltering sounds of someone learning to play guitar could be heard. A delicious smell of coffee and pastries drifted out of the café, which was where the paintings were being exhibited. Heather followed Sean into the room, her hands sweaty now with anxiety. She'd arranged to meet with the director. She managed not to laugh at his hipster beard, curly 'tache and man bun, unzipping her portfolio and passing the paintings to him. This was as nerve-racking as her interview to get into Goldsmiths; Jonathan Finch was perusing her work slowly.

'Suishnish Bay from Hermit's Point?' he asked.

Heather nodded.

'This is the Isle of Tara from Kirklochy Beach,' she explained, as he turned to the next painting.

'I like this very much,' said Jonathan, his whispery voice becoming even more sincere, referring to a watercolour of fishing boats in Kirklochy Harbour at sunset.

'And this,' he added, turning to a painting of two puffins on Keel Island.

Finally he looked up and smiled.

'Yes, you're in,' he said.

Heather decided that Jonathan Finch was actually rather nice.

'I can't believe he liked my paintings,' she said, almost skipping as they walked towards the art shop, where she would get her work framed.

'Heather: you're very good. You just have to believe it.'

The framer's was down Marine Terrace, a narrow lane off the main road. They walked past the inevitable outdoor pursuits store, and Heather stopped to browse in the window of a shop which sold Celtic jewellery and hand painted glazed pottery.

'I think we deserve a lovely lunch,' she said, as they came out of the art shop. Sean led her across the road to a seafood restaurant.

'This place is worth a whole galaxy of Michelin stars.'

Sitting at a corner table, they ate chowder followed by salmon with green beans and new potatoes and drank some white wine. Heather's blood zinged with warmth and well-being. Sean's phone rang.

'Yes, I'm having a good time. Are you having a good time?' By the tone of his voice, she knew he was talking to Katie, and she could hear her shrill voice on the other end of the line.

'Okay, I'll see you later,' said Sean, in valediction. 'Love you,' he added, and Heather liked that he spoke with sincerity and without self-consciousness.

'I'll be ruined,' he said, as he terminated the call.

'Cara's so good with Katie, isn't she?'

'She's amazing. She's done more than anyone to help her deal with Meg's death.'

It was the first time Megan's name had been mentioned between them.

'It must still hurt so much.'

'Sometimes,' said Sean slowly. 'Sometimes I feel normal and then it hits me again.'

'You don't mind me talking about it?'

'No – but I'd rather we could just hang out. It's hard being pitied all the time. I don't want what… happened to define me.'

Heather nodded. In the village, his and Katie's names were always prefixed by the word "poor", and they were seen as tragic. In London, they could have slipped away into soulless anonymity. She suppressed a shiver – it was truly chilling that Sean and his child's lives had been irrevocably damaged within a few minutes.

'So,' she said, 'if you did get hold of a crystal wand and you could vanish anything, what would you choose?'

'Apart from Hitler and Donald Trump?'

'Of course. I'm taking them as read. Room 101.'

Heather: the Northern Line, *Baby on Board* signs, facial hair but especially beards, People who Know About Wine, Doctor Who.

Sean: People Who Can Cook, The Hobbit, bottled water, the Scottish Tories, reality TV.

'Good call,' said Heather. A little giggly with the wine, she high-fived him.

'Yeah. If I wanted to watch boring people doing boring things I could just stay at home.'

Over coffee, though, she became more serious.

'I just fell into advertising,' she explained. 'But now I'm not sure if I want to spend the rest of my life trying to persuade people to buy things they don't need.'

Sean smiled. 'I guess I'm one of the few people who get up in the morning actually looking forward to starting work,' he said.

When they left, the afternoon was well advanced, and the sky an ominous dark grey. Heather collected her paintings from the framer.

Next time she was here, they'd be on display, she thought, in excitement.

They returned to the Arts Centre to deliver the paintings, then hurried up the road towards the station. The rain, never far away in the Highlands, had started, and they broke into a run. Heather stumbled, falling against him, and suddenly he was kissing her – or she was kissing him. She could hear the soft fall of the rain on the trees, smell the wet grass and his musky aftershave. She shouldn't be doing this, but she didn't seem to be able to stop. Her arms wrapped round his neck and pulled him closer, his hands were in her hair. They kissed on and on, while Heather tried to summon the will to push him away. She liked Cara, she was becoming a friend and anyway, it just wasn't her style. Absolutely not.

'Get a room,' called a hill walker, and the spell was broken. Heather at last pulled away.

'I can't do this,' she cried. 'What were you thinking of?'

She shook her head.

'What was *I* thinking of?' she added, more quietly.

'Heather –'

'I can't do this,' she said again. 'You're in love with someone else and so am I –'

There. She'd admitted it. She was still in love with Aidan. Mentally, she slapped herself – she could be the lead in a Hollywood rom-com.

'Heather,' yelled a voice. She spun round to see a shiny black four-by-four pull up, Euan hanging out of the window. 'Jump in,' he added.

They both climbed into the car and Rowan, who was driving, revved up and roared off.

'So, what brings you here?' asked Euan, turning round in his seat.

'I'm exhibiting some paintings at the Arts Centre,' Heather said. A few minutes ago, this had delighted her, but now the excitement was gone. She was so aware of Sean sitting beside her and she was determined not to touch any part of him. She kept her eyes firmly fixed on Rowan's shimmering mass of auburn hair. Even the knowledge, which had so enchanted her yesterday, that Rowan was suffering from an acute dose of cystitis, no doubt brought on by too much sex (hidden behind a rack of hair ornaments, she'd heard her discussing this with the pharmacist), failed to cheer her up.

'Fantastic. Well done. I'll have a look next time I'm there,' said Euan.

'Thanks,' Heather managed to mutter.

Fortunately, conversation was difficult, because Rowan had some kind of quadraphonic sound system and had cranked up her iPod to a volume which fell just short of blowing the windows out. How long had Rowan been there? What had she seen? Heather bit her thumbnail. She trusted Euan but wouldn't put it past Rowan to stir up trouble with Cara. Then again, Rowan hadn't taken the opportunity to throw her any knowing looks or make any smart comments, which she might well have done if she'd seen anything. Cautiously, Heather relaxed a little.

As the four-by-four powered along the single track road, she looked out at the rain-soaked and bedraggled countryside, still berating herself. How could she have kissed Cara's boyfriend? How could she? At last, Rowan swung round and drove down the hill into Kirklochy's main street.

'Rowan,' she improvised, 'could you drop me off at the shops, please? I've a couple of things to get.'

Rowan screeched to a halt, allowing Heather just enough time to slither down onto the pavement and slam the door shut before she roared off again.

Inside the village store, she threw chocolate croissants, the best ever comfort food, and a couple of trashy magazines into her basket and went up to the till to pay. Sandy was talking to Gregor in Gaelic, and she was so para that she was convinced they were talking about her.

Back at the cottage, Treeny was sitting in the living room with Mrs Gillies and Mrs Peden, all of them sipping tea out of china cups.

'He's influenced by some of the Manchester bands,' Mrs Peden was saying. 'Stone Roses, Inspiral Carpets, Happy Mondays, and Oasis, of course.'

'You've been spending altogether too much time with Craig, Mrs P,' Heather said, trying to sound normal.

'We were just talking about this Sheepstock festival thing,' Treeny explained.

'Oh, it'll be fab. Just like having Glasto or T in the Park on our own doorstep. It'll bring loads of tourists into the village. The pub, the B&B and the shops'll make a fortune –' She stopped dead as she realised that Treeny and Mrs Gillies were looking stonily at her.

'The village will be overrun with young people having orgies, drinking, taking drugs and I don't know what else,' said Mrs Gillies. Heather almost giggled at the old lady's primly Highland tone, but was quelled by her grim expression. 'That's to say nothing of loud music playing at all hours of the night.'

'I'm going to open my back door and sell real ale,' said Treeny. 'Make a packet.'

'Why stop there, Catriona?' asked Mrs Gillies. 'You could start a commune.'

'We're going out tonight, by the way,' Treeny went on.

'Where?' asked Heather. She wasn't aware there was anywhere to go out *to*.

'The village hall. The mobile cinema's there tonight. *Ladies in Lavender.*'

'Lovely film,' put in Mrs Peden.

You know you're in trouble when your great-aunt has a better social life than you do, reflected Heather, as she ran a bath later. But she was glad to get some privacy. Sometimes Treeny saw too much and knew too much.

⤸

'Well, I never, Muriel, what *is* her poor mother going to say?'

Heather slid past Mrs Crombie and a group of her cronies, who were standing by the frozen food cabinets, wondering vaguely whom they were discussing. She paid for her wine, class in a glass at £3.99, and walked the short distance to the small, untidy flat above the chandler's that Euan shared with his brother.

'Hi, Cal.'

He looked taken aback as she leaned up and kissed him on the cheek.

'Sorry: I forgot air kissing wasn't the done thing here.'

'You won't get any complaints from me,' said Callum, with easy gallantry.

Following him down the hall and into the front room, which took all of a couple of strides, she was relieved to note that neither Rowan nor Sean seemed to be here tonight.

'Hi, Heather.' Misty patted the sofa beside her and Duncan and she sank down on it gratefully. She was touched to have been included in this get-together, feeling that she'd been welcomed back into the fold – other than Cara, the "crowd" had all been at boarding school together, Kirklochy being too small and remote to have a local high school. Cara and Sascha also greeted her warmly, and her heart eased slightly – Rowan didn't seem to have said anything to Cara about herself and Sean, although that didn't stop her from feeling terribly guilty.

She was wearing tight, sexy low-rise jeans with a bright blue halter-neck top. When she'd looked in the mirror earlier, she'd been pleased to see that her shoulders and arms were sun kissed and her strip of midriff slim and tanned.

'What would you like to drink?' asked Callum, taking Heather's bottle of red and heading for the kitchen with it.

'A cosmopolitan,' cried Sascha, who was obsessed with *Sex and the City*. Heather glanced at her. Her hair, which had last week been an aubergine bob, was now short with a longer fringe and dyed metallic silver.

'I'll have a Screaming Viking,' Heather called.

'Do you want the cucumber bruised or unbruised?' said Euan at once.

'Bruised,' giggled Heather, high fiving him. 'Cheers.'

'The choice is Stella, Stella, Stella or wine,' said Callum.

'I think I'll have –' Heather pretended to consider. 'Stella.'

She sat back on the grotty, but comfortable, sofa, sipping her beer as the banter crackled back and forward. Euan, who boasted that he never, but never, cooked, later went out for fish suppers. Heather tucked into hers with relish, licking her fingers, the newspaper soggy with vinegar. Again, she reflected that the fish and chips here were inordinately delicious.

After they'd eaten, Gregor put on *SexyBack* by his idol, Justin Timberlake, and everyone watched in admiration as he danced and spun across the laminate flooring. Then he pushed back an imaginary hat and recreated Michael Jackson's iconic Billie Jean dance, complete with moonwalk.

Despite having downed several beers by now, the other men were too inhibited to join in, but Heather and Sascha dragged themselves out of the sofa and were soon helpless with laughter as Gregor – who made it seem so easy – tried unsuccessfully to teach them to backslide.

Later still, as inevitably happens when a few people are met together and one of them plays guitar, however badly, they had a sing song.

'Caledonia?' said Euan to Gregor, after Callum, whose guitar it was, had exhausted Ed Sheeran's greatest hits. Gregor nodded. He had a beautiful tenor voice and began to sing what was obviously his party piece. It was such a moving song that Heather felt tears well up in her eyes, and was glad of the subdued lighting. In some ways, she did feel as if she'd come home. She looked round at her old friends – Misty and Sascha were swaying in time to the music while Cara wiped a tear from her eye. Guilt and shame swept over her again as she remembered the kiss and, worse still, the fact that she'd enjoyed it so much. What on earth had Sean been playing at? And she was just as bad. How could she cheat with another woman's boyfriend, especially when she'd been cheated on herself and knew how much it hurt? She'd just have to put it behind her and hope that Cara never found out.

The evening began to wind slowly down into the small hours. Heather found herself sitting next to Euan on the sofa, sipping coffee, the constant, restful sound of the dark waves washing onto the shore in the background, the stars bright in the sky. Again, she felt sadness creeping over her, wishing that Aidan was with her to enjoy it. She'd always wanted to show him around her second home, point out all the places which had been special to her as she grew up, share it all with him, watch him spellbound at the beauty of it all. As if he sensed how desolate she felt, Euan turned to her with a smile and touched her arm.

'Having a good time?'

'Lovely. Thanks so much for inviting me.'

'You're welcome,' Euan said, still smiling. She felt a wave of warmth for her old friend, for caring, for looking out for her. She gave him an extra tight hug as they all stood in the hall, saying goodnight. Euan was so lovely. But why was he with Poison Ivy – horrible Rowan? Love, she thought, as Callum helped her into her jacket. She was well out of it.

8. *The Secret of My Success*

A few days later, Heather fetched oars and rowlocks from the garden shed, filled Treeny's rowing boat with a travelling rug, food and a flask, and set off for Jamie's Cove. She remembered her brother's excitement when he'd discovered the small strip of beach. It was only accessible either by sailing along the Minch or by scrambling down a steep rock face thick with thistle and gorse, and, in all her visits there, Heather had never encountered anyone not invited by her family. In their early teens, she, Jamie and Kirsty had paddled in the sea, investigated rock pools, thrown a frisbee to each other and eaten their picnics in the shelter of a long outcrop of rock. Once they'd even seen some seal pups. Kirsty had collected shells, the colour and shape of which still influenced her designs. In later years, along with the crowd of local teenagers they'd befriended, they'd have a party every evening that weather permitted, barbecuing their food, laughing, talking, flirting, drinking and watching the sunset reflected on the water.

It was a warm day and Heather sweated in her Wellingtons and life jacket as she rowed along the coast. Passing the tiny island of Keel, she paused, crossing the oars and examining through her field glasses four puffins perched on a rock, one with some fish dangling from his beak. Grabbing her iPhone, she took several shots of the birds, which would form the basis of another painting.

Before very long, she was dragging the rowing boat up onto the beach, the water lapping gently around her boots. It would be some time before the tide came in and she was going to have some quality time to herself before returning to London. The cove was the only place in Kirklochy where she was confident she could get some privacy.

She paced about for a while, her hands in her jeans' pockets. She felt so let down by Sean – really, he was no better than Aidan. She paused, gazing out at the horizon, the familiar stab of pain hitting her as she thought again about her ex-boyfriend. Had she been second best? Had he been secretly longing for Savannah all the time they'd been together? Had Savannah clicked her fingers and he fallen back into her arms as soon as she returned from Singapore? Heather closed her eyes tightly, trying to block out the picture in her mind which kept taunting her of the two of them together, locked in each other's arms, kissing passionately. The loud shriek of a gull broke the spell.

Yesterday evening, she'd had to go to the village hall to work on the scenery for Brigadoon. Afterwards, she and Sean had silently washed their brushes in the tiny kitchen. It had felt claustrophobic to be standing next to him.

'Heather, I wanted to talk to you about ... the weekend. I need you to know it wasn't just –'

'Well, I *don't* want to talk about it,' Heather snapped. 'It was a mistake and we should just forget about it.'

Sean reached out and took her hand and she snatched it away, trying to ignore the electricity of his touch.

'I can explain if you'll just give me the chance –'

I can explain. Where had she heard that before? If only he knew, those few words were guaranteed to wind her up all the more.

'I don't want to hear it.' She cast around for a way to convince him. 'Anyway, I told you, I'm in love with someone else.'

'What's going on?' came a voice from the door. 'Valissa wants to lock up.'

Heather jumped. Rowan Galloway was leaning on the door-frame. In ancient, faded purple cut-off jeans and a washed out grey tee-shirt with a rip in the shoulder, she was an anthem to "I could look good in a bin liner". A smile crossed her face. Impossibly restless, terribly spoiled, she was always looking for the next distraction.

'You're not getting it on with *Essex Girl*, are you?' she asked.

'That's none of your business, Rowan, now please *go away*,' said Sean, quiet but deadly.

'*Woooh*,' said Rowan, but, surprisingly, she turned and sauntered off down the hall.

'What's going on? Valissa wants to lock up,' said Gregor, sashaying into the room in pink camouflage trousers. Heather ran her hand through her hair in despair. What a place! It was like perpetually living in the *Big Brother* house.

'Nothing,' she said firmly. 'We were just about to leave.'

She followed Gregor out into the light, drizzly night.

'The pub?' he suggested. 'There's a G & T waiting with my name on it.'

'No, thanks,' said Sean, and set off in the opposite direction. Heather and Gregor hurried through the light rain over to the Claymore, and, a few minutes later, were sitting cosily in a corner near the fire, sipping their drinks. Gregor wanted to talk about his new boyfriend.

'So, where did you meet him?' asked Heather, reflecting that there wasn't exactly a thriving gay and lesbian scene in Kirklochy.

'On the internet,' admitted Gregor, twisting his thumb ring. 'But I went to Inverness to meet him at the weekend, and he's every bit as gorgeous as his photo. *Unlike* this other guy I met... there must have been mucho airbrushing going on there. More the pits than Brad Pitt in the flesh.'

As Gregor went on talking, Heather cheered up, helped by his inane conversation and the alcohol. This reminded her so much of those nights after work when she and the girls would sit and chat in their local prior to going clubbing. Analysis of current relationships was always high on the conversational agenda. Then, as now, Heather hadn't contributed much, as she was happily in love with Aidan, but she'd always enjoyed hearing about her friends' latest crushes and their strategies to hook their men. She'd always been ready to listen and give out hugs when one of the gang got dumped. Thinking about that now, she bit her lip. She must've been unbearable, and she hadn't realised how much it hurt until Aidan had broken off with her.

'And, I can exclusively reveal –' Gregor was now saying. 'Or, maybe not *so* exclusively,' he added, 'that Rowan Galloway is a terrible kisser. *Terr-ible.* I swear, it's like making out with a dead cod.'

'For that, you deserve another drink,' said Heather, getting up to go to the bar. At this moment in time, she felt that Gregor was the only man she could trust.

⤺

There was a squall overhead – a chorus of seagulls, but otherwise it was quiet here in Jamie's Cove, ideal for doing some thinking. Relishing the solitude, Heather folded her waterproof jacket and sat down on it in the shelter of a rock. She put on her headphones and switched on her iPod, gazing thoughtfully across the glittering water to the horizon.

Later, feeling stronger and somewhat refreshed from the time spent in her own company, she headed for the Claymore. The first people she saw as she walked to the bar were Euan and Rowan, sitting on a banquette, clasping hands and with their foreheads touching. They didn't notice her pass; they were too engrossed in each other. Rowan's hair looked as if it hadn't even been combed, cascading down her back like autumn leaves down a branch, and she managed to look stunning nonetheless.

She ordered a glass of red and sat by the fire, sipping and thinking about her life in London. Rain began to spatter against the window and, as cosy as it was in her little nook, she felt a shiver of unease about tomorrow. She was bound to see Aidan again. What if she lost control and burst into tears right in front of everyone? She gulped down the last of her wine and stood up, slipping on her oilskin.

'Hey, Heather,' said Euan, who was passing on his way to buy another round. 'Didn't see you hiding in the corner. You going?'

She nodded.

'Yeah. I'm flying to London early in the morning and I've still a few things to sort out.'

'Right.' Euan's expression was serious. He reached out and pushed back the hair from her face. 'Are you okay with this? I mean, it's going to be hard seeing your ex.'

She nodded again.

'Yeah, but I've got no choice, and I suppose I'd have had to face him sometime.' She tried a smile. 'I'll be back before you know it.'

She turned her head slightly, aware of eyes boring into her; Rowan had fixed her with an icy stare.

'Euan,' she murmured, touching his arm. 'Rowan's waiting for you.'

Euan continued looking at her.

'Well, good luck and, listen, phone me if you need a chat, whatever time, okay?'

Her face broke into a smile – it would be so good to hear his cheery voice if she was feeling low.

'I will.'

'When do you get back?'

'Late Monday.'

'Okay – debriefing in here, Tuesday night, 20.00 hours precisely.'

He touched her cheek briefly, then turned away and carried on on his way to the bar.

⟟

The next day, after taking the coach to Inverness, then flying to Luton, she unclipped her seat belt and lifted her laptop case out of the overhead locker.

'Thank you for travelling with Albatross Airlines,' said the stewardess, whose make-up, in common with that of the rest of the cabin crew, seemed to have come courtesy of Pollyfilla – masses of blue eyeshadow, pink lipstick and thick peach foundation which ended in a line halfway down her neck.

Heather began to descend the stairs, her hair flapping in the wind, the rail cold under her hand. She looked out at the expanse of grey concrete on all sides. The sky was like a bad mood.

Inside the terminal, she passed a crowd of tanned holidaymakers clutching duty free bags, straw hats and stuffed donkeys.

She didn't have to wait to retrieve any luggage – she'd only brought her laptop with her. All her London clothes were still at the flat in Bayswater – she had no need for power suits, killer heels, designer handbags and little black dresses in Kirklochy.

Before she'd moved to Scotland, she'd put all her possessions into the tiny windowless box room in the flat, in which there was an ancient sofa-bed, and sublet her bedroom to a student cousin of Ben's.

She sat on the train, suburban gardens scrolling past. The smell of vinegar drifting over from the McDonald's meal of the hoodie opposite tickled her nose. Her stomach rumbled. Albatross was a budget airline which didn't run to refreshments and she'd eaten nothing since a plasticky cheeseburger at Inverness Airport.

Later, she stepped from the windy station platform onto the underground train, the doors whooshing shut and enclosing her, reducing the known world to a dirty black tunnel. She'd forgotten how claustrophobic it was. She stood, swaying like an exotic plant, trapped between a grey suit with empty eyes and a bearded backpacker, smelling garlic breath and perfume, hemmed in by a wall of unfolded broadsheets. As the train rattled along, she imagined what the flat would now be like after several weeks of two Walker boys cohabiting unsupervised. With every stop, her imagination became more lurid – the fridge would now be purely a receptacle for cooling beer, the coffee table would be all but buried under back copies of *NME* and *FHM*, there would be Betty Blue and Nirvana posters in the bathroom, there would be dirty plates in the kitchen, muddy football kit in the bedrooms. In short the scene would be similar to that in Ben's *Men Behaving Badly* DVD box set.

Soon she was walking down Prestwick Street towards her flat. Outside The Grapes, a group of young people, obviously released from the office for the day, were drinking beer and enjoying the few brave rays of sun which had penetrated the cloud. An endless parade of black taxis and red double decker buses streamed by out on the main road. A dispatch rider roared past, in counterpoint to the scream of an ambulance. She breathed in, almost tasting the fumes. The aroma of coffee drifted out of Starbucks. A rasta mooched by, dreads piled under an enormous tam – she could just make out a reggae beat coming from his iPod.

In the hallway, there was a menu for the Bombay Ruby and a leaflet advertising an Albanian taxi firm, as well as two letters for herself. Heather pocketed those and went upstairs.

The flat was quiet as she closed the door softly behind her, her trainers sinking blissfully into the pile of the carpet. Dropping her laptop and jacket on the sofa-bed, she went into the living room. A young man emerged from the kitchen.

'Hi.' He smiled shyly. 'I'm Paul, Ben's cousin. And you must be

Heather. At least, I hope so.'

He gave a nervous laugh. With his fair hair and old-fashioned glasses, he looked like the Milky Bar Kid, all grown up. A techie, a Trekkie, with a mental age of forty five, she guessed. The kind of boy who could make a fair stab at answering the question: what is the purpose of wasps? Or: why is the sky blue?

'Nice to meet you,' said Heather.

They shook hands.

'Ben'll be back in a minute; he's gone to the Ruby for a takeaway. I'll just warm the plates.' Paul ducked back into the kitchen.

Heather looked around. The flat was amazingly tidy. The CDs and DVDs were arranged in alpha order, every surface was clean and shining, and the carpet was determinedly hoovered – she hadn't realised before that it was patterned. Paul would make a far better wife for Ben than she would.

She sank down on the sofa, closing her eyes, but opened them moments later when Ben burst into the room, a delicious, spicy smell of curry mingling with the synthetic scent of Shake 'n' Vac – Alpine Forest, if she wasn't mistaken.

'Heather,' he cried. 'You made it.'

'Yeah.' She smiled. 'Just a bit jet-lagged.'

Paul reappeared, wearing oven gloves, and minutes later they were sitting at the table, feasting on korma, patia, naan bread and poppadoms.

After gossip about friends, family and work was exhausted, a wary look crossed Ben's face and he began to speak hesitantly:

'I saw Aidan Whatsit... Murphy the other day.'

Heather froze in the act of breaking off another piece of poppadom. Familiar surroundings, the boys' undemanding company, a bottle of beer and a full stomach had all worked their magic and she'd felt relaxed and happy. Until Aidan's name was mentioned.

'Where?' Her voice came out low and faint.

'Camden Market. He was asking for you.'

In spite of herself, Heather felt a spark of excitement at the thought that she'd been on Aidan's mind. When they'd been together, they'd spent many happy hours at Camden Lock, walking hand-in-hand along the canal tow path, browsing leisurely around the stalls, sipping beer outside the Ice Wharf as the water lapped below.

'Was he with his girlfriend?' Her voice came out as if her mouth were full of cotton wool.

'Yes,' said Ben, serious for once, his voice soft. Out of respect for her feelings, she presumed, he didn't comment on how "hot" Savannah was.

'Did they look all loved-up?' Heather was torturing herself now.

Ben took her hand, his expression still sombre.

'Heather, don't do this. Listen. I've got your fave ice cream. Chunky Monkey.'

Heather shook her head. Ben looked concerned: she'd never refused a bowl of Ben & Jerry's in her life. She shuffled off to bed. Despite the fact that she'd felt exhausted when she'd arrived back at the flat, now she couldn't sleep. She lay on the lumpy sofa-bed, looking up at the arcs of light crossing the ceiling as traffic passed in the street below. It was clear from Ben's shifty looks that Aidan and Savannah were madly in love. Heather had only ever had a brief glimpse of her, but, from an old photo pinned casually to the corkboard in Aidan's kitchen, she knew her to possess the dark, sultry beauty of a young Demi Moore. As if that wasn't enough, in her fevered mind Aidan's girlfriend combined the style of Kate Moss with the business acumen of Karren Brady and the wit of Sarah Millican. She imagined the two of them drifting along the canal tow path as she had Aidan had done, holding hands and stopping now and again to kiss, or standing on Primrose Hill, looking out at London spread before them. Perhaps she'd just been a substitute as Aidan hankered after the one true love of his life. Heather began to cry softly then, so as Ben and Paul wouldn't hear, the tears sliding down the side of her face to seep into her pillow. That meant that Aidan hadn't truly loved her: it had all been a sham.

⌐

She finally dozed off in the early morning, meaning that she'd only had about two hours' sleep. It took all her skill in applying her makeup to cover her tired and grey skin, but eventually all that showed on her face of last night's grief was a slight puffiness around her eyes. She studied her reflection in the bathroom mirror. She saw a slim, tallish woman, dressed in a tailored willow green trouser suit, with discreet gold jewellery, her hair neatly twisted into a tortoiseshell clasp. Slipping her feet into her high-heeled pumps and picking up her laptop, she must look the epitome of smart professionalism.

After a lengthy delay at Goodge Street where a suspicious package had been found, she walked towards Bright Sparks House, wishing she could run away and go back to the haven of her flat. She remembered how, at one time, she'd practically skipped towards the office every morning because she'd see Aidan there.

⁔

After her first ever weekend with Aidan, she'd hurried from the tube to the office, for the first time in living memory looking forward to Monday. She'd walked out of the revolving doors and into the impressive marble floored hall of Bright Sparks House, which was big enough for a game of basketball. She'd headed with a crowd of other people towards the lifts. Aidan, looking totally different than he had on Saturday, in a business suit, walked towards her, accompanied by Mike Bright. He gave her a smile and a barely perceptible wink and walked on. It was exciting to think that no one else in the firm knew, except, of course, for Matilda and Lucie. She'd confided in them both the previous day, over a long, lazy brunch in Caffe Lucia. She and Aidan absolutely hadn't wanted to be the subject of talk around the water coolers.

Bright Sparks was rife with gossip about the chocolate launch party: how J-Lo, determined not to be upstaged by the exquisite Chloé Marsden, had turned up more than two hours late, brazenly ignoring the all-white rule in a backless mini-dress of an outrageously bright scarlet, guaranteed to grab everyone's attention; how Chantelle, the office junior, had ended up in A & E; how Dave Sparks and Alex Day, who had long been suspected of having an affair, had been overheard having a blazing row on deck; how Mike Bright's wife had got drunk and nearly fallen overboard.

'It was a great night,' said Lucie, unwrapping a salad roll.

'You think, do you?' said Matilda, who was wearing aviator sunglasses. 'It'll be all around the mailroom by now.'

'Everybody'll have forgotten about it in a couple of days,' Heather soothed.

'No, they won't,' hissed Matilda. 'People keep looking at me.'

'Maybe that's because you're wearing sunglasses indoors.'

Matilda was mortally embarrassed because, carried away by the moonlight and a good few too many White Ladies, she'd kissed Dane, a spotty nineteen year old from the mail-room, who had a Burberry baseball cap and wore more gold jewellery than a crack dealer, all the way home on the night bus to Barking.

'Hi, girls,' said J-Lo, appearing by their table.

'Hi, Jessi,' they chorused.

'Mind if I sit down?' said J-Lo. Without waiting for an answer, she pulled out a chair, set down her tray, and began delicately picking at a green salad and sipping from a glass of sparking water, exuding great wafts of Allure.

'Great night on Friday, wasn't it?' she said. Matilda groaned. 'So embarrassing,' J-Lo went on. 'I completely forgot the dress code was all white.'

Complacently, she tossed her hair back over her tanned shoulders. What time must she have got up this morning to look like this, Heather wondered. Her dark hair, streaked with bronze, was set into curls which rippled down her back. Her tan was set off by a cream dress, accessorised with scarlet sandals with killer heels, her toenails also painted a sexy fire engine red.

'So did Heather,' said Lucie.

'Really?' said J-Lo, turning her huge brown eyes on Heather. 'I didn't see you there.'

'I had to leave early,' said Heather. She absolutely didn't want to tell J-Lo about herself and Aidan. 'I didn't feel so good. I was...sea sick.'

'Sea sick?' J-Lo sounded slightly surprised, but was intent on reliving Friday evening. The others listened as her voice ran on, punctuated by her bewitching husky giggle. No one would ever guess she came from Dagenham. Gradually, Heather tuned out, remembering her Saturday with Aidan.

↬

Heart thumping, she walked up the stairs, the wide glass doors opening automatically, and across the foyer, her high heels clacking on the marble floor. She nodded to the receptionist and then stepped into the lift, which powered smoothly up to the tenth floor, feeling relief that she hadn't yet run into Aidan. She walked into the meeting room with some trepidation, after so long away. The room boasted a view of the BT tower and the bustling central London streets. It was large with a shiny white laminate floor and teal feature wall. The rest of her team was sitting round the square perspex table, on stylishly uncomfortable bright purple chairs.

'...right in the heart of the Cotswolds. It's got a spa. I've already booked my treatments – seaweed wrap and hot stone massage,' Rachel was saying.

Whatever, thought Heather – she found herself thinking she'd rather walk through the pine forest behind Sean's cottage, where the air was clear as crystal, or swim in the freezing salty water of Kirklochy Bay.

'Heather,' cried Sarah, noticing her standing there.

'Hi, guys.'

'Where is it you've been staying?' said Rachel. 'I heard it was Nowheresville, the Back End of Beyond.'

'It is,' agreed Heather. 'That's what I like about it.'

'I quite fancy it, actually,' mused Sarah.

I know, thought Heather, *you'd like to opt out of the rat race and enjoy a better quality of life.*

'I'd like to opt out of the rat race and enjoy a better quality of life,' explained Sarah.

'You look well, Heather,' said Suzie Lock, her boss, sweeping into the room. She took a seat at the head of the table. Heather did feel that she looked healthy – her skin, dusted with freckles, was as clear and brown as barley sugar. She used to straighten her hair ruthlessly into submission and use so much product that it was practically toxic, but nowadays it was much thicker and shinier since she'd let it revert to its natural waves and colour. However, she knew that the lean and hungry Suzie meant that she looked fat, but in this all-female gathering it was virtually against the law to say so.

'Thank you.'

A brainstorming session then took place, where they all discussed USPs, and positive and negative product qualities, ending in a weighty discussion about how to make a well-known brand of support tights a "must-have".

'See it as a challenge,' said Suzie, as Heather had known she would. 'Okay, guys, well done, inspirational, it's a wrap.'

Heather closed her laptop and stood up, remembering the game that she and Aidan used to play at meetings, when they'd each make up a word and use it as often as they dared, scoring a point for every time they dropped it into the discussion without anyone asking what it meant. Aidan, she remembered with a pang, had been marginally in the lead, 927 to Heather's 924 points.

She walked down the corridor, sunlight flooding in the skylight windows. Suddenly, a door opened and Aidan came out, accompanied by two other men. Her heart practically shot right out of her mouth and she was shaking. He looked beautiful. He'd had his hair cut and this served to accentuate the lean line of his jaw and heighten the deep blue of his eyes. She just couldn't face him right now. He hadn't seen her; she was shielded by Suzie, who was walking in front of her. Her boss, who was in her late forties and was an eighties' throw-back, provided good cover, having the widest shoulder pads seen outside an American football game, and hair so big that it must need planning consent. Heather cowered behind her for a moment, then opened the nearest door and stepped inside.

Dave Sparks, in an immaculate aubergine pinstriped suit, was pacing up and down the carpet, remote in hand, mid PowerPoint presentation. Around the long, polished table sat several more suits, laptops and bottles of Perrier in front of them. Next to the seat vacated by Dave was Gianni di Giacomo, head of exclusive menswear label *Zoot!*, camply handsome and Italian, dressed in a patterned suit which looked like it had been made up from a pair of bedroom curtains Treeny once had.

'Heather, can I help you?' asked Dave, ice in his voice. She'd realised by now that she'd stumbled into his latest big pitch. *Zoot!*, she'd read in *Campaign,* was branching out into aftershave, and he hoped to land the account.

'Hi, Dave,' she improvised. 'I was in town and I thought I'd just look in and say hello.'

'Hello,' said Dave flatly. Then he rallied, smiling round at the assembled suits. 'I like to think of all my staff as being part of the Bright Sparks *family*,' he said. 'It's more than just a business.'

Dave Sparks, so smooth you could skate on him, was an expert at, as he put it himself, turning a problem into an opportunity.

'I'll just... be off then,' Heather faltered, groping for the door handle. Back out in the corridor, she saw Aidan and the other two men had paused by the water cooler. Quickly she ducked behind a conveniently placed cheese plant, flattening her back against the wall, her green suit an excellent camouflage. After what seemed the longest time but was probably only a minute or so, Aidan got into the lift and she watched the doors close behind him. She breathed a sigh of relief. This was like a scene straight out of *The Secret of My Success*, one of her favourites from the Golden Era of Film – the eighties. She was still shaking. A door banged behind her – there was another conference room there.

'Hev, what on *earth* are you doing?'

She jumped, turning round to see J-Lo standing there, looking like a Bond girl in a tightly fitted black suit, pointy toe shoes and a Wonderbra, just a hint of lace peeping out from between her lapels.

'Hey, Jessi.'

J-Lo was still looking at her in astonishment, but she'd thought of a brilliant distraction.

'Nice suit, Jess. *New Look*, isn't it?'

'It's Prada, actually,' said J-Lo. 'Justin bought it for me.'

'Good taste. I'm meeting Matilda and Lucie for lunch. Do you want to come?'

No way was J-Lo a girl's girl, Heather knew, and for a moment she was touched by the way her face brightened at the invitation.

Ten minutes later, she was pushing open the door of the Coffee Bean, breathing in the delicious smells of chilli and garlic.

Her friends were sitting at a table by the window, both deeply tanned from sunbathing in the park at every spare moment.

'Guess what?' said Matilda, when they were huddled round the rather small table, sharing a huge platter of nachos. 'I'm coming to

Scotland to visit you.'

'When?' said Heather.

'When I can get the time off,' said Matilda.

'I'd love you to visit me, Tills, you know I would,' Heather said. Invasion of the Essex Girl *would* be brilliant fun. 'But, I told you, Kirklochy's a very small place –'

'Smaller than Clacton?' said Matilda.

'*Much* smaller than Clacton,' confirmed Heather. 'We don't have a branch of Harvey Nicks up there. Or Top Shop. You can't just nip out for a McDonald's –'

'But you do have Scottish men,' said Matilda, her eyes lighting up. She had a long-term crush on James McAvoy, and had also been unduly influenced by the hunky, kilted, caber tossing would-be Scots who'd starred in a recent Bright Sparks commercial for beefburgers.

'Yes, Tills, I give you that. There will be some Scottish men.'

'Hotties?'

'Yeah, one or two, I guess.' Sean, of course, with his thick, dark hair and silvery eyes, she thought – but so not available. Then her heart warmed as Euan's face popped into her mind, tanned from so much time spent outdoors, his rich brown hair windblown, his laughing, deep-set brown eyes never leaving her face as they chatted. Her lovely friend: she wished he were here now.

'Then what are we waiting for?' said Matilda.

'Try to get time off at the beginning of August. There's this big music festival, like T in the Park, the first weekend,' said Heather, with sudden inspiration.

'I'm there,' promised Matilda.

After lunch, as she was freshening her make-up in the loo, Heather's phone buzzed with a text: *Hey, how r u getting on? Hope all OK. Will call u 2nite, E x*

She was humming as she dashed off a reply. Spending time with her girls, looking forward to talking to Euan tonight, had made her feel much, much better – so much that she thought she could cope with facing Aidan.

⌐

'We're going to have such a brilliant night,' said Lucie, as the girls sat over Saturday lunch at Camden Lock, resting from a morning's shopping. Matilda and Lucie were eating mounds of fragrant saffron coloured paella, while Heather had chosen a deliciously spicy jerk chicken wrap, a delicacy she would never have been able to enjoy in Kirklochy. She ate with relish as the Regent's Canal lapped below. In Monsoon, after her exile in the land of waterproof trousers, tweeds and Aran knits, she had suffered a touch of vertigo as she perused the new autumn fashions, all silk and velvet and jewel colours.

'We're only on the guest list for Ice,' cut in Matilda. 'Wiiiith... DJ Scooby.'

Heather knew about Ice, a new and achingly hip club in the West End, from her reading of the celebrity magazines which proliferated in Sascha's salon. *Big Brother* contestants and minimally dressed glamour models were forever being papped staggering, much the worse for wear, from door to taxi. Ideally, underwear would be on display. Even more ideally, no underwear would be on display. Rumour had it that it was easier to get into the Diplomatic Corps than to get into Ice.

'How did you manage that?'

'Justin. J-Lo's new boyfriend. He did the PR.'

After a pleasant couple of hours browsing among delicate jewellery, Indian bedspreads, cushions embroidered with mirrors, handmade soap, retro clothes, second hand books, vinyl records and a million cheap, sloganed tee-shirts, the girls, loaded down with bags, headed for home.

～

The sun was shining with a pale, late afternoon light as Heather walked down Prestwick Street to her flat. The Grapes, festooned with hanging baskets frothing with yellow and purple flowers, looked welcoming so she went inside, weaving her way through packed tables to the bar. She ordered a gin and tonic and took it outside; she'd noticed a couple vacating a table as she went in and it was still free. As she sat down, her phone began to ring.

'Hi, Euan.' She could feel a big smile spreading across her face.

She settled comfortably in her seat and took a sip of her deliciously cold drink, warm against the back of her throat.

'Hi, how's it going? Have you seen your ex?' In the background, she could hear birdsong and the rush of the waves.

'Yup. Yesterday.' She took another belt of her drink.

'You all right?' She could hear the concern in his voice.

'I'm –' Weird. The stab of pain which always accompanied thoughts of Aidan didn't come; it had faded to a slight ache. It must be down to the alcohol. 'Yeah,' she said cautiously. 'I'm good.'

She heard seagulls shrieking at Euan's end.

'Where are you?'

'I'm sitting on the seawall, eating chips with gulls dive bombing all around me.'

'You're lucky,' she found herself saying. Then she told him all about seeing Aidan, ducking behind the cheese plant, gate crashing Dave Sparks' presentation and J-Lo's bewildered expression. Euan was laughing. She loved his uninhibited laughter, the way he threw his head back.

'Good grief. It's like something out of *Friends*.'

That led them on to a discussion about their favourite ever episodes.

'The one where Rachel gets a job in Bloomingdale's and Ross feels threatened by her new colleague,' Heather said. 'So he sends so many love tokens she doesn't have room for them on her desk.'

'Then a barber's shop quintet shows up,' Euan said.

They both laughed. The young waiter had come out of the bar to clear some glasses so Heather ordered another drink. As she sipped it, feeling the warmth spread inside her, Euan filled her in on gossip about Sheepstock and the bands he was most looking forward to seeing.

'I can't wait,' Heather said, and she realised that she really meant it. 'Ooh, and my best friend Matilda's coming too. All the guys are going to love her –'

'Euan.' Heather heard Rowan's voice in the background.

'Listen, Heather, I have to go,' Euan said. 'We're going to a gig. See you in a couple of days.'

'Yeah, see you. Bye, Euan.'

Letting out a little sigh, she slipped her phone back into her bag. Glancing at her watch, she realised that she and Euan had been talking for nearly an hour.

⌒

At eleven o'clock, the three girls climbed out of a taxi into the bustling streets of Soho. The queue outside Ice stretched down the street and round the corner. The door, matt black, was surprisingly discreet.

Heather and Lucie followed Matilda as she swept up to the forbidding looking bouncer and had an intense conversation with him.

'What does he want, a password?' whispered Heather. Lucie giggled, but, just then, the bouncer nodded curtly, just once, and they were admitted entry to the hallowed portals.

The inner sanctum was behind a silver door. Matilda pushed it open.

'Ooh, I've just seen Ryan Wright go into the VIP lounge,' she said, as they were swallowed up into a sweating sea of bobbing heads. Footballers were obviously royalty here, beautiful young girls throwing themselves at them, desperate to become WAGS, inspired by the likes of Coleen Rooney and Alex Gerrard. Heather thought they set the Women's Movement back a hundred years.

DJ Scooby stood on a podium, scratching, mixing and rapping.

Suddenly, it was three in the morning. Heather weaved her way to the bathroom, passing Matilda, who was engaged in a marathon snogging session with Dane from the mailroom, whom she steadfastly refused to acknowledge as her boyfriend, and Lucie, who was sitting with another guy on one of the low black leather sofas, their heads close together.

Inside all was black marble and silver, with ornate mirrors around the walls. Heather looked at her multiple reflections, dressed in her can't-go-wrong dress: black, short, slinky, sweetheart neckline. A girl with metallic hair and razor sharp cheekbones came out of one of the cubicles, her nose dusted in white powder. She looked at herself in the mirror and buffed it off.

Desperate for some air, Heather opened a side door and stepped outside into a narrow alley. She took deep breaths of the pollution and the sickly sweet stench of garbage. A shout rang out, followed by the screech of a siren and what sounded like a gunshot. She'd either have to walk home in her gorgeous, but crippling, red high heels, wait about seven hours for a taxi, or brave the night bus. In Kirklochy, she'd be strolling up the hill to Treeny's under the stars, listening to the soft swell of the sea and breathing in the fresh, tangy air.

9. *White Lace and Promises*

Heather disembarked from the train at East Croydon Station and jumped on a bus that would take her home – as in, her parents' house. It was a sunny day and her street looked its usual summer self, neat lawns bordered by red and yellow blooms, hydrangeas in every shade of blue, pink, wine and purple, clematis climbing the white-washed walls.

'Hi, Heather,' called Steve from number 26, who was polishing his car. 'Hear you've been living in Kirklochy?'

'You've heard of it?' said Heather, pausing by his gate.

'Oh, yeah,' said Steve. 'When I was at Bristol Uni me and some of the lads went hill walking in the Highlands. Ben Lochy was one of the first Munros I ever did. We stayed the night at Crappa Bothy. Stunning around there. Really peaceful.'

'Certainly is,' agreed Heather. Steve carried on talking about the blue mountains, the night sky, the sunsets, the wonderful seafood and the malt whisky.

'Quite envy you, actually. The missus and I've always fancied dropping out of the rat race to enjoy a better quality of life.'

She bid Steve goodnight and carried on down the street. The weather had brought the neighbours out and Mrs Copper from number 30, her fleecy half on, was dragging a beautiful, golden haired child towards her Volvo, while the girl's equally angelic looking twin sister tore round the front garden, demolishing most of a flower bed.

'Callista! Cassidy! Get in the car!' she screeched. Ever since Heather had known her, Mrs Copper had been teetering on the verge of a nervous breakdown.

She stopped to greet Mrs Bacon from next door, who was trimming her hedge. She'd known Mrs B, a sweet elderly widow, all her life. She'd always seemed old, and, consequently, never seemed to age.

Then she was putting her key in the lock of her childhood home, and stepping into the hall, with its familiar smell of vanilla furniture polish. A bowl of cream roses sat on the hall table.

Although there were two other rooms downstairs, the family always hung out in the kitchen/diner. She pushed open the door. Dad was sitting in his usual seat, a green tweed chair with some stuffing bursting out of one arm. It didn't at all match the chintzy furniture in the rest of the room, but he refused to part with it. He was engaged in reading the *Glasgow Herald*, which he ordered specially, from cover to cover, as he did every evening. Kirsty was sitting in her favourite corner of the sofa, sewing sequins and pearls onto oyster coloured silk.

'Hey, sis,' she said, neatly biting off thread and looking up with a smile.

'Hi, Kirst. That's gorgeous,' said Heather, watching as her sister's needle flew in and out of the delicate fabric. 'I'd buy it, anyway. How's business?'

'Good.' Kirsty grinned. 'I'm stocked at Rosanna's now. You know, the boutique in the high street.'

'Wow. I love her clothes, but they're really expensive.'

'Yup. Might be able to move into a flat in town soon.' She giggled. 'But I'll be back here every Sunday for Mum's roast and Dad's free book keeping service.'

Heather sank into the sofa beside her sister. Pansy, the family dog, padded over and shoved her cold nose into her palm. A delicious aroma of chicken chasseur wafted out of the kitchen. She could hear Mum crossing and recrossing the kitchen floor and there was tension in all that movement.

She flickered her eyes at Kirsty in a *What's up?* gesture.

'Whatever you do, don't mention Eleanor Gladstone and the Mothers' Union,' murmured Kirsty. 'There's been a huge bust up about the coffee morning.'

'They're not exactly topics forever on my lips.'

'Eleanor Gladstone's getting far too big for her boots,' called Mum, from the kitchen. The front door opened and Jamie strolled in, whistling, a copy of *Private Eye* under his arm.

'Ah, Jamie. You're here. Now we can eat.'

They took their usual places round the kitchen table, Heather between Dad and Kirsty.

'How's Aunt Treeny?' asked Dad, as they ate their melon.

'Good,' said Heather. 'She's on quite a lot of medication but she's much better. I've arranged for Mrs Peden to stay with her for a few days.' She giggled. 'She'll have the two of them bopping around the front room to Inspiral Carpets,' she went on, and told the family about Mrs Peden's recent introduction to the Madchester scene.

'How's Mrs Gillies?' said Dad.

'Fine,' said Heather. 'She hasn't really mellowed with age.'

They chatted about family news for a while longer. Kirsty was over the moon about her autumn collection being on sale at the super-chic Rosanna's. Their cousin, Tim, the black sheep, whom Heather had always rather liked, had scandalised his parents by not only dating a "wildly unsuitable" girl, but also having her name – Madison – tattooed on his right arm.

'Catherine's absolutely incandescent,' said Mum.

Heather and Kirsty exchanged smiles. Aunt Cathie, their mother's sister, was so uptight that she made Mum herself seem relaxed to the point of coma.

'So, Heather, have you got your outfit for Rebecca Green's wedding?' asked Mum, as Heather polished off the last crimson spoonful of her summer pudding.

'Huh?'

'Rebecca Green's wedding. It's on Saturday.'

'I haven't been invited,' said Heather, in some relief.

'You *have* been invited. I ran into Val Green in Sainsbury's. And, what's more, I assured her you were going.' Mum had assumed her frostiest Morningside accent.

'You had absolutely no right,' fumed Heather. Strange how, within the four flowery walls of 36 Shirley Lane, she was forever frozen at the age of 14.

'I had every right. I was extremely embarrassed that you hadn't even bothered to RSVP.'

'I tell you, I never got the invitation. It must have got lost in the post,' insisted Heather, guiltily remembering a thick creamy envelope with her name and address written across it in a flowing violet ink. It had been waiting for her at the flat and she'd shoved it in her jacket pocket. It was still there. 'Anyway, I can't go. Not without a partner.'

'Your brother'll go with you. Won't you, Jamie?'

'Er –'

'I can't go with Jamie. Everyone knows he's my brother. I might as well get *Single and Desperate* tattooed across my forehead.'

'I'll go with you,' said Kirsty. 'It'll be a laugh, if nothing else.'

Heather looked hard at the table cover, her eyes following the pattern of twining stems and leaves. When she'd been in sixth form college, there had been a boy called Jason. He'd moved from somewhere in North London – lunar miles away. This gave him an intrigue and mystique that the other boys, whom they'd known since before their voices broke, lacked. He was taller than the others, with dyed black hair and blue eyes and a long black coat. He kept a journal. He wrote poetry and letters for Amnesty International. He knew about politics and the music of the eighties – the Smiths, the Cure and Joy Division. He talked about books – *Fear and Loathing in Las Vegas* and *The Beautiful and Damned*. Heather wasn't part of the in-crowd but still he chose her. *There's just something about you*, he'd said. Now, she recognised him as a pretentious git, but it was heady, at seventeen, to sit in his messy bedroom and have deep conversations while *Faith* played in the background, or walk hand in hand around Addiscombe all dressed in black, or turn up at parties with the best looking boy in college. That was until he dumped her for Becca Green. Huh. She didn't know then that that was to be the story of her life.

'Marcy, if she really doesn't want to go –' Dad was backing her up as usual.

'I don't know why you let Eammon slip through your fingers. He seemed a delightful young man –'

'... and a total hottie, although he was a scumbag,' put in Kirsty.

'Ai-*dan*,' snapped Heather. 'He dumped me, *Mother*, as you well know. And just because he's charming and has a good job doesn't make him a delightful young man.'

'You don't have to go if you don't want to.' Dad put his big, hairy hand over hers.

'It's okay, Dad. The Hammers are away to Everton on Saturday. Ben'll come with me.'

Jamie, who'd been intent on demolishing his second helping of pudding, looked up and grinned.

'He owes you, after Nicole's party. I heard you didn't even last the night.'

'You're not funny, Jamie.'

'What?' giggled Kirsty, sensing a chance to take the piss.

'I pretended to be Ben's girlfriend at his ex's engagement party a few months ago,' Heather explained stiffly. 'Halfway through the evening, he met a girl he fancied and chucked me, and I had to make my way home alone from deepest, darkest Essex on the train, accompanied by a crowd of football supporters and a sozzled bunch of girls who were swigging champagne straight from the bottle.'

'Classy.' Kirsty was leaning forward, clearly enjoying the story.

'I'm glad you both find me so amusing,' Heather sniffed, but then she found herself giggling, seeing the funny side.

⌒

'You look really good today,' Ben said. Heather's head spun round at 180 degrees – she and Ben didn't do "nice". However, she did appreciate the ego-bolstering. Becca Green was one of those effortlessly capable, stylish and blonde women who knocked her confidence for six. She was wearing a dress which Kirsty had made for her, based on one worn by Samantha in *Sex and the City*, and she'd spent the morning and the best part of a week's salary at Michel of Bond Street, having her hair straightened, her nails French manicured and a professional make up.

'Bride or groom?'

'Er, bride.'

She and Ben sat on a pew at the back, behind a row of big hats. The church was beautiful, with a high, vaulted roof and an arched, stained glass window behind the pulpit. Sun shone through this, splashing the ancient grey stone with diamonds of jewel colours. There were two flower arrangements with blooms in every shade of pink and also smaller posies at the end of each pew.

'Ben,' she hissed. She'd just spotted the telltale wire hanging from his ear. 'You can't listen to your iPod in here.'

'What?' said Ben, too loudly.

One of the hats turned round, with a haughty, over made-up face below it. Furiously, Heather mimed removing the earplugs and Ben sulkily complied. After a few moments, they were joined by an enchantingly pretty girl in a wide brimmed hat covered with pink roses. Ben brightened slightly.

The groom and his best man were now standing at the altar, both in tails, and looked a little lost. Heather glanced at her watch. She bet that Becca would exercise her prerogative to be late, and make an entrance.

She was right. The congregation, she could sense, was beginning to get twitchy by the time the organist began to play *Wonderful Tonight*.

'I hate that song,' hissed Heather. 'It's so predictable, the lyrics are so smug and there's no melody. Just saying. Not that I'm bitter, or anything.'

'It's just an ordinary blues riff,' agreed Ben.

There was Becca, walking stately past on her father's arm, followed by six bridesmaids and a flower girl. Her hair was an intricate coil haloed in fresh flowers, and under her veil, her profile was serene and perfect. As Becca and Josh took their vows, Heather had to clasp her hands and bite her tongue to stop herself from crying, although her own wedding fantasies had involved a very quiet ceremony in Florence, her favourite city. Just herself, Aidan and close family and friends, her buddy Lewis playing acoustic guitar by a fountain. She'd wear a simple cream dress and they'd write their own vows (Heather was already word perfect on hers) and afterwards have a long, lazy lunch sitting outside in the sun and then take in a gallery. Then the honeymoon could commence.

'I now pronounce you man and wife,' said the vicar. 'You may kiss.'

The sun was shining brightly as they all filed out, the stone sprinkled with pastel coloured confetti.

'Congratulations, Becca.' Heather managed quite a fair show of sincerity as she kissed the air beside her cheek.

'Hi, Heather, hi, Ben,' said Becca. 'Oh, Venetia,' she exclaimed. Venetia, who was wearing a tight, shocking pink dress and a huge black and white hat, which could have had someone's eye out, was obviously a more important person then they were, Heather reflected, as she and Becca embraced fondly and then began to shriek at each other. Heather slipped away, glad that Act 1 of the ordeal was over.

Next, they moved on to a plush hotel, making their way up a wide, gracious flight of stairs towards the ballroom. Heather slipped into the ladies', checking her reflection in a large, gold-framed mirror. Her hair had remained on the straight and narrow and her mascara was still in place. The dress was so gorgeous. In a rich turquoise, it was floor length and backless. She put on another coat of rusty coloured lipstick and sprayed on more Allure, then she went out to rejoin Ben.

He took her arm as they walked over to consult the seating plan, which was written in elaborate, flowing calligraphy.

'Jennifer Anderson,' Ben read. 'That's who I'm sitting next to. Oh, well, maybe she'll be fit.'

'Don't you dare,' hissed Heather, punching his arm. 'You're my date for tonight. Remember, I have access to all your vinyl records, and I will bake them, along with your *Godfather* box set. Oh, hi, Oliver,' she added, plastering a smile on her face as an old school acquaintance strolled by.

'Great nosebag,' Ben conceded, tucking into a delicate salmon paté. Heather sipped her, admittedly chilled and delicious, white wine and looked around. There was Becca at the top table, with her two best friends from school, who were her chief bridesmaids. Further down her own table was a smattering of merchant bankers, competing as to who earned the biggest bonuses and worked the longest hours.

'I think you know what I'm thinking. It rhymes,' said Jennifer Anderson, who had turned out to be a neighbour of Becca's. She wasn't at all "fit", being on the wrong side of sixty and in possession of teeth which would have looked better on a horse, but she was a very nice, funny woman who was helping to make The Ordeal a little more bearable.

'This corset is absolutely killing me,' she confided, in a low voice. 'I've a good mind to go to the loo and fillet it, but I need it to hold me together.'

Heather shivered, suddenly, although the room was warm to the point of being tropical. She'd had a premonition of her future as a single woman. Obviously, she'd have several cats: that went with the territory. She'd develop a menopausal crush on a boy half her age who wouldn't look twice at her, and she'd become seriously addicted to knitting and send her nieces and nephews too small, too patterned hand knitted sweaters at birthdays and Christmas, earning the reputation as an eccentric old maiden aunt. Basically, she'd *become* her batty old Great-Aunt Allie.

Later, they watched Becca and Josh take the floor for the first waltz. Scarlett O'Hara herself would consider the dress – a low cut, tight bodiced, huge skirted southern belle style, to be over the top.

'Hi, Heather, hi, Ben,' said a tubby, prematurely balding guy, passing their table on the way to the bathroom.

'Who on earth was that?' asked Heather.

'No idea.' Ben looked puzzled for a moment, then his face cleared. 'Allan Walton.'

'No way,' breathed Heather, trying not to giggle. All those not in Jason's camp considered the more conventional Allan Walton to be school cheesecake. With his big, long lashed brown eyes and dark shiny hair, he'd been traditionally tall, dark and handsome, to the extent that he could wear leather trousers and actually not look ridiculous. Every year, the number of Valentine cards he received ran into double figures. Further enhancing his reputation was the fact that he was a bad boy, who took for granted his success with girls and tended to treat them badly.

'Yes way. There is some justice in the world,' Ben said. Heather giggled. She could see, now, that Ben was right. The height, the full lips and the dark eyes were still there. He'd just peaked too soon.

'Never fancied him much,' Heather remarked. 'With those big lips it would have been like French kissing a St Bernard.'

'Hi, Heather, hi, Ben. Didn't know you guys were an item.' It was Clare Court, another school acquaintance, hand in hand with a scruffy looking bloke with thick brown hair.

'Oh, very much so,' said Ben, slipping his arm round Heather's shoulders and kissing her on the cheek. A wicked twinkle came into his eyes. Heather had to struggle very hard not to laugh. 'I'd be crazy to let this lovely laydee slip through my fingers.'

'Sweet,' said Clare. They chatted to her and her boyfriend for a while, before snatching up a couple of glasses of champagne. Waiters were drifting around with flutes on silver trays.

Out of the corner of her eye, Heather caught sight of Mr Wells, her old English teacher. Teaching at her school had been his first job and she'd been in sixth form, so she assumed he was only about five or six years older than she was. She'd had a monumental crush on him at the time, he'd just seemed so intense and soulful, with his knowledge of all those passionate novels and the way he read romantic poetry. She'd found out that his first name was Daniel and she would write it all over her exercise books in flowing handwriting. He was coming over. She waited for her heart to start fluttering and a blush to rise in her cheeks the way it always had before, but nothing happened. Extensive doses of Aidan seemed to have inoculated her against all men.

'Hi, Mr Wells. Having a good time?'

'Danny. Yes, I'm having a great time.'

They sipped their drinks and talked for a while. Mr Wells (she couldn't think of him as "Danny") was still in teaching and still at St Diarmid's.

'So, Heather, what about you? You wanted to be an artist. How's that going?' he asked, after they'd discussed Ben's nursing career. Heather smiled, touched that he'd remembered.

'Good. I've been living in Kirklochy in Dreichndrookit for a few months, and I've sold quite a few local views at the arts centre.'

'Well done,' said Mr Wells. 'Quite envy you, actually. I've always fancied dropping out of the rat race to enjoy a better quality of life.'

Conversation was interrupted, then, as Josh went up on stage, said a few words to the lead singer in the band, and then took over the microphone, proceeding to launch into a rendition of *I Don't Want to Miss a Thing*. He gazed directly at Becca throughout, who, in turn, blushed prettily. The experience was so cringe-worthy that it was all

Heather could do not to put her head in her hands.

'Okay,' she whispered to Ben. 'We've mingled, most people have clocked our boats, let's go to the pub.'

Giggling with relief, they ran down the sweeping staircase, Heather holding up her skirt, across the wide, thickly carpeted foyer, and out into the still bright streets.

'Freedom,' bellowed Ben, in his best Scottish accent, as he punched the air.

Ridiculously overdressed, they squeezed into a corner table in the pub, Ben sipping a pint of Stella and Heather a gin and tonic, chatting non-stop as if they'd never been apart.

↩

On Monday, Heather again crossed the huge, marble concourse which was the reception area of Bright Sparks House.

There was Aidan approaching her, looking business-like in a suit and carrying a laptop. This time, she was ready for him. Best outfit? Check. She was wearing a well-cut suit in amethyst with a nipped-in waist and short, tight skirt. High heels? Check. Her purple shoes weren't Blahniks but looked like them, and had four-inch heels, perfect for swivelling round on, and then tapping sharply away. Good Hair Day? Check. It was still shampoo advert shiny, sleek and straight from Michel's ministrations. Her make-up was a work of art. She was confident that she looked her best. Yesterday, she and Matilda had had a leisurely walk and a long talk in Holland Park, then gone to see the latest Bridget Jones film, and ended the day with a curry in the Ruby. With her bestie's support and the warm friendship of Ben and Euan, she felt stronger. She walked steadily towards Aidan, trying her best to seem composed, although her heart was beating so fast she felt sick.

'Hello, Heather.' Aidan's expression was warm. 'It's great to see you.'

Close up, he looked beautiful, familiar. There was the scar above his right eye. She remembered kissing it, asking how he'd got it. Emotion welled up inside her; she was terrified that she would burst into tears but she mustn't.

'Good to see you, too.' She was impressed that her voice sounded relaxed and casual – it could so easily have come out as a croak. In her mind's eye, she saw Matilda holding her thumbs up. Aidan's eyes were of the mesmerising deep blue that she remembered. Her palms were sweating and her heart racing, but she must stay strong.

'Listen, Heather, are you still here for a couple of days?'

She nodded, wondering what was coming next, her heart racing all the faster.

'I'd really like to see you… meet up for a chat?' Aidan spoke in a low voice, as the receptionist and the biggest gossip in the firm, who appeared to have bionic hearing, was within earshot.

'Could do.' She managed to sound off-hand, although she thought there was a chance she might actually faint. Aidan's face burst into a big, relieved smile.

'Okay. Fabrizio's, tomorrow night at seven? I'll book a table,' he said.

'Great.' Heather recalled many happy nights at the cosy Italian restaurant.

'See you then.'

Aidan walked on, heading for the door. Although she had imagined making a big, dramatic exit, Heather stood still in the middle of the marble foyer as smart, dynamic men and women and Cameron, one of the creatives who was an alcoholic genius, scurried around her. She'd never seen Aidan look so sexy.

A few minutes passed and then she walked shakily towards the bathroom, where she leaned on one of the sinks, looking at her ashen face in the mirror. Why had Aidan asked to meet up? Did he just want to smooth things over with her, to make up so that they could work together amicably on her return? Or could he maybe, possibly, want her back? Perhaps he and Savannah had split up and he missed her. Her heart soared, but she tried to push down the tingle of excitement and her elated feelings: she wouldn't know what Aidan wanted until they talked. She'd just have to be patient and wait until tomorrow night. More than twenty-four hours. She took a deep, quavering breath and headed for her office, but, as the lift powered her up to the tenth floor, she couldn't help running a mental reel of all the good times she and Aidan had had in Fabrizio's: meeting up there on a Friday night, letting their hair down after a busy week at work, ordering a sticky toffee pudding and two spoons. She could hardly wait to see him.

10. *What Kind of Man?*

'Hi, babe.' Kirsty had responded to Heather's SOS and bustled into the flat carrying a pink and purple leopard-spot vanity case. The sisters kissed and Heather led Kirsty into her bedroom, which Paul had loaned her back for the evening. The large picture of the Tardis above the bed and the Star Wars figures congregated on the dressing table looked incongruous alongside her pretty lilac wallpaper and floral bedspread.

'You look amazing,' she told Kirsty. Her sister was wearing a dress in a zingy lime colour, striking against her creamy skin, black hair and scarlet lips, and deepening the green of her eyes.

'So do you,' Kirsty said. 'I think living in the village suits you.' For a moment, she seemed wistful. Heather looked at herself in her full-length mirror. As well as being tanned from her outdoorsy lifestyle, her arms and legs were toned from rowing and walking along the beach. She noticed with surprised pleasure that her "derrière" (as Treeny called it), had never looked so pert – again due to all that walking, and her hair had grown so that it now reached almost to her waist. She'd been so busy being heartbroken that she hadn't really noticed her new figure.

She'd showered and washed her hair earlier, so Kirsty began to dry it for her, but making the most of her curls instead of straightening it as she always used to when they were getting ready for a night out.

'Best just to let your hair do what comes naturally,' she advised, above the noise of the dryer.

When she'd finished, Heather's hair was a mass of gleaming waves and ringlets flowing down her back. Kirsty painted her lips in a caramel colour, made up her eyes in bronze and etched her cheekbones in just a dusting of russet. She had subtly enhanced her features and colouring while keeping it natural.

'I love it,' she squealed.

'Just like yourself but better?' Kirsty said, going over to the wardrobe and throwing open the door.

'Maybe a skinny jean?' she suggested, glancing critically inside. 'Your legs are really toned. Plus, you don't want to look as if you've tried too hard.'

After a pleasurable half hour going through Heather's clothes, they settled on a casual look: black denim mini to show off her flat stomach and long, bronzed legs – and her bum – and a sleeveless top in bright red to give her slender arms maximum exposure and reveal just a glimpse of ripped abs. Then, a spritz of Allure and she was ready to go.

'You look great,' Kirsty said, from where she was sitting on the bed. For an instant, she looked hesitant. 'Heather, you're not hoping that you can get back with him, are you?'

'Of course not,' Heather said, although she felt another spark of excitement at the thought. 'I just need closure – and to let him see what he's lost.'

'In that case – you go, gal.'

'Ooh. I think that's my taxi.' The throbbing of an engine could be heard in the street below. They clattered down the stairs, Heather stepping out carefully in her scarlet shoes – maybe she was starting to lose the art of sashaying in killer heels since those days she lived in trainers and walking boots. Out on the street, the sisters hugged briefly then Heather climbed into the cab.

'Where to, darling?'

'Fabrizio's, Charlotte Street.'

Heather barely heard the cabbie's chatter about West Ham and the celebs he'd driven last week: her mind was taken up by thoughts of Aidan. Why had he asked her to dinner? Was it possible that he and Savannah were no longer together and he was going to beg her to come back? And, if he did, what would she say? She'd be cool at first, make him really work for her, that was for sure. Then her brain clicked over and she thought that of course he and Savannah were still together and he was just trying to salve his conscience and smooth things over with her. One way and another, she'd soon know, as the taxi was pulling up outside the restaurant. Heather paid the driver, over-tipping him, then stood on the pavement, trying to nerve herself to go inside. She glanced at her watch; she was a little early. There was a pub across the street where she and Aidan would often go for a nightcap after dinner. She hurried towards it, pushing open the heavy stained glass door.

'Gin and tonic,' she ordered. She'd just have one drink to give her Dutch courage, but absolutely no more – she didn't want to be drunk when she met Aidan. She took a seat at the window. Fabrizio's looked as welcoming as ever, with its cheery red frontage. Two women of about her own age were sitting at a table outside, sipping white wine from large goblets. Her heart raced: there was Aidan, walking along the road. He was wearing faded jeans and a grey wool sweater. She watched the two girls looking appreciatively at his back-view, as he reached the door and went in. She took another sip of her drink, trying to calm down – she absolutely didn't want him to know how nervous she was. She'd be just a few casual minutes late. She finished her drink and stood up, breathing deeply. She walked out into the street and crossed the road. Just then, she felt her phone vibrating against her leg and pulled it out of her bag to see Euan's smiling face.

'Hi, Euan.'

'How's it going?'

'I'm just outside.' She took another deep breath. 'Wish me luck – I'm going in.'

'Best of luck. Listen, Heather, phone me later and let me know how you get on, okay?'

'Sure. Speak to you soon.'

She found she was smiling as she pushed open the restaurant's door – talking to Euan had somehow propelled her over the threshold. Probably due to his training as a journalist, he was interested in everything that was going on in her life and was a great listener – so she knew he'd really meant it when he'd asked her to report back.

'Can I help you, madam?' A doe-eyed Italian waitress had approached her.

'Yes, thank you. I'm meeting Aidan Murphy.'

'Mr Murphy is already here. Follow me.'

The girl led Heather to a table in a secluded alcove. Aidan rose to greet her.

'Hello.' His expression was grave as he stooped slightly to kiss her cheek. She could smell fresh cotton, citrusy aftershave and the scent of his skin.

'Hi,' she murmured, completely overwhelmed.

A waiter appeared by her side as if by magic and pulled out her chair for her. She sat down, and, at last, she was again alone with him, face to face. She waited for the pain and loss to hit her, the old yearning to come flooding back; he was as handsome as ever, a curling lock of dark hair falling over his forehead, his electric blue eyes on her... but nothing happened. All she felt was a bittersweet ache: sadness that she'd once loved him so much but now it was all over. She felt relief, too, at the closure: she was free to get on with her life. She accepted now that they could never go back: she no longer trusted him.

Aidan lifted the leather-bound menu and glanced at it. Perhaps he was more nervous than she was. He looked up.

'Good to see you,' he said, as if they'd just been colleagues. 'How've you been?'

'Good, really good.' Her voice sounded up-beat and she wasn't acting. 'I love living in Kirklochy; I love the pace of life. I've got some great friends and I can't stop painting. It's so inspiring there, and the light –'

'Phew.' Aidan grinned at her. 'That's a load off my mind.'

'What do you mean?'

Perhaps he'd heard a sharp note in her voice; for a moment, he looked flustered.

'I thought you'd gone off to the Highlands because of me.' His expression was sheepish.

Heather laughed. 'No. No. It was because of Aunt Treeny's hip. But, I must admit, it's great to get the chance to live in the village for a while.'

'How is your aunt?' Aidan asked, evidently keen to move the conversation on.

'Well, her old bones'll never be the same again, but she's over the moon to be out of the care home and back among her friends.'

Just then, a waiter came over to take their order. Heather chose what she always did – bruschetta followed by salmon tagliatelli.

'My treat,' said Aidan.

'Why did you ask me to meet you tonight?' Heather asked.

Aidan reached out and took her hand, fixing her with his mesmerising blue eyes.

'You were so important to me, Heather, never think you weren't. I thought you deserved an explanation – face to face, not over the phone.'

Heather nodded.

'Okaaay.'

'Everyone thought Savannah had a great life out in Singapore,' Aidan began. 'A great career. She even had her own maid.'

Heather nodded numbly. Of course she did.

'But she was working sixteen hour days and she was terribly homesick. So, when she split up with her boyfriend, she decided to come back to London.'

'Go on.'

'But she found it more difficult than she'd expected. Jobs were much harder to find than they had been when she'd left and her friends were all in couples or had moved on. She stayed with some mates for a while but felt as if she really needed to let them have their flat to themselves again –'

Heather imagined that the exquisite, über-successful Savannah would have been completely floored by a failed relationship, unemployment and sleeping on a friend's sofa.

'She turned to me for support,' Aidan said, looking uncomfortable again. 'She was in a pretty bad way, what with the break-up and losing her career. She'd lost touch with most of her friends, too.'

'Why didn't she move in with her mum and dad?'

'Because they're in Bristol and the work's in London.'

'Savannah comes from Bristol?'

'Yes.'

Heather almost smiled. Savannah had a Bristol accent! Ah ha. Evidence at last that she wasn't perfect.

'You lied to me,' Heather said. 'You told me that Friday night that you were meeting an old friend from university.'

'I was,' Aidan protested. 'Savannah *is* an old friend. I've known her since first year at uni. That's nearly ten years.'

'Okay. So you didn't lie, technically. But you misled me. It's called "being economical with the truth".'

She and Aidan had always met up on a Friday evening, no matter what. They'd kick off with a couple of drinks in Camden Town, winding down from the stresses of the week, then they'd have dinner, maybe go to the cinema, a club or a gig, maybe stay in with a DVD, wrapped around each other on the sofa.

'I know. I know.'

Aidan held her hand more tightly.

'Savannah phoned me at work on the Friday afternoon. She still hadn't got a job and couldn't find a decent flat. She was skint –'

Heather raised her eyebrows.

'Didn't she have savings from her job?'

'No way. Savannah's terrible with money. She's got hundreds of pairs of shoes and masses of clothes, but she's permanently broke.'

Heather was surprised. In her fevered mind, Savannah was close to perfection – barely a human being at all.

'She sounded really down. She begged me to meet up with her after work, sounded really desperate. She said she couldn't bear to be alone that night – it would've been her and Nigel's anniversary. I said I would meet her at Noho because it's near the office and it was neutral – I didn't want her to come up to the flat.

'She was sitting at the bar when I got there. She'd had a few drinks and was very upset. Then, right in the middle of the room, she started to cry. Everyone was looking at her and trying to look as if they weren't. I put my arm round her, tried to calm her down –'

'You kissed her.'

Aidan nodded.

'I'm sorry, Heather. She just seemed so lost and vulnerable. I realised I still had feelings for her. First cut is the deepest and all that. I tried to fight it because I was with you and we'd always been so happy together, but she'd got right under my skin and I couldn't fight it any longer –'

'It was too big for the both of you?' Heather asked perkily, but then her composure slipped as she again relived the day she'd found out about his infidelity. 'Aidan, how could you? How could you let me find out from Jessica Lomax, of all people? How could you be seeing Savannah at the same time as you were seeing me? I could never do that. If you don't have trust –'

'I'm sorry,' Aidan said again. 'At first, in Noho, I thought it was just a moment of madness and there was no need to hurt you over it, but she kept phoning me up and, in the end, I just couldn't resist. But I really cared about you, too.'

'Torn between two lovers?' Heather asked, just as the waiter placed her starter before her and poured Chianti into both their glasses. She bit into her bruschetta with relish, washing it down with a few gulps of wine.

'Well –' Aidan again looked sheepish. 'I *was* torn. And, you have to believe me, the last thing I wanted to do was to hurt you.'

'Just going to the loo,' Heather said. She stood up and wove between the tables to the ladies' room, a little drunk and with the same crazy feeling of liberation she'd had when she'd realised she was over Aidan. Once inside, she sank onto a padded chair, took out her iPhone and speed-dialled Euan.

'Hi. What's going on? Why did he ask you out?'

'He feels really bad about breaking my heart and forcing me to run away to the back of beyond, and he thought I deserved a proper face-to-face apology and explanation.'

'No! The arrogant git.'

Heather giggled.

'He so is. And he always has just the right thing to say.'

'So, how do you feel about it all?' Euan's voice had become serious.

'I'm fine, Euan. Honestly. Seeing him again made me realise I wouldn't have wanted him back even if he'd asked me. I can't be with someone I don't trust. I really think I've got closure, and it feels gooooood.'

Euan laughed.

'I'm glad to hear it, and so are all my listeners. You do realise you're going out live on Kirklochy FM? The phone lines are going mad and you're trending on Twitter.'

'Well, I'm sure all six of your listeners will be absolutely riveted.'

'Eight, if you don't mind,' sniffed Euan, and it was Heather's turn to laugh.

'I'm not really going out live, am I?' she asked.

'Nah. I'm in the studio, but I've put on *Like a Hurricane* – all glorious seven and a half minutes of it. It's the track I use when I've got to take a wazz.'

'Speaking of which, mate, I should get back, before Aidan thinks I've developed a heavy cocaine habit.'

'Ha. So, see you in a couple of days.'

She bid Euan goodnight, freshened her make-up, and walked back into the restaurant. She found herself smiling as she approached their table – the chat with Euan had put her in great form – which must have confused Aidan no end.

Conversation was somewhat strained as Heather ate her pasta, taking frequent gulps of wine, then a wedge of tiramisu. No one made it quite like Fabrizio and she felt she deserved the mouth-watering treat. Now she felt sad again, her emotions zooming up and down the scale, as she remembered how well they used to get on, how effortlessly the conversation used to flow, bubbling along, punctuated by laughter, shouts of recognition and Woody Allen quotes. There was sorrow, too, in the fact that something which had once been so good was now over and they would never get it back.

They'd parted amicably – such an anti-climax, but she supposed that it would now be possible for them to work together when she returned to Bright Sparks.

Aidan had offered to call a taxi for her, but it was a warm night and she preferred to walk and have some thinking time to clear her head. She was exhausted from the strain of meeting up with Aidan and with the conflicting emotions running around her head. When she got back to her street, she went into The Grapes before going up to the flat, needing some more time to collect her thoughts. She ordered a latté and took it over to a table by the window. No two ways about it, she reflected: her friends and family had got her through it all. They'd always be there as men came and went. Again, she thought about her chat with Euan.

11. *Suddenly I See*

Back in the village a few days later, Heather again boarded the train to Inveralan. Again she sipped coffee and looked out of the window at the golden and green scenery, but this time she only had the latest Jojo Moyes book for company.

The sky was brightening as she walked down the main street towards the arts centre, butterflies starting up in the pit of her stomach as she followed the smell of coffee and pastries down the hall towards the gallery. She jumped as she heard voices raised in anger, but then realised it was only Inveralan Rep rehearsing a play.

She pushed open the heavy door, hardly daring to look at her paintings, but, when she did, she saw at once that many of them bore red spots.

'Heather,' said Jonathan Finch, walking towards her.

'I can't believe how well they've sold,' she told him, truly delighted.

'Yes, they've been very popular with the tourists. You'll be rich.'

'That would be nice, Jon, but at the end of the day it isn't about the money, it's about doing something I love.'

Jonathan leaned on the wall next to one of her largest canvases, obviously in the mood for a chat.

'We ran a modern art exhibition last month,' he said, with a grin. 'I had to restrain our cleaner from throwing out a pile of coffee-stained old magazines. She didn't realise that they were an exhibit.'

They both laughed.

'What were they meant to represent?'

'God knows – urban alienation, I think. So, have you got any more paintings ready?'

Heather nodded.

'Loads of local views. I've just been on fire since I've been living here.'

'Excellent. A pleasure doing business with you.' Jonathan held out his hand in mock formality.

Heather did some more gazing at her rash of red spots before leaving. The sense of achievement was enormous.

She strolled back down the main street, buoyed up by her success in the gallery. The sun was still just managing to hold its own against the gathering clouds as she turned into Marine Terrace. There were some gorgeous shops here. Apart from her crazed assault on Monsoon whilst she was down in London, she didn't often get the opportunity for retail therapy. In the first shop, she bought a soft angora sweater in her favourite leaf green, in the second a hand-painted bowl with a bluebell pattern, and in the third a cute sheep with a woolly coat for Treeny. It was Matilda's birthday next month, so she bought a beautiful pendant – a Celtic cross set with aquamarines – to match her eyes, or, at least, her tinted contacts.

Happily swinging her bags, she headed back to the square. It was market day, and she bought organic soap, mushrooms, pearl potatoes, Scottish strawberries and tablet laced with whisky. She was really enjoying having some time to herself, where she knew no one.

Just then, she saw Cara, striking in her bright red coat. She was about to call out to her friend when she noticed that she wasn't alone. She was with Paolo Fratelli. They were holding hands as they bent over a stall selling jewellery. She watched as Paolo paid for a delicate silver necklace then fastened it round Cara's neck. Cara smiled at him and they kissed and walked on, hand in hand. They passed right by Heather, but were so engrossed in each other that they didn't even see her. What on earth was going on? Cara was meant to be Sean's girlfriend – she lived with him, she thought of Katie as a daughter – so what was she doing with Paolo? It was obvious she was with him: Heather had seldom seen a couple so besotted, and they were making no attempt to hide it. Maybe she wanted to break off with Sean but was frightened to hurt him and Katie?

'Cara,' she shouted – it just wasn't her way to back off from a confrontation. Cara turned to her with a smile. Heather was taken aback; she'd expected her either to blanch or else to turn purple.

'Hi, Heather.' Cara pulled on Paolo's hand and he, too, turned to her. 'Isn't this lovely? Look what Paolo just bought me.' With her free hand, she gestured to the necklace, a delicate silver crescent moon and star on a slender chain.

'Gorgeous,' Heather managed to mutter, her head still spinning.

'So, what brings you here? Just come to shop at the market?' Paolo asked.

'N...n...no,' said Heather. 'Some of my paintings are on exhibit at the arts centre. Just came along to see how many I'd sold.'

'Wow,' said Cara. 'I told you Heather was a brilliant artist, didn't I, babe? Let's go and have a look, then we'll get a coffee in the café. Do you want to come, Heather?'

'Errr. Thanks, but I should get back to Treeny.'

''Course,' said Cara.

'Good to see you again, Heather,' Paolo added.

She stood frozen for a few seconds as the couple walked away, still holding hands, then she hurried away across the square. Facing her was a tearoom, the Spinning Jenny, so she pushed open the door and went in, a bell announcing her entrance. Inside, it was even more chintzy, lacy and Spode-ridden than Maggie's, and full of twittery women.

'No, no, put your money away, Elspeth,' one of them was saying. 'My treat.'

Heather took a seat in the corner and dropped her bags on the floor.

A waitress swooped immediately.

'What would you like, Madam?'

'Er... tea,' said Heather. She hadn't thought that far ahead.

'We have a range of speciality teas. Earl Grey, Lady Grey, Assam, Darjeeling, English Breakfast, Chai, Lapsang –'

'Earl Grey, please,' ordered Heather randomly.

'Anything else? We have scones, crumpets, Danish pastries, cup-cakes –'

'Just the tea, thanks.'

The waitress left her and returned a few minutes later with a tray bearing a china cup and saucer, teapot, strainer, slices of lemon, jug of milk, silver spoon and bowl of sugar lumps complete with tongs.

She vaguely registered that this establishment would be her mother's idea of Heaven on earth. Then, at last, she was alone. She shook her head at herself, not caring how strange she must look to the other customers. Her hand trembled slightly as she lifted her cup. None of this added up – Cara and Paolo had been so open about the fact that they were together, seemed so happy and innocent. So, wasn't she with Sean? Come to think of it, Sean had never actually said that Cara was his girlfriend – Heather had just assumed she was, because they lived together. She must be a friend and some kind of nanny – which meant that Sean was available. And she'd felt so guilty about kissing him. He must've thought she was mad when she'd rejected him. And been hurt. What if he hated her now? Suddenly, she felt tired and despairing. She gathered up her bags, threw a fiver down on the floral tablecloth, and hurried up the road to the station.

❧

Later, she sat opposite Treeny, eating homemade rhubarb crumble with thick, fresh cream from Galbraith's farm. Usually this was a real treat, but tonight she was having to force it down.

'What's up with you, lassie? You're sitting there in a dwam,' said Treeny.

'I'm fine, Treeny. I've just got to come up with a new product concept for a brand and I can't seem to crack it,' said Heather, hoping to blind her aunt with science.

She wasn't sure that Treeny believed her, but luckily the door bell rang just then and Treeny got up to answer it, returning a moment later with Mrs Peden, who was going to be part of a bridge four that evening. Quickly, Heather washed the dishes. Treeny was now sitting back at the table with her friends, deftly dealing them a hand each.

'I'm just going up to the B&B,' Heather told her aunt.

❧

The foyer of the B&B seemed to be, if it were possible, even more kitch than it had been the last time Heather visited. There were posters up advertising Sheepstock and a new stage production of *The Prime of Miss Jean Brodie*. A herd of china cows had joined the rest of the menagerie on the windowsill. A poster advertising the Mod – a festival of Gaelic music and culture – had been squeezed into what little wall-space was left. A panpipe version of the *Massacre of Glencoe* was shrieking across the hall.

'Hi, Heather,' said Misty, emerging from the dining room. 'How did you get on today?'

'Huh?'

'Heather! Your paintings. I thought you were going to Inveralan?'

'Oh, yeah. Good. I'd sold quite a few.'

'Well, fantastic,' said Misty, seeming surprised by her low key response.

She helped Misty to set out fresh tartan table covers and clean plates and cutlery for breakfast the next morning, watched over by large paintings of Rob Roy McGregor and Robert the Bruce.

'I know it's all a bit cheesy,' admitted Misty. 'The tourists love it, though. 'Specially the Americans.'

Grabbing a bottle of Merlot and two glasses, the girls went up to Misty's bedroom, where they settled comfortably, Heather curled up in an armchair while Misty sat at the top of her bed, leaning on the padded headboard. Misty stretched over and put on the radio, a rich, bluesy voice drowning out the now faint sound of the pan pipes.

'And that was K.T. Tunstall with *Under the Weather*,' came Euan's voice. 'I'd like to dedicate it to my Granny Fay, who's not feeling so good. Get well soon, Gran. Next up is Travis with *Why Does it Always Rain on Me?* See what I did? This show isn't just thrown together –'

'He's right up there with the greats when it comes to crap patter,' remarked Heather, over the catchy intro. Misty giggled, swirling the wine around in her glass.

'Have you seen Euan lately?' asked Heather. She hadn't seen him herself for a few days and really missed their chats.

'No. Rowan's mother's filming in Venice – some period drama – and her father's gone over there for a couple of weeks. So Euan's been staying up at the castle.'

'Wooh. Posh,' said Heather. She felt a slight pang as she imagined the two of them, their intimacy, but pushed the feeling away, telling herself that she was bound to feel a little wistful when she thought about happy couples.

'Have you ever been there?' she asked Misty, to distract herself.

'Yes.' Misty smiled wryly. 'I've been to the Hogmanay Ball a few times, and, when it was Rowan's father's fiftieth birthday last year, me, Duncan and a few others from the village went to the party to act as waiting staff, handing round champagne and canapés.'

'What was it like?'

'The curtains and carpets and all that are pretty faded and worn, but it's still beautiful, all high ceilings and wooden panels and sweeping staircases.'

Heather nodded. Rowan's home sounded like Rowan herself – her natural beauty and grace and the confidence that was her birthright needed no adornment.

'Rowan was absolutely off her face, but she looked amazing.' Misty bit her lip. 'I wish he'd finish with her. He deserves so much better.'

'Babe, Euan's infatuated with Rowan now, but it'll burn out eventually – those things always do.' Although she was trying to cheer up her friend, Heather felt comforted by this thought – Misty was right. Euan did deserve someone who really cared about him.

'You think, do you?'

'I know.'

A shaft of sunlight slanted in the window, turning the wine in Misty's glass to glowing purple. She giggled.

'He doesn't exactly fit in up there, does he? He's probably eating his fish and chips off silver platters, and drinking Irn Bru out of antique crystal goblets.'

Heather smiled and sipped her wine, turning to the subject she'd been bursting to discuss.

'When I was in Inveralan today, I saw Cara,' she said carefully. 'With Paolo.'

'I know,' said Misty, rolling her eyes. 'Sickening, isn't it? They're *mad* about each other.'

She leaned forward and refilled both their glasses.

'At first, you know, I thought she was going out with Sean,' Heather ventured.

'With *Sean*?' said Misty. 'No way.'

'Well, they do live together, that's why I assumed –'

'Yeah, but only because of Katie. Anyway, it would be really spooky.'

'Spooky? Why?'

'Heather, Cara is Meg's sister. And, you never met her, but they look very alike –'

Heather nodded. That explained the photo of Sean and Cara embracing that she'd seen in the cottage. It wasn't Cara after all – it was Meg.

'I can't believe no one's told you.'

'I never asked,' said Heather. She hadn't wanted to betray too much interest in Sean in case anyone suspected her of having feelings for a man who was involved with someone else.

Misty shifted into a more comfortable position.

'Sean met Meg at art school in Glasgow,' she explained. 'When… after the accident, Katie was taken into Yorkhill Hospital. Sean stayed with the Frasers – Meg's mum and dad – for months to be near her. Cara's a nurse and she helped look after Katie when she was well enough to leave hospital. I guess she wanted to do something for Meg. When Sean and Katie came back here, Cara came with them. She got a job at the cottage hospital in Inveralan, and then she met Paolo and decided to stay. It's a shame they don't see so much of each other, but he's working all hours in the pizzeria.'

Heather was silent. She felt foolish and bitterly ashamed of her earlier suspicions. Poor Cara. Not only had Sean lost his wife and Katie her mother, but Cara had lost her sister. She tried to imagine if she'd lost her own sister. If she'd lost Kirsty. But her mind closed down – it simply didn't bear thinking about. Now she could see why Cara was so devoted to Katie, why she loved her so much. She put her head in her hands.

'Heather, it's awful, I know. But they've got each other. And Paolo's been so patient and understanding.'

Heather lifted her head and nodded. She'd known the Fratelli brothers since childhood and had always especially liked Paolo, who was living proof that a man could be smoulderingly handsome and nice with it. Misty divided the last of the wine between them.

'So, has Sean ever gone out with anyone since – ?' She tried to keep her voice casual.

'No, I don't think so. Why, are you interested?'

''Course not. I don't date men. Not since Aidan.'

'Think he had a fling with Rowan, but then, who hasn't?' said Misty, with some bitterness. 'Although, hopefully, not while she was seeing my big cousin.'

Heather drained her glass. Rowan! Honestly, the woman should never be allowed to leave the house. She was a walking disaster area. She should be issued with a government health warning. She should be wrapped in barbed wire.

12. *Raintown*

From Treeny's front room, the roof of the Stagecoach could be seen as it passed along the coast road. Heather stood at the window, ready to hurry down to the bus stop to meet Matilda. Her ETA was six fifteen, so, give or take a few sheep, she should be here in about ten minutes.

'Matilda's here,' she cried to Treeny, half an hour later. She hurried out of the cottage and walked briskly down the hill, seeing the village with new eyes as she imagined what Matilda would think of it. She claimed she had never been further north than Watford.

As she reached the stop, the coach had just pulled in. Matilda, her blonde hair lifting in the breeze, was stepping down carefully in her high heels. She was followed by Ben. Heather's face broke into a huge grin. She hadn't realised he was coming.

'Kirsty,' she screamed, then, so loudly that a couple of horses on Galbraith's land looked up in surprise. She hadn't known her sister was coming either.

'It's *so* good to be back,' said Kirsty, stretching and taking deep, appreciative breaths of the tangy sea air.

Heather hugged her, then both of her friends in turn, and they all stood, talking at the same time, as Lachie, the driver (real name Derek: Lachie was his professional name), retrieved their suitcases from the hold. Ben, who just had a backpack, took Matilda's acid green one, leaving her to carry her vanity case and hot pink holdall.

A few minutes later, they were back at the cottage.

'Hi,' said Matilda, tottering into the living room. She looked good enough to eat but totally out of place in her tight white jeans, teal leather jacket and turquoise stilettos. 'You must be Aunt Treeny. I'm Matilda Jaye.'

Treeny's lips twitched, but she managed to answer gravely: 'Hello, Matilda Jaye.'

Everyone was talking at once again, Ben and Kirsty running forward to hug Treeny.

'Ooh, a television,' said Matilda. 'Have you got Sky Plus?'

'Thought you'd come here to get away from it all, Matilda.' Ben glanced up from the *Kirklochy News*.

'The mobile cinema's coming round soon,' Treeny offered.

Ben consulted the paper, then looked up.

'It's *Armageddon* on Thursday,' he said.

'I certainly hope not,' said Matilda. 'Sheepstock doesn't start until Friday.'

⤶

Later, Heather sat on her bed, drinking milky coffee and eating chocolate digestives while she, Matilda and Kirsty chattered non-stop. Treeny had two ancient camp beds which Heather had put up in the room. She filled Matilda in with a brief biog of each of her Kirklochy friends.

'Oh, and there's Gregor, my hairdresser, who's a honey and you know about Euan, who's one of my best mates. His girlfriend's horrible, though,' she added, with a grimace.

'Is that this Rowan you keep mentioning in PMs?' asked Matilda.

'Yeah,' agreed Heather gloomily. 'She's got that beautiful *and* brainy thing going on. You know, she's got the body of Kelly Brook and a first class honours degree.'

'Hotter than Jessica Lomax?' asked Matilda. J-Lo was their yardstick for babe-dom.

'Well, she doesn't have to try the way Jessi does. She can just throw on Euan's old jeans and a shirt and look amazing. She doesn't wear make-up –'

'She doesn't wear make-up?' Matilda squeaked. She herself never went beyond the duvet without full-on slap and half a can of Elnett.

'She's five-ten, skinny, with auburn hair all the way down her back, she's a member of MENSA, oh, and she can sing and act, too.'

'Big tits?' asked Matilda.

Heather nodded wearily.

'There's no justice,' said Matilda. She paused, a hopeful expression on her face. 'No hot guys in the 'hood?'

'Well –' Heather was reluctant to go on: her feelings were too jumbled. Another time, in different circumstances, she might have pursued her attraction to Sean. 'There is Sean, the artist who's been helping me, but –'

Matilda's eyes gleamed.

'He's cute? He's available? Yes?'

Heather nodded.

'And he likes you?'

'I think so. We kissed –'

'Heather, why don't I know about this?' Kirsty interrupted.

'Because it's complicated.' Heather wished she hadn't said anything.

'How?' cried Kirsty. 'You like him, you're both single –'

'Because he was married but his wife died. I think he still has feelings for her and I'm sort of off men at the moment.'

Matilda lifted a lock of her hair and twisted it round her fingers.

'Babe, just because one man let you down doesn't mean that they're all like that –'

'Anyway, we've fallen out,' Heather interrupted. 'Which was entirely my fault.'

'Well, make it up, then,' Matilda urged. 'Apologise. Give him a chance.'

'Maybe,' Heather muttered. Matilda was right in one respect at least; she still needed to apologise to Sean.

⁓

Heather watched as Matilda unpacked: cream silk baby doll pyjamas and cerise silk wrap; fluffy, pink, high heeled mules straight out of Ann Summers; black lacy thongs; black balcony bra with rosebuds stitched across it; vest tops of every colour of the rainbow; pairs of skin tight, low rise jeans; tiny dresses, black leather mini skirt and corset top; leopard skin look stilettos with pointed toes and, last but not least, gold lamé shorts. Those turned heads in every nightspot in Barking, but Heather had a feeling that they would turn heads here for quite a different reason. The only two things she could guarantee about this holiday were midges and rain.

'Tills, the weather can get quite wild here. Haven't you got anything more... suitable? You know – practical. Trainers, warm sweaters?'

'Certainly not,' said Matilda, sounding quite insulted.

Everyone was exhausted from such a long journey, so they spent the evening sitting by the roaring fire. Treeny had a proper toasting fork, so they feasted on buttery toast and marshmallows.

⌒

The next day, the girls all went to Sascha's salon for a few treatments. Ben had ambitions to climb Ben Lochy, so Heather had re-introduced him to Euan and Callum, whom he had met years ago whilst on holiday with her family. The three men had hit it off immediately and the Buchanan brothers were experienced and knowledgeable hill walkers so Ben would be in safe hands.

It was a happy, girlie scene, as they bonded over different shades of nail polish, the salon steamy and ammonia fragranced. Matilda and Gregor were getting on famously, her eyes closed in ecstasy as he gave her a shoulder massage. Gregor was very easy to get on with.

'You're very tense,' he told her.

'I have a very stressful life,' Matilda sighed.

This was true, thought Heather – although most people thought that Matilda's idea of stress was getting a zit on her nose or breaking a nail. She and Gregor were now avidly discussing their mutual passion for Ryan Gosling.

Later, as Heather lay on her back, eyes tightly closed, having her pale eyelashes dyed, she heard Matilda confide in Gregor about how, just before leaving for Kirklochy, she'd finally broken off her romance with Dane from the mailroom.

'He was ever so upset,' she said.

'Best to make a clean break,' advised Gregor sagely.

'I suppose he'll get over me in time,' sighed Matilda.

While Matilda was getting a fake bake, Heather and Kirsty sipped cups of coffee and leafed through the celebrity magazines, Kirsty running a critical eye over the fashion pages. Chloé Marsden was featured in most of them "frolicking" with a "mystery man" in the waves off the romantic island of Phuket. No doubt this was her PR company's response to last week's *Hello!* magazine, in which her former boyfriend Ryan Wright had "presented" his new love, glamour model Natalee, a woman whose breast measurement was larger than her IQ. Both couples were reported to be blissfully happy/on the rocks, depending on which magazine you read.

Later, heavily supervised by Treeny, who was sitting at the kitchen table sipping sweet sherry, Heather cooked a huge meal of salmon, new potatoes and fresh vegetables, followed by bread and butter pudding laced with Drambuie and accompanied by thick, fresh cream straight from the farm. Ben, ravenous from his day on the hills, had seconds of everything, and even Matilda ate heartily, making it her first square meal since Christmas.

'So – what are we doing tonight?' Kirsty asked, sipping tea. She and Matilda were both desperate to go out – there was no point in looking their best if there was no one there to see them.

'Well, to be honest, there isn't much of a Kirklochy scene, but it's karaoke night at the Claymore,' offered Heather. 'It's a good laugh,' she went on. 'Alfie Bolt's wonderfully awful.' She giggled at the memory of Alfie's rendition of those two karaoke classics, *My Way* and *Delilah*.

'Shall I book a taxi?' said Matilda, producing a hot pink iPhone from her handbag.

Heather giggled.

'I don't think that'll be necessary,' she said, pointing at the pub, which could be seen from where they were sitting.

'Oh,' said Matilda, putting her phone away.

'Matilda, are you anywhere near ready?' Heather asked, some time later. Matilda was standing in the middle of their bedroom, wearing only a coffee coloured Wonderbra and matching thong.

'Look, I'll catch you up,' she said, looking distractedly at the pile of clothes on her bed. She hated to be rushed when preparing for a night out and also, Heather suspected, wanted to make an entrance.

'Will that be all right?'

''Course it will. I'm not exactly going to get lost, am I?'

Linking arms, Heather and Kirsty followed Ben down the hill and along the road to the Claymore. Inside, it was as warm and bright as ever. It was a chilly evening and the real fires blazing and crackling on either side of the room looked cosy and welcoming. She breathed in the smell of beer and listened to the buzz of excited chatter as they managed to bag a large table in an alcove. Ben fetched pints of Old Sheepshagger for everyone.

'Slàinte mhath,' cried Heather, and they all clinked glasses.

'Next up, the one and only... Mr Alfie Bolt,' said Murdo, who was compère for the evening.

Alfie moved to the makeshift stage in the corner of the room, bowed from the waist, his wavy hair falling forward, took up the microphone and launched into *All By Myself*, everyone laughing in appreciation at the exaggerated emotion on his face. His voice was, well... powerful, thought Heather, that was the best that could charitably be said for it, but he was an entertainer and finished his song to loud applause. Again, he bowed theatrically from the waist before returning to his seat.

'Thank you, Alfie,' shouted Murdo, over the uproar of praise. 'The next act up is the very lovely Ms Rowan Galloway.'

Rowan, who'd been leaning against the bar, walked languidly forward. She wasn't usually seen at the Claymore of an evening, mixing with the hoi polloi – she must have reached new levels of boredom. She wore jeans and an amber coloured tee-shirt exactly the same shade as her hair, which was tied up in a high ponytail, showing off the beauty of her long swan-like neck and her lean jawline. Scorning to use the Karaoke machine, she accompanied herself on the clarsach, singing a haunting version of *Wild Mountain Thyme*, her voice sweet and true. There was total silence in the pub. No one spoke, no one got up to order a drink or use the loo. There was rapturous applause when she finished, and everyone begged for more. Rowan obliged with three other songs, switching tempo with ease, swapping her clarsach for a guitar. She acknowledged the applause with a brief bow, then returned to her place beside Euan at the bar. Euan smiled proudly, slipped his arm round her and kissed her cheek. Heather winced at the display of affection.

Damn, Rowan was good, she thought, by no means for the first time. Rumour had it that she'd been a star of the Cambridge Footlights. Heather wouldn't be surprised if she'd dashed off a symphony over breakfast, then redefined the theory of relativity before lunch.

Rowan was a hard act to follow, but there were other talented singers – Valissa belted out a couple of big Barbra Streisand numbers, then Craig, Mrs Peden's grandson, a quiet and surly youth most of the time, made his way to the stage. He wore the inevitable beanie hat and ill fitting jeans which revealed a portion of shapely buttock. Grabbing the microphone, he began an impassioned version of *Don't Look Back in Anger.*

The applause was just dying down when the door opened and silence fell, as if Billy the Kid had just walked in. Heather looked round. Actually, it was Matilda who stood in the doorway, enjoying the impact she was making. With her waist length blonde hair, delicate features and slender figure, Matilda had always been a good looking woman, but tonight, with her false eyelashes, tinted contact lenses, smooth golden tan and French manicure, she looked amazing. She wore her gold shorts, a black vest and her leopard skin stilettos, her figure enhanced by her wonderbra and her height elevated to Amazonian by her five inch heels, which made her bare brown legs seem to go on forever.

Alfie Bolt choked on his pint.

'Put your eyes back in,' snapped Shanice, his wife.

'Matilda, over here,' called Heather, raising her hand.

'I'll just get a drink.'

Matilda, her antennae perfectly attuned to sighting hot men, began to make her way towards the bar, winking at Euan, who was still standing with Rowan. Rowan laid her drink down and stared at her in disbelief.

'Do I know you, love?' she asked, in purest Barking.

'What *are* you wearing?' Rowan managed to splutter, after a moment.

''Ot pants, darlin',' explained Matilda kindly. 'Don't s'pose you know too much about fashion up here, do ya?'

'I would never go out dressed like that.'

'Well, not everyone can carry it orf, sweet'eart,' said Matilda sympathetically.

For once, Rowan seemed to be lost for words.

'Soo-perb.' Heather heard Cara say.

Matilda sauntered over to the bar, Heather following.

'A Cosmoplitan, please,' she ordered.

'Er, make that a dry white wine, Murdo,' cut in Heather. She was certain that Miss Carrie Bradshaw's favourite cocktail was well beyond Murdo's ken.

There was still a frisson running round the room as Heather and Matilda returned to join the others in their alcove. Everyone was in tearing spirits. Cara and Misty pulled their chairs over and they all budged up to make room, Misty insisting on shaking Matilda by the hand because she'd humiliated Rowan. She and Euan were standing close together, whispering, then they went out.

'Trailer park trash,' hissed Rowan, as she passed, but Matilda just smiled sweetly.

Heather almost felt sorry for Rowan. What with the Bolts (five of them, if you counted Destiny, Sheree-Jade's two year old daughter), herself and Kirsty, and Matilda and Ben, the London contingent very nearly outnumbered the locals.

'Put your hands together for Ms Cara Fraser,' called Murdo, over the excited chatter, as Cara took the stage, performing a sultry version of *Fever*. Next up was Gregor, who delivered *Somewhere Over the Rainbow* in his rich tenor voice. He was followed by Matilda and Ben, neither of whom could sing a note, camping it up wildly on *Don't Go Breaking My Heart*, and looking to be hugely enjoying themselves.

'Who's your friend?' said Gregor, later, grabbing Heather's wrist as she was on her way to the bar for another round.

'Oh, that's just Ben, remember, I told you –'

'He doesn't look like "just Ben" to me. He's gorgeous,' hissed Gregor. 'Is he single?'

'Well, yes. But, Greg, sweetie, Ben isn't gay.'

'You think, do you?' said Gregor ominously.

'Anyway, I thought you were all loved up with Robbie.'

Gregor tossed his head.

'I am, but a boy can still window shop.'

Heather and Kirsty, billed as the Fabulous McAndrew Sisters, were the last act up. Although their performance was 10% talent and 90% enthusiasm, everyone in the pub seemed to be singing along and clapping in time to the music. Kirsty looked beautiful in her lime green mini dress, teamed with over-the- knee black suede boots and a pink fur shrug. When they had the same Scottish forebears, why did she, Heather, have to be afflicted with red hair, while her sister's was sleek, black and shiny?

As the evening raced on, Heather began to feel that she really did belong here, that she'd been totally accepted. Many people came over to chat and to meet Matilda and Ben, some to renew their acquaintance with Kirsty, and, at closing time, she was swept into a laughing, shouting crowd, strolling along the front, the waves silvered by moonlight. Outside Treeny's cottage, Matilda and even Ben paused to admire the starscape.

Later, the three girls sat on Heather's bed, drinking hot chocolate and chatting softly about the evening.

'My feet are killing me, but I haven't had such a laugh in ages,' said Matilda, taking off her shoes and massaging her toes.

Much later, Heather tiptoed out of the room and into the kitchen to get a glass of water. She could hear Ben's deep breathing as he slept on the sofa. She pressed the glass against her cheek, enjoying the coolness of it, then sipped slowly, looking out of the window. A small, quick movement in the grass caught her eye: a fieldmouse, she guessed. Further up the hill, at Shell Cottage, she could see a light was still on, its yellow glow leaking out into the garden. Sean must still be up. She leaned on the windowsill. She wondered if it were true that he'd once been involved with Rowan but knew deep down that it was. Rowan's casual possessiveness told her so. Rowan, she was aware, wanted to keep Euan dangling on a string but also liked to feel that all the other men in the village were under her spell. Besides, she reflected, apart from her beauty and her notorious sensuality, she was so arrogant and self-absorbed that she wouldn't be intimidated by Meg's memory and would treat Sean in her usual offhand way, and, probably, that was why he liked her. Thoughtfully she rinsed out her glass and crept back to bed.

13. *Devil Woman*

'You don't mind us all descending on you like this?' Heather asked Treeny, as they sat outside in the pale, early morning sun, eating breakfast. She looked out at the vastness of it all, the fields and the tall dark pines of the forest which, in turn, were dwarfed by the mountains.

'Not at all, lassie,' said Treeny. 'I like having you all to stay, makes me feel twenty years younger.' Her eyes twinkled. 'In fact, if I *was* twenty years younger, Ben would have to watch out. I'd be right in there.'

Heather giggled. Having known him most of her life, she was impervious to his looks, but, she supposed, if you liked spiky blond hair, beaming smiles and big blue eyes, he was handsome, as if he wouldn't look out of place in a boy band. He'd clocked up two admirers in as many days, but Heather preferred her men dark and sultry. Yet again, she wondered why Treeny had never married, why there had never seemed to be a great love in her life.

'Aunt Treeny –' she began, but, just then, Kirsty, stretching and yawning, came out of the back door and collapsed beside them on the bench. Her face was chalk white, her green eyes bloodshot, her hair tousled.

'Didn't know the cottage was haunted, Treeny,' said Heather.

'I'm out of practice,' groaned Kirsty. 'Old Sheepshagger. What do they put in it?'

'Alcohol. The Deil's own urine,' said Treeny, accentuating her Highland accent, but her lips twitched.

Matilda wandered out next, wearing a floor length pale blue dressing gown borrowed from Treeny – her baby doll pyjamas had been shoved back into her suitcase.

''Morning,' she yawned.

''Morning. I'll get you some breakfast,' said Heather. With the help of Treeny's trusty old spurtle – a kind of wooden spoon without the bowl – she was becoming a dab hand at making porridge, although Treeny was appalled that she flavoured it with honey, or jam and cream, instead of salt.

Ben was easy to entertain, she thought, as she stirred the thickening oats in the pan. He'd been bitten by the Munro-bagging bug and, as long as he had the hills and the pub, he was quite happy. She'd been worried about keeping Matilda amused for two weeks, but today the Lammas Festival, which would culminate in Sheepstock, kicked off with a village fayre. All money raised would go to the orphanage in Malawi sponsored by the people of Kirklochy.

'This is fantastic,' said Heather, later, as they walked round the village square, her arm in Treeny's. Bunting criss-crossed, flapping in the light wind, balloons floated above every stall. Out of the Brigadoon orchestra, Valissa had pulled together a band, which was playing the *Skye Boat Song*, while the prettiest teenager in the village skipped through the crowds, tawny hair flying, charming everyone and holding out a green velvet hat which was quickly filling up with notes. Stalls were set out on trestle tables all round the edge of the square. Miss Munro, Treeny's friend from the post office, had a serious knitting habit, and her stall was piled high with adorable matinée jackets and bootees in lilac, apricot and lemon. Next to this stall was one selling handmade cards painted by Heather and Sean. Matilda happily snapped up some rose scented soap infused with red petals, which, she declared, was better than that sold at the market in Covent Garden, but half the price. Shortbread, fudge, tablet, organic vegetables, haggis, neaps and champit tatties, and ice cream supplied by the Fratelli brothers were also for sale. Sascha and Gregor had even set up a nail bar, where they were giving the local women French manicures for £5 a time, while their husbands drank real ale from plastic cups.

'Treeny,' said Matilda suddenly. 'There's a geezer stood over by the ice cream stand eyeing you up. Well fit, too, for an older bloke.'

'Where?' said Kirsty, wheeling round.

'Don't be so obvious,' hissed Matilda.

'Well, I don't see anyone,' Heather said.

'He's gone now.' Matilda grabbed Treeny's sleeve. 'Don't move from here, so he knows where to find you –'

'Don't be so silly, girls,' said Treeny. 'He's probably just short sighted. Let's go and get some lunch.'

Matilda was persuaded to try haggis, and, after a few tentative bites, decided that she liked it.

'Look, Heather,' she said, then, her butterfly brain jumping onto a new topic. 'We can have our fortunes told.'

At the end of the row of tables was a circular structure draped with purple and pink velvet and what looked like gold tinsel. Outside was a sign, gold writing on a midnight blue background:

Madame Esmeralda
Tarot and Palm Reading
Fortune Telling

'Lot of mumbo-jumbo,' said Heather.

'Oh, come on. It'll be a laugh. And it's for charity,' said Matilda, walking towards the tent and pushing back the heavy purple curtain.

The ladies of the Rural were supplying the teas and Mrs Gillies poured Heather, Kirsty and Treeny each a cup. It was getting chilly, and Heather cradled hers gratefully, warming her hands on it, as she waited for Matilda to come back.

'That was blinding. I'm going to travel, get a big promotion at work, and meet a sexy new guy,' she beamed, as she walked towards them. She pressed her hands together. 'I've applied for Rachel Lott's job – you know she broke both her legs in that ski-ing accident, which was a bit of luck. Plus Lucie and I've been talking about going to Ibiza on holiday.'

'Amazing,' said Heather drily, as Treeny handed her teacup back to Mrs Gillies and walked towards the tent. The girls drank more tea and chatted while they waited for her to return.

'What did she tell you?' said Kirsty, when she'd rejoined them.

'I'm going to be well enough to go on holiday abroad next summer, and it'll be a place I've always wanted to visit.'

'Where, where?' said Matilda.

'Rome,' said Treeny, a determined look in her eyes. 'Your turn, Heather.'

A wall of subtle, expensive perfume hit Heather as she pushed past the velvet curtain, and took a seat on what was obviously one of the terminally uncomfortable beige plastic chairs from the village hall, covered in thick, coral coloured material.

Madame Esmeralda, sitting behind a table with black sugar paper taped over it, was an exceptionally beautiful young woman, with long black hair and a high-cheekboned face on which were painted moons and stars in mauve kohl pencil. Her eyes were large and emerald green and she was wearing a black lace dress and huge gold hoops in her ears. An onyx cross hung between her full breasts. She looked vaguely familiar. She waved her heavily beringed hands over what was unmistakeably a goldfish bowl, upturned and sprayed with glitter.

'Cross my palm with silver,' she intoned, in husky broken English. Heather passed her a tenner, which she snatched up in slender fingers with long nails lacquered purple. She closed her eyes, appearing to meditate for a few moments, then began to circle her hands over the goldfish bowl.

'I sense you have come through a time of great upheaval, great internal conflict,' she said, in the same mittel-European accent.

Heather nodded grudgingly, but then, her nails were bitten down and her lips chapped, so it wasn't that hard to tell. Suddenly, a giggle erupted inside her and she laughed out loud.

'Rowan, it's you, isn't it?'

'That's Madame Esmeralda to you,' snapped Rowan, in her normal cut glass English accent. 'Do you want your fortune told or not, Heathah?'

'Yes. Yes, I do,' said Heather, trying not to laugh again. For the first time, she warmed slightly to Rowan, that she seemed to have a sense of humour buried deep down, and that she was willing to spend her day masquerading as a fortune teller to raise money for the charity – and had really thrown herself into the part.

'You have travelled far. Very far,' said Rowan, reverting to her pseudo-Polish accent. 'And, before the planets are again in alignment, you will find a place to call home.'

'Okaaay.'

Rowan wafted her hands around over the crystal ball once more.

'Your artistic career will take off,' she said, in portentous tones. 'I sense a fierce creative spirit within you.'

She closed her eyes again, as if concentrating deeply.

'A man has entered your life –'

'I don't want a man in my life –' protested Heather.

'Hush, I can only tell you what I read in the stars. A man has entered your life. He is tall, dark and handsome –'

'Can't you be more specific? Like, what letter does his name begin with?'

Ludicrously, Heather's mind began to range over the tall, dark and handsome men she knew: Aidan, of course, who was probably strolling hand in hand with Savannah right now, totally loved up, and Sean, who wasn't even speaking to her. She perked up as she thought about Euan, with his laughing dark eyes. Oops, Rowan really had goofed with this prediction.

'I can only tell you what the bowl reveals, I mean, the ball reveals. He is tall, dark and handsome and he is of sorrowful countenance –'

'Thanks, Row... er, I mean, Madame Esmeralda. Very *illuminating*,' said Heather, as she got to her feet.

'Well, what did she tell you?' Matilda asked, in excitement, as Heather emerged from the tent, shivering slightly.

'Oh, I'm going find my place in the world, my career as an artist's going to take off, and I've got a handsome man in my future –'

'Brilliant,' said Matilda, and she actually clapped. 'Things are really looking up for both of us.'

Heather didn't have the heart to tell her that the soothsayer was Rowan, wearing a Hallowe'en wig, tinted contacts and purple lipstick.

'You've got to love her, haven't you?' said Kirsty. They waved over to Katie, who was sitting with her little friend Eilidh, both of them having matching tiger faces painted on.

It was late afternoon when they returned home, laden down with parcels. Out of loyalty, Matilda had purchased most of Heather's handmade cards.

'You didn't need to do that, Tills,' said Heather. 'Honestly.'

'I wanted to; I love them,' said Matilda. 'Anyway, I've worked out I won't have to buy another birthday card for three years.'

Ben, back from another day on the hills, put his head round the kitchen door. He was wearing Treeny's white lacy apron.

'Ooh, are we interrupting a private fantasy?' said Matilda.

'I'm cooking tonight, guys. Moroccan. Lamb tagine with couscous,' Ben said, ignoring her.

'Sounds fab,' said Matilda, sniffing the air. 'We'll just leave Nigella to it, shall we, girls?'

Treeny opened a bottle of wine and poured out a glass each, then she settled on her favourite chair with the latest Caro Ramsay novel. Matilda produced a book with a lurid pink cover: *How to Get Him and Keep Him*, by Dr Brandi La Puma. From the shiny cover photo, Dr La Puma looked like a cross between a bespectacled Jennifer Aniston and a shark. Heather put on her Shaun the Sheep slippers, curled up on the sofa, inspected her shiny new pink nails and sipped her wine until a delicious aroma began to drift out of the kitchen.

᠆

'My round.' Gus the Taxi stood up, reaching into his pocket for his wallet. Gus didn't often join them in the pub – usually he was working.

'Hey, Gus,' Heather called, as he pushed his chair in. 'Will you go outside, walk round the building twice, then come in the side entrance and go to the bar via the loo?'

Kirsty, Matilda and Ben laughed. A guffaw came from Alfie Bolt, who was propping up the bar, but Gus looked puzzled.

'I think that joke lost something in the translation, babe,' Kirsty said.

As Gus returned and began to transfer pints of Old Sheepshagger from the tray to the table, Treeny's friend Miss Munro passed by carrying a glass of sweet sherry. She seemed to be here alone. Heather opened her mouth to invite her to join them, but Euan got in first.

'Hey, Flora,' he called. 'Come and sit with us.'

They all shuffled along and Euan moved a chair over for the older woman, who sat down next to Gus.

'We were just talking about budget films,' Euan told her. 'Your go, Kirst.'

'Men in Black Polyester,' Kirsty said.

'Lethal Curry,' suggested Gus.

'From Here to Next Tuesday,' said Matilda.

'What about you, Flora?' Euan asked. Miss Munro pondered for a moment.

'Fifty Shades of Earl Grey.'

Heather giggled. 'Good call.'

She and Miss Munro high fived.

'That was a nice thing you did,' she whispered to Euan, later, when Miss Munro had gone to the ladies'. 'I think she's been quite lonely since her sister died.'

Euan nodded, his expression serious. 'She has.'

Heather leaned in and kissed him on the cheek.

'What was that for?'

'Just for being lovely.'

14. *The Girl in the Painting*

'I think, maybe, a progressive Canadian Barn Dance was a tad ambitious for your first time,' said Heather. Rain lashed against the window of Fratelli's. Waves leapt over the sea wall onto the pavement. A young girl hurried past, seemingly dragged by an inside-out yellow umbrella. The sky was the colour of charcoal. At the Lammas ceilidh the previous evening, Matilda had gone completely the wrong way during the Canadian Barn Dance, and then, later, during Strip the Willow, she'd tripped over her Jimmy Choos and caused a pile up.

'It was a right laugh,' she said. 'Nearly as good as the caber tossing competition.'

She had been thoroughly over-excited by the sight of so many hunky men with kilts, six packs and rippling muscles.

The big fifties' jukebox in the corner pulsed and rippled with rainbow colour, cheering up the grey of the afternoon. Treeny had selected her favourite record, The Teddy Bears' *To Know Him is to Love Him*, and was teaching Kirsty to jive on a small square of chequered floor. Ben, who had a six-year old's passion for them, was digging into a Knickerbocker Glory. Heather and Matilda sipped Fratelli's signature vanilla lattés. By this stage in the holiday, Matilda was wearing Heather's jeans and a faded Red Hot Chili Peppers tee-shirt left behind by Jamie at Easter. Treeny had contributed a pair of walking boots and a bobble hat and the outfit was completed by a fleece Matilda had bought for a fiver in Altitude Problem, the outdoors shop on the promenade.

'I look like a train wreck,' she moaned.

Heather opened her mouth to protest – even the hat looked supercute – but Ben was too quick for her.

'You don't, Tilda. You look beautiful.'

Heather glanced at him: *Tilda*?

Without heavy make-up and hairspray, Matilda had an almost Scandinavian prettiness, with her long blonde hair, delicate features and tanned skin.

'I don't know why you wear all that gunge on your face anyway,' Ben was saying. 'You don't need any of it.'

Matilda laughed.

'I'm an Essex girl. I've got to look blingtastic; it's in my DNA.'

Ben was still looking at her, his face serious.

'Makes me feel more confident, I suppose,' she said, hesitantly, after a moment.

'We love you anyway, whatever you look like,' said Heather, putting her hand over Matilda's. Only close friends knew that Matilda's mum was an alcoholic, and that her dad had left home when she was just thirteen, when she'd become head of the family, trying to protect and care for her two younger sisters. That she'd missed out on college and taken an office job because she'd had to start earning money as soon as possible. Only close friends knew that her obsession with presentation and detail was her way of maintaining order and control, of not stepping over the line into chaos.

'Here,' Kirsty said, approaching with a tray bearing five tall glasses of hot chocolate. Somehow, she, also, managed to look glamorous with her wildly windblown hair and wearing a grey lamb's wool sweater and two colourful scarves wound artfully round her neck. She winked. 'Asked Tino to put a splash of Bailey's in.'

'Cheers.' They clinked glasses and each took an appreciative sip.

'Hi, guys,' said Euan, who'd just bustled in, amidst a cold blast of air.

'Come and sit with us,' called Heather. Euan slipped off his dripping jacket and hung it over the back of his chair, while Kirsty went to fetch him a coffee. Heather's breathing quickened: the rain had soaked right through his jacket and his tee-shirt was quite wet and clinging to his chest and abs. He'd pushed his dark hair back flat against his head, drawing attention to his face: his long-lashed dark eyes and the lean line of his jaw. Surely every red-blooded girl around the table was, like her, recalling the wet shirt scene in *Pride and Pre-*

judice. Heather shook herself: Euan was her *mate* – she really shouldn't be thinking those impure thoughts about him.

'Thanks, Kirst,' he said, as Kirsty placed a steaming coffee and a rocky road in front of him.

'You're welcome.' Kirsty threw him a luscious smile. Heather exhaled: her sister was such a little flirt.

⮑

'I'm sorry, Ben, but "lairy" isn't a real word,' challenged Treeny. The previous evening, Ben had discovered, in the sideboard, a cache of games – Monopoly, Cluedo, Trivial Pursuit and Scrabble in battered, tattered boxes which had been produced summer after summer when Heather, Jamie and Kirsty were younger. He'd immediately proposed a game of Scrabble. From the kitchen, where she was peeling potatoes, Heather could hear the others arguing cheerfully.

'Oh, and "havers" is?' said Ben.

'Chrissie, I'm going to need a judge's ruling, but I think you'll find it is,' called Treeny to Mrs Gillies, who was sitting on the nearest easy chair, a Scrabble dictionary on her lap.

Heather put the potatoes in water, ready for boiling later, and, pulling on Treeny's oilskin, slipped out the back door. She had decided to visit Sean. There had been a bad vibe between them since they'd argued and she wouldn't feel right until she'd apologised. She'd been putting it off for too long, using her guests as an excuse. Outside, there was a high wind blowing, but it wasn't far to Shell Cottage, so she decided to press on. She started to walk up the hill, the wind rising and so strong that it almost blew her back down again. Behind her, she could hear the waves crashing onto the rocks and, above, the sky was turning black. She was about to go home when the rain started: cold, heavy drops splashing onto her face, which instantly turned to sheets, soaking through all but her oilskin jacket. As she turned back for Thistle Cottage, sleet stabbing her cheeks, the wind rose still higher and she lost her balance and crashed to the ground.

Her arm was sore, jolted when she'd reached out a hand instinctively to break her fall, and a stone was digging into her hipbone.

Rough shrubbery scratched her face. She lay on the ground as the elements raged around her, more swathes of icy rain sweeping across her face and seeping into her jeans. She'd been coping very well, so far, she realised. Too well. Treeny's illness, Aidan's betrayal and the subsequent messy break-up, the leaving of her job, her family, friends, flat, future and all that was familiar to come as an outsider to this tiny village on the outside edge of the back of beyond – she seemed to have taken it all in her stride. Until now. A wild sob came from deep inside her. She curled into a foetal position on the marshy ground and cried and cried. No one would hear her howls above the wind and the rain pouring down would wash away her tears.

～

'Heather. Heather, can you hear me?'

Sean was bending over her, his hair lifting in the wind. The storm had abated somewhat.

'I fell,' she managed, hoping he hadn't witnessed her meltdown.

'Can you sit up?'

Painfully, she manoeuvred herself into a sitting position, mopping ineffectually at her wet face with her palms.

'To your knees,' said Sean, taking her hands. Gingerly, she moved until she was kneeling, sinking into the damp ground.

'Can you stand up?' Slowly, Sean pulled her to her feet.

'I'm fine,' she said, having carefully put her weight on each foot to make sure nothing seemed to be broken.

'Heather, you're not fine. Come on.'

She allowed him to put his arm round her in support for the short distance to Shell Cottage, and, leaning against him, smelt lemon soap and white spirit. Slowly, they made their way across the marshy ground and through the gate.

In the hall was a rack with Sean and Cara's outdoor shoes and a pair of tiny red wellies and beside them pink and white trainers of the kind that light up. She hung up her jacket and put her mud-encrusted boots next to those.

'You need to get out of those wet clothes,' Sean said, and, despite his soft Scots accent, those words had never sounded less erotic.

'Sorry,' he blurted, in realisation, 'I didn't mean it that way.'

Now they were in Katie's room, a dream bedroom for a little girl, with murals of Disney princesses and fairytale heroines painted all over the walls – Meg's handiwork, Heather guessed.

Sean directed her to the bathroom and handed her a soft, fluffy white dressing gown printed with candy pink hearts, which she hoped and presumed was Cara's, and left her alone to change.

It was with great relief that she stepped into the shower, enjoying the feel of the jet of hot water washing the mud and twigs out of her hair. She lathered her limbs with the lemon soap she'd earlier smelled on Sean's skin and washed her hair with Cara's strawberry shampoo which smelled good enough to eat, then she dried off quickly, wrapped the dressing gown around her and stepped out into the hall.

'Heather, we're in the living room,' called Sean.

She sat on the sofa, tucking her hairy legs up under her. Now that she didn't have a boyfriend, she didn't think that the agony of getting them waxed was worth it. Sean went into the kitchen to make her some tea and throw her clothes into the washer-dryer.

Then, at last, she came face to face with Megan McAllister.

The painting dominated the room and the dark eyes seemed to be on her whatever angle she chose. Meg was sitting on a stool, just wearing jeans and a sweater, and Heather could see how like Cara she was – the same long, shiny brown hair and heavy fringe, the same bright, alert face. Close up, there were myriad details – the amber flecks in the hazel eyes; the glow where the sun touched her hair; the tiny, gold studs in her ears; the bright sparkle of her sapphire and diamond engagement ring. In the background were the same trees and hills Heather could see from Treeny's cottage...she wasn't sure how long she gazed, entranced. As an artist, she could appreciate Sean's talent, but she could also see the love for his wife that had gone into every brushstroke. With a pang, she remembered that Sean had never finished his portrait of her.

'Heather,' said Katie, who had come to stand before her in an adorable wine coloured pinafore dress. 'Are you very sad?'

'I am quite sad,' she admitted. Her reddened, swollen eyes gave her away.

'Why?' asked Katie, her round brown eyes on her.

'Because –' She cast around for a way to explain to the child. 'You know how, when you fall out with Eilidh and you're not talking, you feel miserable until you're best friends again?'

Katie nodded gravely.

'Well, I fell out with my best friend, and I feel miserable because we don't talk anymore.' Again, she felt the ache that the relationship which had meant so much – to both her and Aidan – had failed.

Katie considered this.

'Would you like some ice cream?' she asked.

Heather found herself smiling. Somehow, Katie always did manage to cheer her up a little. She scampered off and returned with a plate piled with chocolate, pistacchio and strawberry.

Heather plunged her spoon into it with relish. Just then, the front door banged, and Cara burst into the room, cheeks red and hair tousled.

'What a day,' she exclaimed. 'Oh, hi, Heather,' she added.

'Hiya,' said Heather, as if it was quite normal to be sitting there in a dressing gown, working her way through a plate of ice cream.

'What happened to you?' asked Cara, flopping down beside her on the sofa.

'Heather fell over,' explained Katie. Heather found herself giggling – it sounded as if she, too, was seven.

Sean came in with the tea, and they sat around talking for a while. Cara pulled Katie onto her lap, stroking her hair.

'I think we'll just get takeaway pizza from Uncle Rocco tonight,' she said.

'Aunt Cara, can I get a pizza with absolutely no meat, now that I'm a virgin?' said Katie.

'Vegan,' corrected Cara, kissing the top of her head. 'Anyway, since when were you a vegan?'

Heather smiled to herself – she detected the influence of Eilidh's mum, the local florist, who taught tantric yoga in the village hall, and was a Buddhist. Cara and Katie went off in search of pizza, and Heather and Sean were left alone.

'I was on my way here because I wanted to talk to you,' Heather began, moving closer to him on the sofa. 'I wanted to apologise for the way I spoke to you... that time. It was out of order.'

'It was,' said Sean, his eyes on her. They were hard and grey like wet slate.

Heather had no wish to talk about Megan and Cara, so fell back on psychobabble.

'I had some issues to resolve,' she said.

'What issues?' asked Sean, not seeming too impressed by her non-explanation.

'Just... stuff.'

'Really, I want to know.'

'I left London because I'd split up with my boyfriend and he was seeing someone else. We worked together and I couldn't bear the thought of seeing him day in, day out. Especially if she was with him.'

'Are you over it now?' Sean asked. She nodded.

'Yes, I'm over it, but it still hurts sometimes. As you saw, I had a bit of a wobble today.'

'Yes.' Gently, Sean traced his finger down her cheek. She rested her head on his shoulder, breathing in the smell of white spirit, lemon soap and fabric softener. It felt warm and comfortable. She closed her eyes. Sean put his arms round her and it felt good to be held. He stroked her hair and rubbed her back.

'Everything's going to work out for both of us, I know it is,' she said.

'Mmm.' Sean murmured. He began to caress the back of her neck. She relaxed into his embrace, her eyes still closed. She didn't know how long they sat there, warm and safe, before the outside door banged.

'Daddy! We're back,' Katie shouted.

Heather opened her eyes, and suddenly she was back in the untidy, book lined and toy strewn living room of Shell Cottage. A Sindy doll looked implacably at her through stiffly lashed eyes. Megan was staring at her.

'Daddy! We got you pepperoni.'

Sean sighed.

'Listen, Heather, we can't talk here. Why don't we go out for dinner, just the two of us? We could go back to The Creel – remember, the place we had lunch?'

Heather's heart beat faster and she could feel the colour rising in her cheeks.

'Yes – it was lovely. I'd…I'd like that.'

'It's a date, then. I'll book a table. Do you want to stay for some pizza? There'll be loads.'

Heather shook her head. As much as she loved spending time with Cara and Katie, she needed some head space to savour the memory of how it had felt to be held by Sean, to recall every detail: his citrus scent, the soft wool of his sweater, the rough maleness of his stubble, the silver-grey of his eyes; to reflect on the change in their relationship and to look forward to seeing him again, this time having him all to herself in the lovely restaurant which overlooked the sea. It would be even more beautiful in the evening, she thought, imagining them looking out as the sun set, pink and apricot, over the beach, and turned the windows of the houses on the curve of the bay to gold. She touched his cheek.

'Thanks, but I'd better get back. Matilda's cooking for us all.'

'I'd put on some clothes first, if I were you.' Sean's lips twitched.

Heather looked down at her dressing gown and the pink slippers she was wearing. Cara's feet must be a couple of sizes bigger than hers and she looked like a less stylish version of Minnie Mouse. The door opened and Katie hurried in.

'Heather, come into my room. I can show you my *Frozen* duvet cover,' she said, taking Heather's hand.

'That sounds uncomfortable,' Heather joked, excitement still bubbling within her. 'Don't you get really cold in bed?'

She allowed Katie to lead her into her bedroom. Cara came in with her clothes, creased but warm and dry, and laid them on the duvet.

'Two minutes till tea, missy,' she told Katie. 'I'm just warming the plates.'

Heather dressed quickly.

'Heather?' said Katie. 'Is it Matilda?'

'Is what Matilda, sweetie?'

'Your friend that you fell out with?'

'No, it's not Matilda.'

'Good,' said Katie, flopping down on her bed. 'I like Matilda, she looks like a princess.'

Heather presumed that, to Katie, a girl who had waist length blonde hair, dripped with diamanté and wore a pink fake fur coat and silver stiletto boots would look like a princess.

'She's going to do my make-up and hair. And my nails. She promised.'

Heather privately resolved to have a word with Matilda about this. She wasn't having the child going about the village looking like a seven-year-old lap dancer.

'You should talk to your friend, say "sorry", make it up, and then you'll be happy again,' Katie went on.

'How did you get to be so wise?' said Heather. Although she had made her peace with Aidan, a part of her would always hurt that they'd no longer be close.

'Sunday school,' said Katie.

'Pizza's out!' Cara called.

Katie skipped out of the room, Heather following. Sean was waiting in the hall. They smiled tentatively at each other for a few seconds.

'How are you fixed for Friday?' Sean asked.

'Friday's great,' Heather said, with another tingle of excitement.

'Brilliant. I'll pick you up at Treeny's at seven.'

⤻

As she approached Thistle Cottage, she could see Kirsty, who had been banished outside to smoke, leaning against the wall. The storm had abated and the grey sky was suffused with a weak yellow light, like an energy saving bulb.

'Hi,' Heather said, pausing beside her. Just a year younger than she was, Kirsty was the wilder side of herself that she sometimes wished she could be. She envied her cool, dark looks: her pearly skin and her shiny black hair. She wore her trademark scarlet lipstick. Her hands were wrapped round a large mug of coffee and Heather noticed that her nails were painted in purple, black and wine alternately. Even in fingerless gloves, an old hand knitted cardigan of Treeny's, and with her hair in a messy plait, she managed to look effortlessly stylish, a bright scarf draped round her neck and a sequinned cloche on her head.

'You look terrible,' she said, blowing a cloud of smoke into the chilly air. 'I mean it. You must have frightened the cows.'

'I fell.'

'I know. Sean phoned Treeny earlier. Did you do it on purpose?'

'Of course I didn't do it on purpose. Do you want to see my bruises?'

'No, thanks.'

'But…' Heather paused for effect. 'It was sort of worth it…drum-roll…because – he asked me out!'

'Oh, my God,' squealed Kirsty, holding up her palm. 'Result. He is sooo cute.'

Heather high-fived her, beaming and again feeling a blush rising in her cheeks. She looked at her sister's dancing green eyes. She was so glad Kirsty was here to talk to and to share her excitement.

'Where's he taking you?' she demanded.

'The Creel – it's the seafood restaurant on the front at Inveralan.' Kirsty inhaled deeply.

'Wowzer. I know it; it's gorgeous. A crowd of us went there for Greg's birthday last year.' Her words were laced in smoke. 'We had the best time.'

Heather gave a little wriggle of anticipation.

'I'm going to make you look your absolute best. Hair, make-up – the works. I'll lend you something fabulous to wear. Sean won't know what's hit him.'

'Thanks, babe.'

'Yup – it's definitely high time you got back in the saddle, so you can totally get over that scumbag, Aidan. That's always been my policy.' Kirsty blew out a last plume of smoke.

'Kirst, if I start taking relationship advice from you, I'll really be in trouble.' Heather gently punched her sister in the ribs.

'What do you mean? I've been out with loads of guys.'

This was true. Kirsty changed her boyfriends more often than she changed her earrings.

'You might want to give that last statement some thought,' Heather said. She slipped her arm round Kirsty's shoulders and together they went into the cottage.

15. *Tonight's the Night*

Only her sister would pack a teal coloured taffeta midi for a few days' holiday in the village, Heather thought, gratefully, as she stepped into the dress, pulled it up and slipped her arms into the sleeve-holes. She felt the zip cold against her back as Kirsty lifted her hair and gently pulled it up.

'Fits perfectly,' she said. 'You absolute bitch – you look better in it than I do,' she went on, opening the door of the antique wardrobe so that Heather could see herself in the mirror inside.

She inhaled sharply as she looked at her reflection – she barely recognised the glamorous, film star vision before her.

The dress clung to every curve, the rich colour turning her eyes to turquoise and contrasting to perfection with her mass of shining hair. Her make-up, which Kirsty had taken the best part of an hour to apply, subtly enhanced her features, and the delicate gold sandals borrowed from Matilda made her legs look long and shapely.

'Thanks so much, Kirst.' Heather was nearly in tears as she hugged her sister. She sprayed on another blast of Allure just as she heard the chap of the door-knocker, and grabbed up her tiny gold bag.

'Don't wait up,' she cried.

'Don't do anything we wouldn't do,' chorused Kirsty and Matilda.

'Sky's the limit, then?' Heather joked, but, really, she just wanted to enjoy being in Sean's company, get to know him better, talk to him.

'Hi,' she whispered, a little shy now, as she opened the door and stepped outside. The sun was shining, but the breeze coming in from the sea was brisk. She shivered slightly, having come out without a jacket. Sean ran his hands up and down her bare arms to warm her and she shivered again, this time with pleasure at his touch.

'You look beautiful,' he told her.

'You, too.' She looked up at his face, his eyes pewter coloured in the evening light. His dark hair was swept back from his smooth forehead. She was touched that he'd also made an effort: in place of his usual paint splashed jeans and tee-shirts, he was wearing black trousers and a grey shirt. The smell of turps was absent for once and she breathed in a mixture of the tang of lemon and of the sea air.

'Let's go.' Sean's words broke the spell, but he put his hand on the small of her back as they walked down the path towards his car. As she climbed in, trying her hardest to do so elegantly, she was sure that Treeny, Kirsty and Matilda would all have their faces pressed against the window.

Then Sean turned his key in the ignition and drove off, and, finally, they were alone, cocooned in warmth. He pushed a button on the dashboard and the music of Ben Howard filled the car. They didn't talk much on the way, Sean concentrating on the road and Heather gazing at the scenery scrolling by: trees of every kind and shade of green, bright yellow fields of rapeseed, still, deep blue lochs reflecting back the sky, flowers of pink, purple, blue and yellow blurring on the verge by the roadside.

⌒

'Follow me, Sir, Madam.' The waiter led the way across the parquet floor to a secluded table by window and tucked into an alcove. He pulled out their chairs for them and handed each a leather bound menu.

'Would you like to see the wine list, Sir?'

Sean glanced up.

'Not for me, thanks, I'll just have a sparkling water, but you go ahead if you want to, Heather.'

'Water's fine for me,' Heather said. She'd noticed his care while he'd been driving, and surmised that he was ultra-conscious of road safety, the day of the accident burned into his brain. She'd noticed, too, that he was wearing a wedding ring, and felt a faint note of disquiet – but, guiltily, she pushed it down. The ring was a symbol of how much he'd loved Megan. She was the mother of the child who meant the world to him. Maybe he could start a new chapter with someone else, but Meg would always be with him – no one could take those memories away.

The waiter left them, returning with two glasses of water, each garnished with one slice of lemon and one of lime.

'Cheers.' They clinked.

The waiter reappeared to take their order.

By the time the starter arrived, conversation was flowing easily. Sean started off by asking her about her exhibition, and she told him which paintings she'd already sold – which was most of them.

'Wow,' Sean said. 'Didn't I tell you how good you are?'

Heather grinned.

'You did.'

That led them on to talking about the panorama before them – the wide beach, the water, calm and blue, lapping gently against golden sand, the ice cream coloured houses beginning to take on a rosy glow, then to other favourite views and walks in and around the village. The waiter cleared away their starters, returning with square white plates of salmon, mash and fresh vegetables, arranged like a work of art in themselves. As they ate, they chatted about everyday things – family, memorable holidays, classic TV shows they'd loved, favourite books and films.

'So, what do you get up to when you're not painting or hanging out with Katie?' Heather asked.

'Me and some of the lads play poker.'

'So do I! Treeny's been teaching me.'

'Seriously? Treeny plays poker?'

'Yup.' Heather grinned. 'She nearly got thrown out of the care home for gambling, which she would've called a result.' Despite the absence of wine, her blood zinged with well-being – it was far too long since she'd sat in a gorgeous restaurant with a handsome, attentive man. She took in the elegant planes of his face, his thick eyelashes, his artist's hands with their long, tapered fingers. His phone lay on the table to the side of his plate – Katie was never far from his thoughts – but he hadn't as much as sneaked a look at it all night.

'Thanks for bringing me here, Sean,' she said. 'I'm having a lovely evening.'

Sean smiled and reached for her hand across the table.

His phone began to ring, strident against the soft classical music playing in the background.

'Sorry – better take this. It's Cara.'

She could see the terror in his face as he listened to Cara's voice, her anxiety detectable even down the line.

'I'll be with you as soon as I can,' he said, then terminated the call. 'Katie's missing,' he told Heather, his voice shaking. 'We've got to go. Now.'

Jumping to his feet, he pulled his wallet out of his jacket pocket, threw down a bundle of notes and swept towards the door, Heather following as fast as was possible in killer heels.

They didn't speak as Sean started up the car and drove off down the coast road. She fastened her seatbelt and caught sight of his set face. How must he be feeling, desperate to get back to Kirklochy, yet conscious of how Meg had met her death skidding across a country road and afraid to drive too fast?

⤳

Probably they'd made good time, but, sick with fear, Heather felt that the journey had taken several hours. Pulling up, Sean tossed her the keys to the boot. Inside was the family's walking gear and she swapped her sandals for Cara's thick socks and walking boots and pulled on a fleecy over her dress.

'Sean,' cried Cara, her voice high with apprehension. She ran towards him and fell into his arms, and they clung to each other, not saying anything.

A number of people had already gathered outside Shell Cottage. There were Matilda, Kirsty and Ben, their faces ashen.

'Cara thinks she went into the kitchen – there was a carton of orange juice lying out – let the dog out into the garden and then followed her. The gate was open. We think... we think she's gone into the forest,' Matilda said.

Euan seemed to have taken charge, and had summoned his colleagues from the mountain rescue team to assist in the search. Phil, short for Philth, the local policeman, was there, with reinforcements having been called in from the surrounding villages. A few professional looking dogs stood, proud and alert, one of them sniffing at the pinafore dress Katie had been wearing the last time Heather had seen her.

Euan was trying to get the sequence of events out of a near hysterical Cara.

'I gave her a bath and then put her to bed at eight o'clock like I always do,' Cara was saying, her voice coming out in long, shuddering gasps. 'Then there was something I wanted to watch on television. About half way through at the adverts I checked on her and she was still awake, sitting up in bed reading. After the programme finished at nine I looked in on her to see if she'd fallen asleep but she'd gone.'

'You didn't hear anything?' asked Euan.

'No,' said Cara, tears spilling out. 'I had the television on.'

'What was she wearing?' asked Euan, his voice soft.

'Pyjamas and a dressing gown. Oh, and she'd put on her Wellingtons.'

'Right,' said Euan. 'Sometime in the last hour or so, she got up, went into the kitchen and let the dog out into the garden. The dog jumps over the gate and runs off, and, worried that she might get lost, Katie follows her –'

Cara nodded, then put her hands over her face, sobbing pitifully into them.

Heather looked out across the landscape. She'd thought so often how vast and majestic the patchwork fields, tall pines and the mountain range were, but now she saw danger in all that beauty, quite different from the dangers facing children in London. Katie was somewhere in the forest, that seemed certain. This was summertime in Scotland, so there was still more than an hour of light left, but it was a chilly evening. At least it wasn't winter, but it would be easy for a child, even a country child, to get lost in that forest, to become disorientated, to become tired. To trip and fall, perhaps. To stumble into the stream that ran through it. To become cold and wet. Especially a child who walked with a limp and who was inadequately dressed. Her heart ached as she thought of Katie's utter panic when she realised that she couldn't find her way out of the woods, that she'd walked around in a circle, maybe, that she was lost, that she was frozen. They had to find her. They had to. If they did not, she wouldn't last the night.

'It's all my fault,' howled Cara. 'I was supposed to be looking after her. If anything happens to her, I'll never forgive myself. It's all my fault,' she cried again.

'It isn't.' Matilda walked towards her, her voice radiating calm. Years of coping with her mother's chaotic lifestyle and unpredictable behaviour while caring for her sisters had made her resourceful, a cool head in a crisis. She kept talking, still in the same measured voice. 'You couldn't know she would do this. She's never done anything like it before. Nobody's done more for her than you have. And, Cara, beating yourself up isn't going to help find her. We're going to search for her, and we won't stop until she's safe again.'

More and more of the villagers had turned up. It seemed to Heather that everyone was here, other than those too frail to leave the house, and those with young children of their own to look after. Alfie Bolt was standing nearby with his nineteen year old son, whose predilection for cannabis was said to be the main reason for the purchase of a Highland bolthole. Craig Peden and his mates, the beanie hat brigade, had forsaken their cider drinking in the bus shelter to assist with the search. They were hunched together, saying little, their hands deep in the pockets of their ill fitting jeans, looking slightly affronted. All the Fratelli brothers were there, apart from Paolo, who was in Edinburgh on business, but would catch the next available flight to Inverness. There was Mrs Lawrie, eighty if a day, in a tweed coat which nearly reached her ankles and a knitted hat pulled low over her forehead, standing with Treeny. Her heart sinking all the more, Heather noticed Hamish Lockhart on the fringes of the crowd, a loud-mouthed know-it-all, who, to make matters worse, was obviously drunk.

Briskly, addressing everyone through a loud hailer, Euan divided the search party into groups, allocating each one a local who knew the area and a portion of the wood to comb. One member of each group would remain outside the wood and keep in touch by mobile phone. Several people, sensible people, the kind of person Heather would never be, had compasses and torches. It was agreed that Treeny and Mrs Lawrie would wait at the cottage, in case the child managed to find her way back.

Heather marched towards the wood with Misty, Ben, Kirsty and Matilda, Misty walking briskly ahead.

'Katie, Katie.' She could hear Cara's wild voice cry across the flat, open land.

16. *Lost*

It was grey in the forest, dead pine needles thickly carpeting underfoot, the trees towering above like the arched roof of a church. Heather could hear the occasional call of a bird, detect the swift movement of small animals in the undergrowth and, further away, the rush of the stream.

'Katie,' she called, they all called, and she could hear the name over and over, a kind of desperate echo through the trees from everyone hunting, hunting for her.

They walked forward slowly, Ben sweeping his powerful torch into every gap in the trees.

'The worst thing we can do is miss her,' Misty explained.

Suddenly, standing staring in front of them, caught in the beam of the torch, was a fox. After a moment, it turned away and slid back between the trees. Heather had always thought foxes were beautiful, but there was danger there, too. If Katie fell, if she lost consciousness, the foxes might have her. She pushed the idea from her mind.

'She must be terrified,' Kirsty said.

'We'll find her,' came back Matilda's firm voice. 'Or, if we don't, the sniffer dogs will.'

Time passed all too quickly. Darkness fell, and, in the forest, it was darker still, eerie. Anxiety tore at Heather's heart. She felt exhausted and her face was scratched by the low branches, but they had to keep going. Her hair caught on another branch, a pain shooting through her head, and she had to pull it free. She'd be frightened to be in this place alone in the dark – a grown woman. She couldn't even begin to imagine how Katie must be feeling. They walked on, saying little, all consumed by the same fear, cones and needles cracking underfoot. Suddenly Heather could hear the whirr of a helicopter above, see strong light pierce the canopy of trees.

'Look.' Kirsty darted forward, lifting something from the ground. It was the belt of Katie's pink dressing gown.

'She came this way,' breathed Matilda.

'Katie, Katie,' they all shouted again, in voices that were hoarse and sore. They walked on, stooping low in case she'd fallen and was lying on the ground, but could see nothing.

'She could have turned back, gone in another direction –' said Ben, in despair.

'In that case, someone else would find her,' Matilda said.

As the night advanced, it was becoming colder. Heather shivered, pulling Cara's jacket more tightly round her. She was so tired, yet her senses were heightened by the terrible fear. She jumped at a noise overhead, then realised that it was only a bird. Nearby she could hear voices, then Hamish Lockhart and a bunch of others came crashing through the trees.

'What are you doing here?' Misty cried. 'You're meant to be searching north of the burn.'

'Let's just get on with it,' said Hamish, his voice terse. This was hopeless, Heather thought, overcome by a wave of exhaustion. They'd never find her; they were lost themselves. It was so easy to lose direction.

It was then that she heard a voice, quite clearly, ringing across the dark quietness of the wood. Her party all stopped dead. No one could mistake that accent.

'It's all right, baby girl,' Rowan was saying, in a gentler voice than Heather had ever heard from her. 'No one's cross with you, we all just want you home and safe.'

A thick beam of light caught Rowan on her knees on the forest floor. Heather watched, hardly breathing, as the small figure emerged from the shadows. Rowan scooped Katie up in her arms and cuddled her close.

'She's here,' shouted Hamish. 'She's safe.'

'Yesss,' said his girlfriend, stumbling towards him and throwing her arms round his neck. Heather found herself hugging Misty.

'Rowan.' Matilda ran towards them, almost tripping, seeming as exhausted as Heather felt. 'How is she?'

'Very tired, very cold and very frightened, I would say,' said Rowan. 'But she'll be fine, won't you?' She stroked Katie's back as the child whimpered.

They made their way back through the trees, Misty navigating. It wasn't a large forest, although it had certainly seemed so when Katie was missing.

A cheer went up from Euan and those people who had found their way back out of the woods. Raising his loud hailer, Euan broadcast that Katie was safe, to call off the search. The people who had waited outside the wood made quick calls by mobile and slowly, people began to appear from the darkness of the trees. Sean and Cara emerged, holding hands.

'Thank God, thank God,' Cara was saying, her face crumpling again, but this time in tears of relief.

Everything seemed a blur to Heather after that. The police helicopter, at deafening volume, descended into a nearby field. Murdo invited the villagers back to the Claymore for a stiff drink, with those who could not be accommodated heading for the B&B, where a restorative dram was also available. Another group walked down to Fratelli's for espresso shots.

Heather and her friends found themselves back in Shell Cottage, where Mrs Lawrie was bustling about, making cups of sweet tea. Katie was still clinging to Rowan like a monkey, as if she'd never let go. Rowan, in turn, was holding her tightly. Euan was looking at Rowan with such love and admiration that, just for a moment, Heather felt lonely. Then she felt guilty about being so self-indulgent.

'Want Rowan,' Katie said, putting her thumb in her mouth. She seemed to have regressed a few years in as many hours. She rested her head on Rowan's shoulder.

'Rowan's going nowhere,' said Rowan, walking confidently towards Katie's bedroom. Sean, who'd seemed almost catatonic, followed her.

Heather sank onto the sofa beside Treeny, Cara on her other side. Cara's mobile phone burst into life, her ringtone an inappropriately catchy Charlie Puth tune, and she had a brief, muttered conversation.

'Paolo,' she said, her eyes shining through her exhaustion and the ravages of her tears. 'He's at Inverness Airport. He says he'll be here as soon as he can, even if he has to get a taxi.'

Through the open kitchen door, Heather could see Ben and Matilda sitting at the table, their fair heads close together, deep in conversation. Trudie, the dog, innocent of her part in the evening's drama, snoozed in her basket in the corner.

Kirsty and Jake Bolt had gone outside to smoke, but that was ages ago, and they were still out there, despite the cold. Heather could see their silhouettes, Kirsty moving her hands around with continental gestures as she talked. Jake, Heather realised, was just Kirsty's type – moody, brooding, quiet, slightly depressive, prone to solitary walks on the windswept beach, and with a faint whiff of scandal. There was a touch of Heathcliff in his long dark curls. There was enough danger and darkness in Jake to appeal to Kirsty's romantic soul.

Just then, Dr McLuskie, the local GP, who'd been summoned from a function, turned up, in full Highland dress. He went into Katie's bedroom to examine her. Sean and Rowan came back into the living room.

'I don't know how to begin to thank you,' said Sean.

Rowan shrugged. 'I didn't really do anything. It was Euan. He organised the search party.'

'You found her,' said Euan.

'Any of us could have found her. I was just lucky.'

'Not half as lucky as she was,' said Cara, with fervour. 'Thank you so much, Rowan.'

'Damn. My dress is ruined,' said Rowan suddenly. She was, Heather now noticed, wearing a black silk maxi with purple Hunter wellies and a Barbour, the skirt ripped, torn and spattered in mud.

'I'll buy you a new dress. Anything you want,' said Sean.

'Doubt it, dahling,' said Rowan, her voice upper class and brittle. 'I got it in Bond Street.'

After a while, Dr McLuskie came out, saying that Katie was suffering from shock and exhaustion, but would recover well.

'We'll stay with her until she goes to sleep, Sean. She asked me to,' said Rowan, looking slightly abashed at having been seen to have a heart. She and Euan went out, Heather following.

'You have the coolest bedroom ever,' Rowan said, gesturing to one pink wall where flower fairies danced, soft as gossamer, towards a castle. 'Did Mummy paint all this?'

Katie nodded, her expression solemn.

'You're a good little artist, too,' Heather said. There was a small easel set up just by the window, to make the most of the natural light.

Katie nodded again.

'And look at all your books.' A dark pink painted bookcase was brimming over with children's classics, many of which Heather remembered enjoying in her own childhood, although they now had funkier covers.

'Heathah and I are so jealous. I want a dressing table with lights round it like yours.'

'Never mind you and Heather. I'm so jealous,' Euan said.

'Cinderella's my very favourite fairytale,' Heather said, looking at another mural of a castle. Behind the windows could be seen princesses in pink ballgowns and tiaras dancing with men in black tie with curling moustaches. 'Isn't she beautiful, with her long, golden hair and her party dress?' Cinderella was dashing down the sweeping staircase towards her coach, her crystal slipper left on the top step.

'She looks just like Matilda,' Katie said, seeming more animated.

'She does.'

'I think the Little Mermaid's better. She's my favourite,' Rowan said. On the opposite wall, the Little Mermaid, perched on a rock, watched wistfully from behind the fronds of a willow tree. Heather marvelled at the attention to detail. Katie would never want this painted over, she was sure, not even when she was a truculent teenager stamping around slamming doors and all dressed in black. To the McAllister family, it must be worth far more than the discovery of an original Banksy.

'Rowan?' Katie stuck her thumb into her mouth again. 'Will you come round tomorrow night? We can watch my Little Mermaid DVD. It's my favourite too.'

'Of course I will,' Rowan said.

'I hope I'm invited too,' Euan said. 'I'll torture you until you say yes.' He reached out and began to tickle the child's ribs, and she squealed with uncontrollable laughter. When she'd recovered, she threw a sideways glance at Heather.

'You've to come, too, and we'll do some painting.'

'I think you're milking it, now, Katie-bubble, but I'd love to.'

Rowan reached out and plucked a book from the nearest shelf.

'One story,' she said. 'Then you need to go to sleep.'

Heather left them to it and slipped into the bathroom. So much had happened since Sean had picked her up only hours ago, she reflected, as she soaped her hands, the now familiar lemon fragrance drifting up. Her face in the mirror was grey, her cheeks lacerated by low branches, her hair a mass of frizz, her make-up smudged, her dress covered in mud – all the glitter and glamour of earlier well and truly gone. She felt unaccountably low, even though Katie had been rescued safe and well. It must be the comedown after the adrenaline high of fear she'd felt during the search. No wonder she was exhausted and flat.

She dried her hands and went back into the living room. Sean was standing motionless before the portrait of Meg. Was he having a conversation with her in his head, telling her about the events of the evening? Begging her for forgiveness? Lightly, she touched his back and he turned to face her, Meg's eyes meeting hers unblinkingly over his shoulder.

'We'll go,' she told him. 'You look done in.' She leaned up and kissed his cheek. 'I can't begin to understand how you must be feeling, or maybe I can, in a small way. I love her too.'

'I know you do,' said Sean.

Touching his cheek once more, she left him alone.

‿

It was a crisis situation: they were nearly out of coffee. Heather, still feeling tetchy and restless after the events of the previous evening, offered to walk into the village and buy fresh supplies.

On the way, she spotted Cara walking on the beach, her scarlet coat making a splash of colour against the greyness of sea and sky, her scarf and hair floating out behind her on the wind. There was something despairing in the way she was trudging with her head bowed. Not surprising, after everything that had happened last night. She, too, must be shattered. Heather crossed the road and climbed over the seawall onto the hard, ribbed sand.

'Cara,' she shouted, but the word was snatched away by the wind. She hurried after her friend.

'Cara,' she said, again, when she was closer. Cara spun round, her eyes red and swollen. 'How are you?'

'Fine,' Cara said, her voice shrill. Heather fell into step with her. Waves swept onto the sand and then retreated.

'We can talk about it, if you like.'

Cara turned to her, tears sparkling in her eyes.

'I hate myself.'

'Babe, don't do this. You didn't do anything wrong and she's fine. Dr McLuskie said she was fine, didn't he?'

Cara nodded, tears running down her face.

'Why don't we go for a coffee and we can talk?'

'No,' cried Cara, seeming panic stricken. 'Not Maggie's and definitely not Fratelli's.'

'Okay,' Heather said gently. As she'd passed Maggie's tearoom, she'd seen Mrs Crombie, the most gossipy, indiscreet woman in the village, sitting by the window with a bunch of cronies. Facebook was less efficient at spreading news than she was. Next door, at Fratelli's, Rowan and Euan had the prized window seats, and were gazing at each other and holding hands across the table. Again, Heather felt a stab of pain – after such a promising beginning, she just didn't know where she stood with Sean.

In London, there would have been any number of Costas and Starbucks and Café Neros, anonymous chains where she and Cara could have holed up. She took her friend's arm and they walked on. The beach was deserted but for a bedraggled looking teenager with a dog.

'It's not just about Katie,' Cara said, at length, and she stopped walking. Heather was silent, giving her time and space. The sound of surf and seagulls was loud. 'I've done something terrible. Please don't ask me, Heather.'

Her hands plunged into her pockets, she turned away and began to march down the beach.

'Cara!' Heather followed her, picking up her pace. 'You can tell me.'

'I can't,' Cara sobbed. 'You'll hate me.'

'Of course I won't hate you. It can't be that bad.'

'It is. After Rowan left last night, Sean and I, we –' She looked down at her boots.

'You slept together,' supplied Heather, thinking how woefully inaccurate this euphemism was to describe the desperate, passionate lovemaking that she imagined.

Cara nodded, briefly, once.

'It didn't mean anything, not in that way,' she said, eager, now, to speak. 'We were just... it was all the emotion, we were comforting each other. After what happened to Meg, we couldn't bear it if we'd lost Katie. I mean, we literally couldn't bear it –' She broke down again.

'I know, babe, I know.'

Heather put her arms round Cara, feeling her soft hair against her cheek, her shuddering body. Her face was wet with Cara's tears.

'I can't believe it, my sister's husband. And…it was your first date with him. He really likes you. I don't want you to think… it honestly didn't mean anything. And it'll never, ever happen again. Please don't let it come between you. Please give him a chance.'

'I don't think you can ask me that.'

Cara sniffed.

'Sorry. It's just… you're really good together. Promise you don't hate me.'

'I don't hate you,' Heather said wearily. Perhaps she'd always known that she and Sean weren't to be. 'Cara – I don't think Sean's ready to move on. He isn't over Megan's death. It's got nothing to do with you and him.'

Cara looked down at her feet, more tears wobbling on her eyelashes.

'Paolo doesn't know?' Heather asked gently.

'No. I was so shattered I fell asleep in Sean's bed, but when Paolo phoned to say he was on his way he woke me up –'

'At least he didn't find out,' said Heather.

'I can't believe that I've cheated on him. I never meant to. I'd never have thought in a million years…Sean and I've talked about it, we've absolutely sworn it won't happen again, but what am I going to do?'

'Caz, you love Paolo, don't you?'

'Of course I do.'

'Then you shouldn't tell him. You shouldn't threaten what you have with him.'

Heather surprised herself by giving this advice, but it felt right.

'But I feel so guilty I don't know how I'll ever be able to look him in the face. We've never had any secrets –'

'If you tell Paolo, it might stop you feeling guilty, but how's he going to feel? He'll be devastated. Put it behind you and move on – with Paolo.'

'It's something I'll have to live with for as long as we're together.'

'It's for the best. You can't throw away all you've meant to each other over a moment of madness.'

The two girls turned back and set off home.

'Heather, I really am sorry,' Cara said. 'It's just... I've always hoped you and Sean might get together. You've got loads in common, with the painting and all.'

Heather shook her head, walking faster so that Cara had to hurry to catch up with her. Sean was in love with Megan but couldn't have her. Cara looked just like her, was the same age now as she had been when she'd died. Heather shivered. Best not to go there.

꙳

Back at the cottage, Heather, hearing voices and laughter from the living room, went straight to her bedroom and sat down on the bed. Wrapping her arms round her knees, she rocked gently back and forward. She needed some time to herself to come to terms with Cara's revelation. In Kirklochy terms, it was worthy of the front page of the Sun on Sunday. If the gossips found out about this, Sean's reputation in the village could be ruined. Paolo might understand, but, then again, he might get all Mediterranean, punch Sean and break off with Cara. If Cara walked out, what would happen to Katie? And, after all that had happened, what would become of Sean?

She wasn't aware how long she sat there, thoughts chasing round her head, but eventually the door opened.

'Did you get it?' asked Matilda.

'What?'

'The coffee, Heather. We're all dying from withdrawal symptoms here.'

'Sorry. Forgot,' muttered Heather.

'How could you forget? You only went out for one thing.'

'I met a friend, we got chatting and it went out of my mind.'

'And this friend wouldn't be the lovely Sean, would it?' Matilda's voice took on a teasing note.

'No,' snapped Heather.

Matilda crossed the room and sat down on the bed next to her.

'Listen, babe,' she began, putting her hand on Heather's shoulder, 'after what happened with Aidan, we really want you to meet someone who'll treat you as you deserve.'

'I know,' admitted Heather. 'Matilda, no offence, but –'

'You want to be on your own for a while,' said Matilda. 'Okay. I'll go into the village and get the coffee. In a bit, babe.'

She left. Heather opened her Ian Rankin novel and tried to return to the dark dampness of Edinburgh's Royal Mile. A handless corpse had just been discovered at the foot of a narrow close.

'Hi, what are you doing?' Kirsty's dark head appeared round the door.

'Just thought I'd read for a while.'

'Helps if the book's the right way up.'

'I've just got a lot on my mind,' said Heather, tossing her thriller aside – even it wouldn't be enough to divert her from her misery.

'What?'

'I can't tell you, Kirst. I wish I could.'

She really did. Kirsty had always been her confidante, pretty much since they could speak, and they'd be holed up in her bedroom or Kirsty's, talking through whatever childish problems occupied their minds.

'Heather, we've always been able to talk about anything.'

'If I tell you this, do you absolutely promise not to tell anyone else?'

'Of course I do.' Kirsty looked hurt. 'Anyway, who would I tell? I'm going back to London in a couple of days, and I doubt if the girls would be that interested in the goings-on in a village they've never even been to.'

Heather nodded. Kirsty's friends mostly believed that, if something wasn't in *Vogue*, it wasn't worth knowing. Taking a deep breath, she lowered her voice and gave Kirsty the edited highlights.

'But, babe, what about you and Sean? I thought you really liked him.'

'I do. I did. And I thought Sean really liked me,' she said, finally, feeling guilty about bringing her own feelings into the equation. In comparison with what Sean and Cara had been through, they seemed so trivial.

'I'm sure he did…look – do you think it's definitely over? I mean, things were pretty fraught last night –'

'I wasn't planning sex on the first date – especially not with another woman.' Heather's voice was harsh.

'Okay, okay.'

'I think he turned to Cara because she's the next best thing to Meg.'

'All this is a bit Jeremy Kyle for me, Heather. I'm sure he was attracted to you, but the timing isn't right.'

'Maybe,' sighed Heather. Once again, she was second best, the consolation prize. That was no surprise, but, even so, she felt depressed.

'It's awful, a real mess,' she said. 'I just hope Paolo doesn't find out.'

'Well, Cara surely wouldn't tell him,' Kirsty said. 'And neither would Sean.'

'I don't know,' Heather said. Who knew what Sean would do, if he felt haunted and desperate enough? She could even find it in herself to feel terribly sorry for him, bereft and longing for someone he couldn't have.

⤺

A few days later, Heather sat at a table in the Spinning Jenny in Inveralan. After a few moments, Cara came in, a jacket thrown on over her scrubs. As she sat down, Heather poured out the tea. She was sure they'd both need a sugar rush, and so had ordered them each a chunk of rocky road.

'How's it going?' she asked, grateful for the relative privacy of being away from Kirklochy.

'Okay,' Cara said cautiously. 'Paolo's being so nice to me – I mean even more than usual – because of what happened to Katie. I feel so guilty. I can hardly look him in the eye.'

'Has he noticed anything?'

'Of course he has, but he thinks it's just delayed reaction to the shock.'

'He's a good man,' Heather said. 'You absolutely mustn't tell him.'

'No, I won't, but I have made a decision. I'm going to move out of Sean's. There's a vacancy at the nurses' home.'

'But what about Katie?'

'Oh, look, Heather, I don't want her to suffer because of all this and I'll still see her a couple of times a week, but me living there was never meant to be a permanent arrangement. Plus, she doesn't need me so much, she's growing up and she's spending more and more time with Eilidh. And Eilidh's mum's happy to have her. She was Megan's best friend in the village –'

She broke off and Heather guessed what she was thinking – that the two young mothers should have been hanging out together with their daughters, enjoying their growing up.

'So I move in at the weekend. It'll be much easier for work, and I'll be able to see Paolo most days.'

Heather drank her tea, feeling more peaceful. There seemed to be some hope for Cara and Paolo at least.

17. *Matilda & Ben*

Heather, Matilda, Kirsty and Ben were in the Claymore, where Murdo was compering the weekly pub quiz. The team comprising the local accountant and solicitor and their wives was marginally in the lead, while Gregor and Sascha's team, who called themselves "Norway" on account of their consistently low scores was, as always, lagging behind.

'Round 4, question 2: what is the name of the engineer who created the map of the London Underground?' asked Murdo. Sometimes he would take pity on Heather and put in a question she might actually be able to answer.

'Harry Beck,' she whispered. Matilda wrote the answer down with a pen topped by a pink feather.

'Question 3: In the periodic table, what is the symbol for copper?'

'Cu,' murmured Matilda, scribbling. There followed a number of scientific questions. Quickly, Matilda jotted down the answers. Ben glanced at her with some respect. Heather smiled to herself. People often wrongly assumed that because Matilda was a blonde babe in a balcony bra that she was not very bright.

'Finally, question 10: In the television series "Doctor Who", for what does the acronym "Tardis" stand?'

'Time and relative dimension in space,' muttered Matilda. 'Used to date a geek,' she explained, jumping up to hand Murdo their answer sheet.

Heather managed another smile. Still feeling down about her stillborn romance with Sean, she was so glad that her sis and best mates were here, helping to cheer her up. What would she have done without them? At least she wasn't second best in their book.

'And, at half time,' announced Murdo, 'in the lead with an amazing 38 points is Barking Mad.'

'Yessss,' screamed Matilda, hugging Heather.

'You answered most of the questions, Tills.'

'Yeah.' Ben grinned. 'Who knew there was a brain underneath all that slap and peroxide?'

'Cheek,' said Matilda, tossing a yard of hair over one shoulder. 'This is my natural colour.' She took a playful swipe at Ben, but then they stopped larking about and just looked at each other.

'I'll get the drinks in,' said Heather.

⌒

'Forgot my –' The words died on Heather's lips. Matilda and Ben were sitting on the sofa, kissing. Matilda's arms were wrapped round Ben's neck, and he was cradling the back of her head in his hand. Heather's heart ached at the tenderness between them. They broke off at the sound of her voice, slightly flushed, Ben's arm protectively round Matilda's shoulders.

'Thought you'd gone out,' said Ben.

'So I see.' Heather's heart was beating fast, so that she felt quite queasy. She snatched up her purse, which she'd left lying on the coffee table. 'I'll leave you to it.'

'C'mon, Hev. Don't be like this. Sit down and we'll talk.' Matilda gestured to the chair beside her.

'How long have you been sneaking around behind my back?'

'Just a few days, honestly. We were going to tell you –'

'Obviously.'

Heather turned and walked out.

'Heather, what's going on?' Kirsty had appeared in the doorway of the bedroom.

'Ask them.' Heather threw over her shoulder. She slammed the door behind her. A chilly wind rose as she walked down the hill.

'Heather, wait up –'

She kept on walking. Kirsty, sliding on the mossy ground, drew level with her. She was wearing only skinny jeans, ballet pumps, several strings of pearls, a black vest top and goose bumps, a few inches of naval visible. Her slender body was shaking, her hair drifting on the wind.

'Kirsty, what are you doing? You'll catch your death of cold,' Heather said, aware that she sounded just like Treeny.

'Well, you shot out the door like a greyhound out of a trap. I didn't have time to wrap up.'

The sisters walked on until they reached the promenade.

'Let's go in,' said Kirsty, who must be freezing by now. They were standing outside Fratelli's. 'I need a caffeine fix.'

'And a sugar rush,' said Heather. She pushed open the door and went in, managing to grab a free table in the middle of the café. It was very busy. The entire teenage population of Kirklochy sat in one corner, drinking strawberry milkshakes out of tall glasses. They had grouped eight chairs all around one table, and were talking and laughing loudly and flirting unsubtly, the boys vying for the attention of a stunning girl with high cheekbones and tawny hair. Gregor and Sascha sat at another table, not talking, as Sascha was reading a magazine called *Hollywood Hair*, while Gregor was engrossed in *How to Get Him and Keep Him*. Heather presumed that Matilda no longer required Dr La Puma's words of wisdom.

Tino Fratelli came to take their order, with the usual warm Italian welcome. Heather ordered two vanilla lattés and, calculating they would give the best chocolate hit, two brownies. The air was, as always, suffused with the aroma of coffee and cinnamon. Behind the glass fronted counter were tubs of ice cream of every colour of the rainbow, next to rows of gateaux and pastries. Heather longed for the innocence of childhood, when a Fratelli's Neapolitan ice cream was all it had taken to put a smile on her face.

'Making out on the sofa. It's just so disrespectful to Treeny,' she huffed, after they had been served.

'Oh, I know,' said Kirsty, licking foam from her upper lip. 'Absolutely. But that's what young people are like these days. No consideration.' She giggled. 'How old are you anyway, Heather, about ninety-seven? What's really wrong?'

Heather bit into her brownie, feeling the rich, heavy sweetness burst on her tongue. Why was she so upset about Matilda and Ben? She supposed it was never easy when mates began a new romance, and she feared the threat to their friendship. She didn't want to lose both her best friends at once. She looked at her sister's pretty, heavily beringed hands clasped round her glass, the nails painted, today, pearl colour. It was because they *were* her best friends that she felt so bereft. She'd always been so close to both of them.

'You think you'll be left out?' prompted Kirsty.

Heather nodded. Ben had had a number of girlfriends over the years, including a brief holiday fling with Sascha, in the days when she was still Morag MacDougall, but none of them had been especially serious. One particularly bitter ex had said that pre-booking a cinema ticket was too much of a commitment for him. As for Matilda, nobody could've described her relationship with Dane-from-the-mailroom as romance of the century. There had been no one to threaten her. But, then, when she'd been with Aidan, hadn't she put him first? She felt her eyes prickle with tears. If Aidan hadn't ruined everything, she'd still be happy, and she'd be happy for Matilda and Ben. Would she and Matilda ever be alone together again, close, comfortable and sharing every thought? Now, if she wanted a heart-to-heart with Tills, Ben would be there in the background, or, if she wanted to sound out Ben on the man's point of view, Matilda would be with him.

'It's early days,' ventured Kirsty.

'I know,' admitted Heather, but, somehow, she sensed that this was the real deal.

Kirsty broke off a piece of brownie.

'People change and move on. Everything's going to be different, but I'm sure you'll all be fine.'

Heather managed a smile.

'All the same, it's really undignified. Like the time Dad caught you and that boy in the garden shed. What was his name again?'

'Damian.'

'Yeah, Damian Moon.' Heather giggled. 'Dad grounded you and threw him out, you said you'd never been so mortified in your life and you didn't speak to him for a week.'

'I was only fourteen,' protested Kirsty, laughing at the memory. 'Er, actually I think I'll just...go and have a word with Greg.'

She slipped out of her seat and approached Gregor's table, just as

Ben came in, bringing with him a blast of chilly air and looking slightly sheepish.

'Mind if I sit down?' he asked, glancing at the seat Kirsty had vacated.

Heather said nothing, so Ben pulled out the chair and sat opposite her. He reached over and took both her hands in his.

'Look, I'm sorry I didn't tell you that Matilda and I'd got together, but *I'm* still trying to get my head round it. I mean, I've known her for years, so it came as a total surprise to me. I used to think she was just a beautiful, blonde babe –'

'That bad?' came a voice from the next table.

'Shut up, Callum,' snapped Heather.

'... I thought she was a lightweight, really into her appearance, but since I've been here and spent so much time with her, I realise there's so much more to her than that. She's been through so much. She's so strong and bright and brave.'

Heather half expected a Whitney Houston song to strike up – *Didn't We Almost Have it All?* Something like that.

'Well, I knew that already,' she said. She sipped her coffee. 'It's difficult when your best friend cops off and you're the gooseberry,' she admitted. 'But both my best friends have copped off at the same time.'

Ben held her hands more tightly.

'It's early days,' he said, echoing Kristy's words. 'But, whatever happens, I promise it won't come between us. We'll still hang out all the time.'

'Ben, you do realise that she's pretty vulnerable underneath?'

'Yesss,' said Ben, soft but firm, and Heather thought that Matilda had probably been very lucky to find him.

'Would you like another coffee?' asked Ben, getting up at her nod and heading for Tino, who was standing behind the counter, polishing a banana boat.

It was then that Heather noticed the girl sitting at the table next to hers. She'd been so engrossed in her thoughts that she hadn't seen Rowan, who was alone, gazing at an empty espresso cup. She looked totally different from her normal self, anxious and careworn, her face ashen. Her eyes were shrunken and red: it was obvious she'd been crying.

'Rowan, are you all right?'

Rowan turned to look at her, but it was a few seconds before she answered, like a foreign correspondent on a news link.

'I'm fine.'

'You don't look fine,' said Heather, sliding into the chair opposite her. She was struck again by just how beautiful Rowan was, although her amazing eyes were today bruised with exhaustion and her face was chalk white. As she pushed back a lock of amber hair, Heather noticed that her fingers were stained with nicotine. She almost wished Rowan would abuse her like she normally did.

'I'm —'

'What is it, Rowan?'

'Hangover,' growled Rowan. She smelt of Obsession mixed with stale smoke. 'I'm sorry, Heathah, I would talk to you, but I can't be bothered.'

Heather let this pass – she'd been touched by the kindness that the other woman had shown to Katie and Sean.

'Look, I know we've not always been the best of friends, but if you're worried about something, you can talk to me, you know?'

Kirsty appeared beside Rowan's chair.

'Heathah, just leave me alone, all right? Get off my case. You're hanging around me like a disease.'

'I was only trying to help -'

'I don't need help,' said Rowan, her eyes sparkling with anger. She got up and pulled on a khaki coloured parka, somehow managing to make the uninspiring garment look as if it were straight from the pages of *Vogue*. She flicked her hair back over the collar and picked up her car keys from the table.

'It's been a joy, Rowan,' said Kirsty sweetly. 'Same time, same place tomorrow?'

Ignoring her, Rowan stalked out, letting the door bang. The sisters watched through the window as she walked away, her titian hair lifting in the breeze. She sat down on the seawall, putting her head in her hands. Heather turned away, not wanting to intrude anymore on Rowan's grief.

'What's up with her?' she wondered.

'Who cares?' said Kirsty, as the door opened again and Matilda came in. Although she was wearing a thick, navy blue fisherman's jersey, old jeans and hiking boots, no make-up and her hair scraped back in a ponytail, she still turned heads.

'Hi, Hev,' she said, seeming slightly abashed. Pulling the table vacated by Rowan beside their own, the four sat down with a coffee each. In an unprecedented move, Matilda decided to order a double chocolate muffin.

'Can I get you anything, babe?' she asked, her voice humble.

'Yes, please. A bowl of salted caramel ice cream,' Heather said grimly, although she'd just devoured a brownie. But, still in emotional trauma, she felt she deserved it. Matilda stood up, her pert tush attracting more admiring glances, and returned to the counter.

'29 across,' said an anorak-clad tourist to his partner. 'Conduct or speech directed against the peace of the state. Eight letters: two blanks, D, five blanks.'

'Sedition,' murmured Matilda, as she resumed her seat. She passed Heather her ice cream. 'We'll go to the Claymore tonight, just the two of us, and we'll have a long chat.'

⌒

Heather didn't usually like music festivals. Not because she didn't like music but because she didn't like mud, wet clothes, flooded tents, no loo paper or sharing a chemical toilet with about 700 other people, but the beauty of Sheepstock was that it was being held on Farmer Galbraith's land, within easy walking distance of the cottage, so she and Kirsty, Matilda and Ben would be able to see all the bands they wanted to, while also being able to shower and sleep in comfort every night.

The Sheepstock festival was to be the highlight of the holiday for Matilda and Ben. By the Friday morning, Kirklochy was overrun with young people in shorts and Wellington boots, walking down the promenade in droves, parking everywhere that could accommodate a car or a van, pouring into the pub for beers, queuing outside the village store for fizzy drinks and junk food and outside the chemist for midge repellent, suntan oil and condoms. There wasn't a single vacancy in the B&B or in any of the hotels for miles around.

'This is fantastic,' said Matilda, who looked like Kate Moss in frayed denim hot pants and pink and black spotted wellie boots. 'I can't believe I'm going to see Paolo Nutini, Richie Girvan and Gus McCourt all in the same weekend.'

Last night, tucked into a cosy corner of the pub with their bottle of Pinot Noir, Heather and Matilda had had a long chat, knees touching under the table, all about Ben, Aidan, Sean and their friendship. They'd been completely honest about their feelings, held nothing back and, after a heart to heart during which both girls had pledged always to be there for each other, always to make quality time for each other, she felt immensely lighter.

The friends made their way to the field where the first concert was taking place and the next few hours passed in a sweaty, excited haze of swaying and singing along to the music along with hundreds of others until they were hoarse and their hands were sore from clapping.

Later, they went to the dance tent to see celebrated DJ, Gus Mc-Court, bopping until they were breathless to the latest dance classics, including a trance version of Flower of Scotland with a driving beat. Over the bobbing heads, Heather spotted Sascha and Misty dancing with Gregor and his boyfriend, Robbie.

It was still light when, much later, the whole group sat down on tartan travelling rugs over a waterproof groundsheet. Heather, proud of her prowess in this respect – garnered from so many summers spent in the Great Outdoors – built and lit a fire, and they talked and laughed softly, sipping beer as they huddled close to the crackling orange glow.

'Heather McAndrew,' said a voice.

They all looked round at the guy who had spoken.

'Lewis Burns,' said Heather.

'As you live and breathe,' put in Gregor.

'Hey, Burnsy,' Kirsty said.

He'd been a friend of Jamie's, always in and out of Treeny's cottage. She'd known him since she was twelve and he was fourteen. The man who stood before the group, a wry smile tweaking at the corners of his lips, bore little resemblance to the gangling teenager she'd once known. Tall and slim, he wore tight, faded Levis and an ancient R.E.M. tour tee-shirt. A guitar was slung round his neck. His hair, just this side of black, was thick and with a slight wave. His eyes were an exceptionally bright blue and his hands beautiful, like the hands of an artist, with long fingers and well shaped nails. She could see that her old friend was a seriously attractive man now and was beginning to understand why Sascha and a few of the other local girls had held a Burns Supper in his honour just before he left for Edinburgh to pursue a career in music.

'Still living in Edinburgh?' Heather asked, as everyone else seemed slightly shell shocked. Sascha was blushing and avoiding his eye, while Gregor was looking at him speculatively, his boyfriend suddenly disgruntled. By all accounts, though, Lewis was 100% straight. Matilda, who was resting her head on Ben's shoulder, barely seemed to notice him.

'Heather, great to see you again,' said Lewis, fixing her with his blue gaze, making her feel all woman and as if she were the only person in the field. 'Yeah, just back here to see my mum. How's Jamie?'

'Fine. Great. He's a vet. He's engaged. He's getting married next year.'

'Wow,' said Lewis, evidently impressed by Jamie's instant transformation to proper grown up.

In a way, Heather reflected, Lewis, with his hypnotic blue eyes, easy charm, and knack of making her feel like the most attractive girl in any room, reminded her of Aidan. It was a poignant thought.

'Why don't you give us a tune?' asked Gregor, indicating the guitar, so Lewis gave an acoustic set, with everyone shouting out requests and joining in as the fire blazed on and dusk began to fall. He had a beautiful voice: he could read out the third division football scores and sound sexy. Heather watched her friends, their happy faces lit by the ripple of the flames. This took her back to all those summer nights on Jamie's Cove. They started an extended version of Sweet Child O' Mine, Lewis duetting with Gregor.

'Euan,' Heather called, seeing him walk towards her group. She patted the rug beside herself and Kirsty and Euan sat down while the music carried on in the background.

'Hey. Haven't seen you for ages.'

'I've been away, covering the Montrose Jazz Festival.'

'Rowan not with you?'

Euan shook his head.

'I'll just have to hang out with my other favourite redhead. She's in Glasgow, auditioning for a couple of roles,' he explained.

'Ooh, what are they?'

'Well, she's reading for the part of a cop in Mean City, a rookie that got accelerated promotion because she'd been to university, so no one respects her.'

'Ah thoat that wee ned wiz loaked up in Bar-L,' growled Kirsty, in a fair approximation of a Glasgow accent.

'Not a cliché at all, then,' said Heather. 'What else?'

'Have you seen Green Place, the soap?'

Heather nodded eagerly. She and Treeny were totally hooked on the Partick-based drama, and every Wednesday at eight p.m. sharp found them ensconced on the sofa with a pot of tea like an old married couple. Heather much preferred it to Treeny's other favourite soap *Thairis Air A Ghleann*, on the grounds that it wasn't in Gaelic.

'I love Green Place! What part is she up for?'

'Effie McKinnon's estranged daughter. She comes back after years away to try to heal the family rift and wreaks havoc with all the men in the area.'

'Bit of a stretch for her as an actor, then?' said Kirsty. Heather giggled, and then put her hand over her mouth. Euan was always unstintingly, and, as Heather thought, undeservedly, loyal to Rowan. But he just laughed and punched Kirsty gently on the ribs.

Suddenly, Heather remembered Rowan's haunted appearance the other day, her tearstained face. She'd thought that Rowan didn't care much about anything and wondered what could possibly have been causing her so much distress.

It was Gregor, bent on mischief and a few Stellas down, who suggested playing "spin the bottle". If Heather hadn't had a few beers herself, she would have refused. Gregor picked up one of the empties and spun it wildly on the travelling rug. It stopped, pointing at Ben, who, of course, chose Matilda, leaning in and giving her a chaste peck on the cheek. The next time the bottle birled, it came to rest pointing at Heather. Diplomatically, she gave Gregor a quick kiss on the lips. After this, Sascha kissed Robbie, Matilda kissed Ben and Robbie kissed Gregor. Then it was Kirsty's turn. What a little minx her sister was, she thought, as she watched Kirsty put down her beer with deliberation, shuffle on her knees towards Euan, throw her arms round him and kiss him passionately, in a way that would put Edward and Kristen from *Twilight* to shame.

'Ding, dong,' said Gregor.

'Hubba, hubba,' added Matilda.

'Get a room,' called Sascha.

'Put him down, Kirsty,' said Heather. She tried to sound jokey, but, in reality, her heart was hammering against her ribs. Kirsty broke away, smiling, and went back to her place.

Heather was fed up with the game by now, but Kirsty spun the bottle once more, and it was Lewis' turn. He winked at Heather, put his arm round her and kissed her gently on the lips. Then he pecked her on the cheek and gave her a quick hug before resuming his place. It was obvious that he felt as she did: he and Jamie had been super-close when they were teenagers and he was as good as another big brother to her and Kirsty.

Soon the fire began to die down to the last glowing embers. The others packed up and got ready to leave, Matilda and Ben beginning to wend their way back home between the rows of tents and camper vans, their arms round each other. Gregor and Robbie followed, hand in hand. Behind them were Sascha, Misty and Kirsty, deep in chat about the hit Scottish reality show *Fly Me to Dunoon*. Heather remained sitting with Lewis, leaning in to hear his soft voice – it was so good to see him. Euan threw them a cool glance and seemed about to say something, but then his phone rang.

'Hi, darlin',' he said, and hurried off to speak privately. What was up with him, Heather wondered, as the fire died. Maybe he suspected Lewis of having slept with Rowan. They both rated sex pretty highly and had a beauty and charisma that set them apart: surely they were bound to have hooked up at some point.

'Will we walk?' Lewis asked, as it was getting cold. Heather nodded and he helped her to her feet. They strolled down to the beach, the water turquoise tonight, the sky streaked with pink and peach. Jeez, he was handsome, she thought, as she walked beside him, her boots sinking into the wet sand. His hair could do with a wash and a cut, but there was no disguising his fine jawline, his chiselled features and his brilliant blue eyes. Gulls shrieked overhead and Heather enjoyed the feel of the light breeze in her hair and the whisper of the surf.

'Remember that party Euan and Cal had when their folks were in Spain?' Lewis asked. 'You and Jamie brought some of Treeny's homemade wine.'

Heather giggled.

'Ah, yes. The bramble wine. It was about 98% proof.'

'Rocket fuel,' agreed Lewis.

'God. We were all completely wasted. I didn't touch a drop of alcohol after that for about two years.'

'Jamie threw up into their mum's wellie boots,' Lewis said.

'And pee'd in the airing cupboard. To think he's a responsible adult now.' Heather laughed. Lewis put his arm loosely round her shoulders as they walked on. 'Still with your girlfriend?' she asked, after a few minutes of comfortable silence. Lewis shook his head.

'I'm sofa surfing. Staying at a mate's for now.'

'And would this mate be a girl?'

Lewis smiled a shade sheepishly.

'Yeah, but there's nothing going on there.'

His smile switched from sheepish to bewitching. Just as well Heather was immune – she just couldn't help remembering the gangling, awkward teenager he'd been before he became such an Adonis.

'You're not still with your boyfriend?' he asked.

'No.'

'Wee shame,' said Lewis. 'But you really like Euan, don't you?'

'Not like that.' Heather's heart was banging against her ribs again. She could feel colour rising in her cheeks, which Lewis seemed to take as proof of her crush.

'Not much gets past me.'

'But… well, anyway, he's got a girlfriend.'

'Trust me. Rowan isn't exactly a keeper. It won't last.'

In spite of herself, Heather felt warm inside, as if she'd just had a few glasses of Pinot Noir by the fire in the pub. Lewis rubbed her upper arm. He was such a nice guy – so long as you didn't do anything silly, like fall in love with him. They'd just reached the footpath that led up to the main road, not far from Thistle Cottage.

'Come in for coffee?' Heather asked.

⌒

Heather and her party came back from listening to Scots rocker, Richie Girvan, unplugged and bought burgers from Café Coli, a van which was parked on the edge of the field. Then they collapsed on the travelling rug, this time positioned under a tree in the shade. The shrill ring of Matilda's phone cut across the buzz of conversation. She groped in her backpack.

'Hi, babe,' she exclaimed. Heather could make out a voice on the other end, which sounded like a parrot on acid – Matilda's sister. At once, the smile was wiped off Matilda's face.

'Delilah,' she was saying. 'Calm down and tell me clearly what's wrong.'

The piercing voice went on.

'And you've phoned all her friends, and the hospitals?' Matilda asked. Some more screeching followed.

'Okay, I'll be with you as soon as I can.' Matilda ended the call. 'Heather, I'm so sorry,' she went on. 'I'm going to have to go home. Mum's gone AWOL. She went out last night and never came back. No one knows where she is.'

'Don't be silly,' Heather told her. 'It's fine. You do what you have to do.'

'I wish I could stay.'

'I'm coming with you,' said Ben.

'I can't ask you to cut your holiday short. You'll miss the Arctic Monkeys,' protested Matilda.

'You didn't ask me, I offered,' Ben pointed out.

'Would you?' asked Matilda, and Heather could see hope flare in her eyes.

'Of course,' said Ben. 'I'm not having you going all that way, alone and frightened.'

Back at the cottage, Matilda and Ben stood in the living room, surrounded by suitcases – all of them belonging to Matilda.

'I've loved it,' she was telling Treeny, looking surprised to hear herself say so. 'Thanks so much,' she added, walking over to her and embracing her. 'I so hope I'll be able to come back some day.'

'Come back at Hogmanay, if your mother's well enough,' invited Treeny. 'The Laird has a ball up at the castle for all the villagers. It's always a wonderful party.'

'I'd love to,' said Matilda. Heather put her arms round her friend. 'Safe home. I hope Nadine's all right. Let me know as soon as you hear.'

'Oh, she will be. She always manages to find her way home somehow.' Matilda sounded desperately sad and tired.

'And you look after her,' Heather added, turning to Ben.

Later, she blinked back tears herself as she and Kirsty stood in the bus shelter, watching Matilda and Ben climb onto the coach which would take them to Inverness Airport.

'Matilda could do a lot worse,' remarked Kirsty, as the sisters made their way back to Thistle Cottage.

Heather nodded. This afternoon proved that there was something strong, something durable between Matilda and Ben.

When they got back to the cottage, Misty was sitting with Treeny, sipping tea out of a china cup.

'I'm just going to have a wee lie-down, girls. Won't be long,' said Treeny, and left the room. Heather and Kirsty collapsed onto the sofa, one on either side of Misty.

'What happened to you on Friday night?' Misty demanded. 'Did you get off with Mr First Degree Burns? Euan seemed to think so.'

'No, I did not,' said Heather. 'He's just like another big brother. And, I must say, I'm glad he's a mate and not my boyfriend.'

'The trouble with Lewis is that he thinks he's irresistible,' Kirsty said.

'The trouble with Lewis is that he *is* irresistible,' said Misty.

'I'll see if there's some wine left,' Kirsty said, getting up and heading for the kitchen.

'Not Treeny's homemade stuff,' cautioned Heather, giggling as she remembered her conversation with Lewis. 'It could power the entire village. A couple of glasses and you slip into a coma,' she told Misty.

She tiptoed into Treeny's bedroom. Her aunt was lying on the candlewick bedspread, her chest gently rising and falling under her cardigan. Heather went out, closing the door over.

Kirsty had produced a bottle of Merlot and some chocolate biscuits she'd brought with her from M&S (since there wasn't a branch within 60 miles of Kirklochy). She poured out a generous glass each, then they settled down for a good gossip.

'Heather, tell Misty what that scumbag Aidan did to you,' Kirsty said, waving her glass around and splashing wine on the carpet. Its only plus point was that it was so hideously patterned that stains never showed up. 'He told her he loved her, then it turned out he was two-timing her –'

'I can tell her myself, Kirst,' Heather said, her mouth full of orange flavoured chocolate. 'He told me he loved me, then it turned out he was two-timing me –'

'He was so blatant about it. He's so arrogant,' Kirsty exclaimed, in indignation. While she and Misty discussed how best to kill Aidan, Heather fell silent, reliving the terrible day she'd found out about his treachery. She valued honesty and sincerity above all else, and she couldn't believe the way he'd managed to deceive her. Yet the memory didn't hurt as much as before. Maybe the passage of time really was healing, as everyone always said.

'…garrotte him with his designer tie,' Kirsty was saying, when she tuned back in.

Later, the wine and chocolate hit seemed to have cheered them all up.

'I'll have to get back to the B&B - I'm working tonight,' Misty said.

'We'll walk you over, babe,' said Kirsty, getting up and wrapping a pale pink pashmina round her shoulders.

The three girls walked the short distance, breathing in the delicious scent of freshly cut grass.

'Heather.'

They turned to hear a man's voice: Euan was jogging towards them. 'Hi.'

'Heather, I just thought you should know that Lewis Burns is seriously bad news. You really don't want to get involved with him. My cousin Dawn was totally messed up by him. He treats women like dirt.'

'I've got no intention of getting involved with him. We're just mates.'

'Really? I saw the two of you walking along the beach, all lovey-dovey, his arm round you.'

'We're mates, I tell you. He's just very affectionate.'

'That's one way of putting it.' Euan's face wore an uncharacteristic sneer. 'When he ditches you, which he will, don't come crying to me.'

'He won't ditch me, because I'm not going out with him. If you really want to know what we got up to on Friday, we had a walk on the beach and a catch up, then we went to Treeny's for tea and toast. That's how rock 'n' roll we were. Anyway, you can talk, going out with Rowan Galloway. Now there's someone who's seriously bad news.'

'We're not talking about me and Rowan.'

'No, well, maybe we should be.'

'Come on, girls,' Misty said. Leaving Euan standing on the grass verge, they headed for the B&B. A panpipe version of *The Bonnets of Bonnie Dundee* could be heard.

'What's up with him?' Misty asked, running her hand through her hair in vexation.

Had Euan been thinking about what might have happened between her and Lewis for the past few days? Was he, maybe, a little jealous? Heather felt a spark of excitement deep inside. Perhaps it wasn't the chocolate, the wine or the passage of time that had lessened the pain of losing Aidan.

〜

Matilda phoned later to say that, by the time she and Ben had made it back to Essex, her mother had found her way home, sans handbag and mobile and with no recollection of the previous night. She'd woken up on the floor of a stranger's flat and had had to make her way home from an area she didn't recognise with no money. Heather shivered at the degrading and downright dangerous things that Nadine had got involved in over the years, all due to her addiction.

'I think it's given her a fright,' mused Matilda, not for the first time. 'Maybe this time she'll sort herself out.'

'Here's hoping.'

'Ooh. In all the excitement I forgot to tell you. I think I know what's up with Poison Ivy,' Matilda cried.

'What?'

'Well, I was in the chemist the other day... did you know they stock Clinique products? I was really surprised –'

'Long story short, Tills.'

'Well, she was in front of me in the queue, and I saw what she was buying –' Matilda paused for effect. 'A pregnancy test kit. She looked pretty freaked out when she saw me standing there.'

Heather choked on a mouthful of coffee. Rowan? Pregnant? It couldn't be. Did Euan know? Suddenly, her heart was thudding. If Rowan was expecting Euan's baby, he'd never split up with her – they'd be linked forever, and she'd have no chance with him at all.

18. *Story of My Life*

It was the opening night of *Brigadoon*. Most people from the village seemed to have turned out and were waiting expectantly outside the village hall. Even old Mrs Gordon, who was 102, was there, in a wheelchair, her legs wrapped in a tartan travelling rug.

Near the door, a stylish crowd stood laughing and talking – more broadcasting, really: Rowan's friends. Heather's heart skipped a beat as she recognised the Orlando Bloom look-alike - or Alex Cornish-Taylor, as she now knew his name to be, aka Xander – equally as attractive in distressed jeans and a leather jacket as he'd been in black tie. Laughing up at him was the golden girl whom she'd seen him with before. Several other Beautiful People surrounded them. Heather recognised two sisters, members of the landed gentry, who lived on several acres of land further along the coast. Very similar in appearance, both had the refined, glacial, blonde beauty of Grace Kelly. The group's presence imbued the production with glamour and sophistication.

'Hi.' Euan rushed up, holding a camera and with his iPhone sticking out of his jacket pocket.

'Come on,' Heather said. Valissa opened the doors of the village hall with a flourish and the crowds began to shuffle in.

She could understand what people meant about the smell of greasepaint and the roar of the crowd: she felt a frisson of excitement as she and Euan grabbed their seats. The orchestra began to tune up, in counterpoint to the buzz of conversation from the audience. It was a capacity crowd – people were even standing up the back, tickets having been sold, it was said, as far afield as Glenstruan. The curtains opened for "Down on McConnell Square", the first scene.

Heather looked at the scenery she and Sean had painted, proud and enjoying seeing it at last in its rightful place, as the backdrop to the musical. As scene after scene unfolded, she felt herself transported into that magical, mystical land and the wonderfully romantic story.

'... almost like being in love,' trilled Rowan, her voice clear and true, making the hairs on the back of Heather's neck stand on end.

Valissa had choreographed a dance incorporating some Highland and country steps. Gregor was a wonderful dancer and Rowan, fluid and graceful, was a match for him.

All too soon, the production ended, to rapturous applause. Heather felt uplifted: it had been a truly wonderful night. As Rowan and Gregor ran lightly to the front of the stage, hand in hand, they got a standing ovation, and Rowan and Valissa were each presented with a bouquet of red roses.

Euan, who had been tapping away on his phone throughout the show, had to interview Valissa, Rowan and Gregor for the *Kirklochy News* also.

'I'm coming backstage to see Greg,' Heather said, following him. Gregor was a primadonna who would sulk for days if she didn't praise him sufficiently. No wonder he didn't get on with Rowan, who was a total diva. She smiled to herself. She wouldn't put it past Rowan to have some outrageous Hollywood-style demands – measuring her dressing room to ensure that it was bigger than Gregor's, maybe, or insisting on melon flavoured jelly belly beans, two dozen orchids, Cristal champagne and enough Perrier water to bathe in.

Gregor's dressing room was, in fact, a cupboard, which had been hurriedly converted by moving the mops, brooms and cleaning materials into the kitchen and replacing them with a mirror.

He kissed Heather on both cheeks in a very continental way and then stood back, waiting to be appreciated.

'Marvellous performance,' said Heather sincerely. 'The singing, the dancing, the acting, all absolutely Baftaesque.'

'Thank you,' said Gregor, graciously, fluffing up his hair. 'I am thinking of a change of career, so I may be up for a Bafta next year.'

He pulled Heather down beside him on the brocade armchair loaned by Valissa, so that they could discuss his triumph in more detail. He was also full of gossip about how, the previous evening at the dress rehearsal, Rowan had turned up drunk and so seriously late that Valissa had lost her temper, throwing her accent to the winds and letting rip in broadest Liverpudlian.

'Oh, my days,' he squealed, in delight. 'She sounded just like Paul O'Grady. *I* would never be late for a performance. *I* am a consummate professional.'

''Course you are, babe.' Heather absently patted his hand. She'd never met anyone she wanted to slap as much as she did Rowan. Rowan would have known that she was indispensable – it was tacitly agreed that she was streets ahead of her understudy, who, besides, was on the wrong side of fifty.

Euan carried out his interviews and also took several photos – he was the newspaper's star photographer as well as everything else. Rowan, in a green velvet dress which brought out the colour of her eyes, looked gorgeous. Before long, a spontaneous party had started in her dressing room, which had been invaded by the Beautiful People, Xander expertly opening bottles of champagne without spilling a drop and splashing it into paper cups, and everyone standing round knocking it back and talking in ringing voices.

'Fabulous performance, my dahling,' said Xander, to a chorus of agreement.

'And guess what? My agent just rang to tell me that I've landed the part of Rosie McKinnon in *Green Place*,' Rowan said. 'It isn't exactly Poldark, but it's one of the juve leads. It'll do to start with,' she was saying.

Heather watched the girl laughing exultantly with one of her friends, as she tossed back her drink and Xander refilled her glass. If Rowan really ever had been pregnant, she reflected, she didn't seem to be now.

She took a sip of her champagne, which was ice cold and utterly delicious.

'I could get used to this way of life,' she told Euan. The party had spilled out of the dressing room and they were standing in the draughty corridor, their backs against a storage heater.

'It chokes me to admit it,' she went on, the sound of applause still ringing in her head, 'but she's good, your girlfriend.'

'She's good,' Euan said, his face as hard as the rock face on the coast. 'Whether or not she's my girlfriend is up for debate.'

'What do you mean? Have you two had a row?'

Euan's mouth set in a tight line.

'You could say that –' He hesitated, and then outrage triumphed over discretion. His face cleared and he went on: 'But instead of staying here to sort it out, she's going to Alex's parents' villa in Tuscany as soon as the show wraps up, and staying until the filming of *Green Place* starts –'

'That'll be nice,' Heather said uncertainly.

'For her, maybe. But I'm not invited. Not good enough for her posh mates.'

'Don't own enough land? No title? Nowhere in line for the throne?' asked Heather.

'Something like that.'

Euan gazed morosely ahead.

'Well, I think she's mad. If you were my boyfriend, I wouldn't let you out of my sight.'

She put her hand over his.

'She went away with Alex and his crowd last summer. To India,' Euan went on. 'To "find themselves". Do you know how long for? *Four* months.' He jerked his thumb towards his chest. 'I'm meant to be going out with her but I hardly saw her.'

'Euan, you don't think –'

'Do I think she's slept with him?' Euan interrupted, although this wasn't at all what she had been going to say. 'Yes, I do. In fact, I think she's probably slept with his girlfriend as well. Maybe both at the same time.'

'Well, when you were on a break, surely?' As far as she knew, Euan and Rowan had had more breaks than an ice hockey team. She wasn't all that surprised at his comments about Rowan. Mrs Crombie and the village gossips, pleasantly scandalised, had long claimed that she was bisexual (or was one of our Sapphic sisters, as Valissa elegantly put it) and there was much speculation as to the true nature of her relationship with one of the exquisite blonde sisters.

'So I've told her – if she goes off to Tuscany, it's over between us.'

The more Euan insisted that she shouldn't go to Tuscany, the more determined Rowan would be to go, Heather thought. She would go, and she would arrogantly presume that Euan would forgive her and be waiting for her return, as he always had been before. Euan was such a lovely man, such a good friend, that she felt protective. She'd never treat him badly or take him for granted. He didn't deserve that. She took his arm, leading him into the deserted kitchen, where they could have some privacy.

'I asked her to marry me,' he said, as soon as he'd closed the door behind them. This is where I came in, Heather thought.

'What did she say?' she asked carefully.

'Nothing, at first. She just laughed.'

'Euan, was Rowan pregnant?' Heather dared.

Euan looked spooked.

'How did you know that?'

'My mate, Matilda, saw her buying the test kit, but, don't worry, I don't think anyone else knows about it.'

Heather watched pain flit across his face.

'What happened about the baby?' she went on, only just breaking the silence.

'There is no baby. We went out for a walk one night to talk about it all and she started to get stomach cramps, really bad. By the time we got back to the flat she was bleeding –'

Heather gave a brief nod, so that he didn't have to say any more. A miscarriage, probably, or else a late, heavy period.

'That must have been awful for you both,' Heather said. As a woman, with warm feelings about motherhood, she felt terribly sorry for Rowan, but for Euan, too. Sometimes, the men were forgotten, she thought.

'How is Rowan now?' she asked.

'I called Dr McLuskie and he came out straightaway. She's fine.'

'I meant, emotionally?'

'I think she was glad.'

'Surely not,' Heather said, remembering the day she'd spoken to Rowan in the café. She'd looked so haunted and strained, and outside she'd actually wept. 'I think she would've been really hurting, but she's handling it badly.'

'Really?' Euan's face was still hard and set.

'Part of her may have been relieved,' Heather admitted. 'She's very young still. And she's just starting out in her career. It wasn't the best time –'

'She said she thought we were just hanging out, having a laugh. She said she certainly didn't want to get married.'

'That's brutal,' Heather said. She put her arms round him, rested her head on his leather shoulder. 'Euan, I know it must be amazing sometimes, but at the end of the day it doesn't sound as if you're very happy together.'

Euan pulled back a little, stroked her face.

'Why can't she be more like you? Sort of... gentle?'

'But, if she was more like me, she wouldn't be Rowan.'

Euan was looking at her with peculiar intensity, his fingers caressing the back of her neck. The moment was charged. Heather couldn't tear her eyes away from his. She felt a flutter deep inside and suddenly she was longing to feel his arms round her, his lips on hers. His dark eyes were tender as he carried on stroking her neck and then plunged his hands into her hair. Her heart was racing.

'Euan.' That was Rowan's voice, uncomfortably close. Her high heels tapped towards the kitchen.

'Euan, where the hell are you?'

Rowan was just outside the door now.

'I'd better go and talk to her, sort things out,' whispered Euan. 'I'll see you tomorrow.'

He touched her cheek, his eyes still fixed on her face, then opened the door, gave her one last smile and went out into the hall. Heather ducked behind the door as Rowan ran forward, kissing him full on the mouth.

'Where have you been?' she said. 'I've been looking for you for ages.'

'No, you haven't, Rowan, you've been drinking with your stuckup mates.' Euan's voice was so cold it could freeze nitrogen.

Heather slipped out of the kitchen and made for the front door, their voices floating back to her as they made their way towards the others.

'I was celebrating. We're going back to my place now for a party.'

Rowan and her friends, it was said around the village, could give Kate Moss a run for her money when it came to hard partying.

'Well, I'm not coming. I'm going back to my place to slum it.'

'Oh, pleeease.'

Outside, Heather began to walk briskly towards the cottage. The living room light was out, so Treeny must have gone to bed. That was good. If her aunt was still up, she'd have wanted to make her a hot chocolate and have a post mortem about the show, but Heather wanted to be alone to think about the events of the evening. She went into her bedroom and sat at the dressing table, looking at her flushed face and bright eyes. Would she really have kissed Euan? Standing with him in that cramped little kitchen, she'd wanted him so badly, longed to feel his mouth on hers, his tongue parting her lips. But she'd felt tenderness flare up within her also. She'd felt both friendship and desire. She needed this time on her own to reflect on the shift in their relationship, but she also felt bereft at being parted from him. She exhaled a long, shuddering breath: she was in love with Euan. He'd helped her to settle into the village, made her feel as if she belonged, helped her cope with her heartbreak. Now, she was well and truly over Aidan and yearning for another man who had a stunning girlfriend also. She couldn't go there again. Even if Euan and Rowan did split up, she couldn't be his second best.

She had to get a grip. Their passionate encounter had been due to the emotion of the moment, she told herself – Rowan's scornful reaction to his proposal and her losing their baby must have been terribly hard on him. She sighed. He'd probably be back with Rowan tomorrow anyway: he just couldn't seem to resist her. Practically the last thing he'd said to her before they parted tonight was that he was going to sort things out.

She felt too wired to sleep, so she made a chamomile tea and sat at the kitchen table, sipping it and warming her hands on the mug. She was fed up with always being the consolation prize – Sean looking for a substitute for his wife, the love of his life, Euan hurting badly and looking for a diversion from the pain. Maybe it was time she went back to London for some peace and quiet.

19. *Mountain High, River Deep*

Misty had persuaded Heather that she couldn't return to London without completing her first Munro.

It was autumn now, and the village looked beautiful, with the leaves on the trees turning every shade of yellow, orange and red. In late September there was an Indian summer with a series of pale gold days. One morning, the grass still soaked in dew, Heather had walked across the fields to the croft where Treeny had been born. It was ruined, now, little more than a pile of stones, but she had walked through where the door would have been and stood in the long grass. She'd felt quite spiritual, standing there, linked to her ancestors, her great-grandparents, to McAndrews stretching back into the past. She'd felt as if she belonged.

On the way to the mountains, she saw Euan and Rowan walking along the coast road, holding hands, their pace slow, deep in conversation, Rowan's amber coloured hair floating out behind her on the breeze. Heather's heart ached. She'd been so sure that Rowan would go off on holiday with her friends, but Euan had told her that, faced with his ultimatum, she'd decided to stay with him and try to get their relationship back on track. It was a relief in some ways, she tried to tell herself. Now she knew that there was absolutely no point in mooning about after Euan, since he was back with his girlfriend – a girlfriend who was gorgeous, bright, exciting and challenging. At least she'd been able to retain her self-respect and Euan's friendship.

When she drew up in the parking area at the foot of Ben Lochy, her friend was already there, a huge rucksack sitting on the bonnet of her car. Once she was confident that Heather was properly equipped for the weather in waterproof jacket and trousers, the two girls set off along the narrow, stony path which made up the first half mile or so of the journey.

'Fawn,' hissed Misty suddenly, grabbing Heather's arm, and they stopped walking to watch the young deer with its long, spindly legs.

All too soon, they began to ascend Ben Lochy, the gradient steepening. Heather followed Misty, who was stepping out with ease, her fair ponytail bouncing on her back. Suddenly, she was very grateful for all those miles she and Matilda had jogged on the running machines at their gym, all the lengths they'd swum, all the body pump classes they'd sweated their way through, and she realised that there was more to all that exercise than remaining a perfect 10.

'Hey, you're really fit,' said Misty, stopping walking for a moment and turning to her, her face glowing. 'I thought you were just a soft southerner.'

'Cheek,' said Heather, but, secretly, she was proud that she was holding her own so far. She also admired Misty's adept way with an ordinance survey map and a compass – so far, her own landmarks had been Monsoon and Costa Coffee in the King's Road.

'Actually, it's a great workout,' Misty said.

They carried on walking. Misty pointed out passing birds: a razorbill and a guillemot.

Despite the fact that the backs of her legs were now aching, as they climbed ever higher Heather could see why so many people had such a passion for hill walking. She stopped, partly as an excuse to rest, partly to take in the view. A ring of peaks scattered with snow rose to her left. Far below, there was a glint of silver as a loch wended its way across a valley. In the glen, she could see a scatter of white houses, tiny from here. Pine trees, tall and straight, hugged the foot of the mountains, which were russet with bracken and sprinkled with sunlight. The fields, from this height, were a green and gold patchwork quilt. In the distance, another range of hills was blue, darker than the sky.

Heather inhaled sharply, breathing in the air which was fresh and pure. Beside her rushed a burn, white water flowing over rocks. She felt a huge sense of release, looking out at the vastness of the scene in front of her. It would be good place to do some thinking, to find some perspective.

She and Misty sat down on a rock, refilling their water bottles from the burn. Heather had been amazed at the crystal clarity of the water here. Two other walking parties passed, obviously having been attracted by the weather, and both stopped to chat. Everyone they'd met on the way had seemed so friendly.

'It's beautiful,' Heather admitted.

'So you'd do it again?'

'Ask me that when we get to the top.'

They set off again, Misty's lithe figure strolling ahead with seeming ease. It was steep at this point, and Heather had a stitch in her side as well as aching feet and calves. They paused again, this time to admire some horses with long, wild manes. Misty fed each of them an apple.

'Are we nearly there yet?' Heather asked.

Misty giggled.

'Nowhere near.'

'How far have we walked?'

'Probably about a couple of miles,' said Misty.

'No way.'

'Yeah, but distance doesn't really count – it's gradient. Do you want to stop for another break?'

Heather nodded gratefully, and they sank down on a low wall.

'I can't believe Euan and Rowan are still together,' Misty said. 'I keep expecting him to see sense and dump her.'

Heather shrugged, not especially wanting to talk about it. Of course, Misty didn't know about Rowan's miscarriage. No one did, other than the couple, the doctor and herself.

'Yup,' she said. She'd heard that Rowan was throwing yet another party at the weekend before moving to the west end of Glasgow, where she would be filming her debut scenes in *Green Place*.

Misty was silent.

'I just wish I could have what you have with Duncan,' Heather said, at length.

'Mmm. Yes. I've been really lucky.'

'A partner who really loves you, and you really love him,' she went on.

'Yeah,' said Misty. 'Babe, I'm sure you'll meet someone lovely soon

– you deserve it.'

'Come on, let's walk,' said Heather, jumping to her feet with a sudden burst of energy. She began to stride ahead, Misty hurrying to keep up. She forbore to say that she'd already met someone lovely, and that he was about as available as Orlando Bloom.

'Be careful at this bit,' Misty called, as the next part of the mountain was strewn with boulders.

Carefully, Heather picked her way across. Murdo had told her last night in the Claymore that Ben Lochy was a comparatively easy mountain for an inexperienced climber, before regaling her with hair-raising stories of clambering over icy mountain passes with a dog on his back, fording rivers which were waist deep, edging along ledges only a few inches wide over a drop of several hundred feet. He'd talked about places called the Lost Valley and the Devil's Staircase, the names of which alone struck fear into her heart.

Round a bend in the road was a bothy. Heather was grateful she didn't have to stay there the night – it looked like a garden shed in the middle of nowhere. It made the current worst night of her life – spent at Luton Airport - look positively civilised.

Suddenly, she seemed to lose her footing. She saw the grassy pathway come up to meet her as if in slow motion. Instinctively, she put her arm out to break her fall, jarring it as she did so.

'Heather.' Misty jogged towards her. 'Can you stand up?'

She looked up. Misty's face was chalk white.

'I think I've done something to my ankle.' She winced at the pain.

Carefully, Misty helped her to her feet. She could stand, but couldn't put her weight on her right leg.

'We'll have to go to the bothy,' Misty said. Heather put her arm round her friend, and, leaning on her for support, managed to limp the hundred or so yards to shelter. Inside, it was Spartan, with just wooden boards on the floor, and two other raised boards for sleeping on. One wall was dominated by a large, empty fireplace. They sat down on one of the boards and both got out their mobile phones to call for help.

'Damn,' said Misty, in frustration, 'I can't get a signal.'

'Me neither.' Heather put her phone down beside her on the seat. 'What do we do now?'

'We'll just have to stay here and keep trying,' said Misty. 'I'm not going back down. I don't want to leave you on your own. Someone'll notice we're missing eventually. My mum and dad know I'm here, and I'm meant to be working tonight.' She managed a weak grin. 'They'll notice I'm not there then, that's for sure.'

'Treeny knows I'm here, too,' Heather said, then grimaced again at the pain in her ankle.

'Is it really sore?' Misty's face was all concern.

'Yeah,' Heather said, faintly, biting her lip.

'Let's see what we've got,' suggested Misty. Both girls opened their rucksacks and produced: a flask of coffee, a flask of tea, a Mars Bar, some jelly babies, ham and cheese rolls and egg and cress sandwiches. Heather managed a couple of bites at a sandwich and nibbled a jelly baby or two. From time to time, they tried their phones fruitlessly for a signal and kept a look out for any other walkers who might pass.

'This is the best tea I ever tasted,' said Misty, obviously trying to keep their spirits up. Heather nodded, although her ankle was throbbing by now.

'Could do with a nip of brandy in it.' Heather winced.

As it looked as if they were there for the foreseeable future, Heather told Misty the full, unexpurgated story of herself and Aidan.

'That must have been so awful,' Misty said. 'So humiliating.'

Heather nodded. Far worse than any level of humiliation was the hurt at Aidan's betrayal. It had been all the more unexpected and painful because she'd been so much in love with Aidan, had trusted him implicitly.

'It was –' Heather began, then stopped immediately.

Her phone was ringing. She picked it up. *Treeny Mobile* flashed up on the screen. Amazing. As far as Heather knew, Treeny had never used her mobile phone before. She snatched up the phone and pressed the "answer" button.

'Treeny,' she blurted, determined to get her message across before she lost the link with her aunt. 'I've hurt my ankle and Misty and I are stranded in Crappa Bothy. Can you let Euan know? Treeny, can you hear me?'

'Yes –' came Treeny's voice, faint before the line went dead.

It was some time before help came. Heather was convinced she might pass out from the pain.

'Can I come and visit you in London?' Misty was asking, trying to distract her.

'Of course. You'll like where we live – it's just near Hyde Park,' Heather said. 'Oh, I wish Euan was here.'

'Yes. He'd know what to do, what with being in the mountain rescue team. He's always a good man to have around. I mean, obvs, he's got a mental age of twelve, but he can actually be pretty sensible sometimes.'

Despite her aching ankle, Heather perked up at the chance to talk about Euan.

'Yeah, like that time Katie went missing and he organised the search parties.'

'Mmm. Yeah, he was amazing.'

'He was really sweet to Katie, too,' Heather said, her heart warming still further.

'He's great with kids. He really loves them.'

Heather winced again, although, this time, not from the throbbing pain. Suddenly, she couldn't hold back any longer. She'd been dying to talk to someone about Euan, and she and Misty were alone, a couple of thousand feet above the village, in the middle of nowhere, no one else around.

'Misty?' She lifted one of her gloves and began to tug at the fingers.

'Mmm?'

'I've been going on and on about how Euan and I are just good friends, but the truth is… I've got feelings for him.'

'Oh, my God,' Misty said, holding up her hand. Half-heartedly, Heather high fived her. 'You should totally tell him how you feel. I know he's with Rowan, but it won't last –'

'I found out…Euan told me that Rowan was pregnant,' she began. Misty's mouth dropped open.

'Rowan? Pregnant? No.'

'She lost the baby,' Heather explained. 'But Euan feels so bad for her that he wouldn't leave her. He even asked her to marry him.'

'*What?*'

'Yes. Even if he does have feelings for me, he'd never hurt Rowan now.'

'Suppose not,' Misty huffed. 'He's just too nice for his own good. I mean, Rowan's probably *glad* she miscarried – a baby would get in the way of her plans for world domination.'

Heather shook her head.

'I don't think so. You didn't see her, Mist. Her face. She looked so unhappy. I could tell she'd been crying. She looked absolutely haunted. I think she's hurting badly, but putting on her hard-as-a-diamond act as usual. No, I'll just have to try and get over Euan – there's no future for us. Rowan was meant to be going to Tuscany with some of her posh mates but she's stayed here to sort things out with him.'

'I'm sorry, Heather.' Misty squeezed her shoulder.

Just then, the door opened and Euan burst in, looking anxious.

'You took your time,' said Misty, fake-cheerily.

'That's enough of your cheek, missy,' he said, then turned to Heather. 'Oh, my God, Heather, are you all right? Everyone's been worried sick about you.'

'I'm fine. I think I've sprained my ankle, but I'm expected to live.' She felt much braver about her injury now he was here.

'Come on. Let's get you home.' His voice was calm and reassuring. He hoisted her over his shoulder in a fireman's lift, as if she was weightless. Then he walked out of the bothy and began to stride back down the hillside, Misty hurrying to keep up. Despite the pain, this had to be the best few hours of Heather's life so far.

20. *Lonely This Christmas*

After September was over, time began to fly towards Christmas.

Heather hobbled around for a few weeks before getting her plaster removed. She'd never spent the festive season in Kirklochy before, but this year she had no choice – the village was completely cut off, and the snow and freezing temperatures meant that, even if she had managed to make her way to Inverness Airport, she wouldn't have been able to get a flight: they were all cancelled.

She'd never seen the village look so beautiful, which was saying something – the pine trees were weighed down with snow, which also was piled thickly on the fields and on top of the dykes and hedges. There was a huge snowman standing at the gate of Shell Cottage, with coal eyes, a carrot for a nose, and a trilby hat. Some mornings, Heather woke to an Alpine scene of a pale blue, pink and gold suffused sky, the branches of the trees etched black against it. Joyfully, she painted the view from Treeny's front room, a perfect Christmas card scene.

Kirklochy was busy again, as young people turned up for the skiing, including Rowan and her friends, who all seemed to have been born with skis attached to their feet. Heather had no doubt that Rowan would excel at the sport.

A few days before Christmas, she and Treeny got out the tree and, fortified with mulled wine and chocolate truffles, began to dress it with fairy lights, baubles and garlands, Heather finding a felt angel which had been hand stitched by Kirsty when she was at junior school and, in a box, all the Christmas cards that she'd drawn herself for Treeny over the years, touched that her aunt had kept each and every one of them, even her earliest attempts.

'Heather,' said Treeny, as they sat by the fire, making paper chains. 'I know you have to go back to London soon. I know you can't stay here forever –'

Heather shook her head with a sad smile – she wasn't sure that she was ready to think about that yet, but her six months of working remotely were nearly up. Did she really need to go back to London? She could just stay here, make Kirklochy her home and painting her career as she'd always wanted. She'd miss the money, of course, her job paid extremely well. But did she really need so much money? It was actually pretty hard to burn plastic here, due to the lack of retail outlets. Life was simpler – she didn't need exclusive gym memberships, flavour-of-the-month-clubs or Jimmy Choos. She had just as much fun chatting with the villagers over a few pints of Sheepshagger in the Claymore Inn. She wasn't ready to be parted from Euan, even though romance absolutely wasn't on the cards. She missed him – she wasn't seeing him as often as before because he was travelling up and down to Glasgow, where Rowan was now filming.

'So I've made a decision,' went on Treeny. 'I've asked Flora to come and live here with me. We get on, and she's been terribly lonely since Mirren, her sister, died. She's retiring at the beginning of March and she's been dreading it. We'll be company for each other.'

Heather nodded, feeling a huge burden drop from her shoulders at the thought of there being someone else to help look after Treeny. Her broken hip was mended as best as it could be, but she'd never be quite the same. She now remembered that, when she was younger, there had been two Miss Munros, always together, who'd shared the flat above McTavish the baker's. Flora and Treeny could help each other.

Being in the village meant that she missed out on the festivities at Bright Sparks. Each year, there were several parties, one for secretarial and administrative staff, one for the graphic designers, and one for the creatives. This last had an obscene budget – Ben reckoned his hospital could pay two nurses for a whole year for that kind of money – and wasn't considered a success unless there was at least one monumental falling-out, a few colleagues ending up in casualty, and half a dozen people getting it on on top of various photocopiers. When she'd first started working in the office, in the innocence of youth, she'd assumed that the white power which always seemed to be present in the bathroom on Fridays was talcum. The ultimate party was one thrown by management for all staff and then, on Christmas Eve, everyone would gather in the boardroom for champagne, canapés and rallying speeches. By this stage in the year, Heather would normally be walking about like a zombie with serious sleep deprivation, perpetually blood shot eyes and a green tongue.

Last year, she'd spent Christmas with the Murphys. It had been fantasy family Christmas. Aidan's mum had cooked a traditional feast and there had been masses of presents, visitors and party games.

Now, the memory caused only a sweet ache.

This year, she went carol singing and saw Katie's seminal performance in the nativity play.

'Let us go forth into –' bellowed one young actor.

'Bethlehem, Iain,' prompted the Sunday school teacher, in a very loud whisper.

Eilidh had the plum role of Mary, while Katie was an angel, but there was no professional jealousy between the two girls, because Katie was enchanted by her outfit, a white, frilly dress sent to her by her grandparents in Glasgow. Gold shoes, gold wings and a piece of gold tinsel, wrapped round her dark curls as a halo, completed the outfit.

'Superb performance,' Heather told her afterwards. 'Do you want to go to Fratelli's for something to eat, or will you be lunching with your agent?'

'Worthy of a Golden Globe, dahling,' added Cara. She and Heather each took one of Katie's hands and they began to stroll towards the café, Katie, high as a kite, chattering excitedly.

⌇

On Christmas Eve, Murdo laid on a party in the Claymore for all the locals, with free mince pies and delicious, spicy mulled wine infused with cloves, orange and cinnamon. Heather was sure he'd more than made up for the outlay because the drink was flowing faster than a mountain stream and the bar takings were bound to be immense. His teenage daughter had decorated the pub in gold, red and green. Fairy lights twinkled round all the windows, a huge tree, nearly reaching to the ceiling and heavy with red and gold balls, stood in the corner. The mantelpiece was festooned with holly, among which red candles flickered, adding another perfume to the air. A large real fire crackled in both fireplaces and mistletoe hung from every light and beam.

Heather leaned on the bar, sipping a glass of mulled wine. The warmth of the spicy drink, the cosy room and her friends' presence had induced a happy, hazy feeling, and she was delighted that one of her own paintings was hanging above the fire: two puffins perched on a rock with Ben Lochy in the background. She could just about cope with the fact that she was alone while Misty and Duncan were sitting, his forehead resting on hers, talking quietly, seemingly oblivious to everyone else, while Paolo and Cara were standing in an alcove, gazing at each other, their fingers entwined.

Her phone started to ring, vibrating in her pocket. She pulled it out.

'Hi, Matilda,' she said, seeing her friend's face on the caller display.

'Hey, babe, how are you?'

'I'm good.' She didn't want to bring Matilda down by moaning about her single status. 'How're you and Ben?'

'We're great,' said Matilda. 'Mum, Delilah and Tallulah love him almost as much as I do. His mum and dad have invited us all for Christmas day. There'll be about twenty of us.'

'How is Nadine?'

'She's fine. Really good. She's sober and she's going into rehab in the New Year. Ben helped to persuade her.'

'That's brilliant, Tills. Really brilliant.' Nadine's sobriety would be the best Christmas present Matilda and her sisters could ever hope for. 'Where are you, anyway?' Heather went on, hearing squealing in the background.

'Granite,' said Matilda, naming a Barking night spot. 'Just wanted to say Merry Christmas and we'll see you next week, at Hogmanay.'

'Merry Christmas to you, too, Tills,' Heather said, smiling at Matilda's use of the Scots word for New Year's Eve. It sounded strange in a broad Barking accent. She said goodnight and slipped her phone into her back pocket, just as someone selected *Love is all Around* on the jukebox. Isn't that the truth, she thought. A long married couple, the worse for drink, began to waltz on a square of tartan carpet. Heather slipped past them, weaving her way between the tables. Out in the hall, she nearly crashed into Euan.

'Hi, Heather.'

'Hi, Euan. Haven't seen you for ages.' She spoke breezily, trying to hide how flustered she felt to see him. Had he always been this handsome? His thick, dark hair had been cut shorter lately, enhancing the line of his jaw. She was standing so close to him that she could see the slight shadow of stubble, the reflection of his long lashes below his deep set brown eyes. Reaching out, he swept the hair back from her forehead.

'Missed you,' he said. For a moment, they just looked at each other. Then he flicked his eyes up at the bunch of mistletoe hanging directly above their heads, his lips twitching slightly. Then she was in his arms and they were kissing, long and deep. Euan's kisses were urgent and searching and Heather kissed him back with all her strength, their passion driving everything out of her mind except her need for him. Right now, she could only think about the two of them, put Rowan out of her mind, lose herself in him. They kissed on and on, the music, laughter and the tinkle of glasses fading into a background blur.

Then her phone began again to vibrate in her pocket. She broke away from him.

'Leave it,' he whispered, but Heather was already pressing "answer", the spell broken.

'Are you all right, Treeny?'

'I'm fine,' Treeny said, but her voice sounded weak and scared. 'I've just had a wee fall…stupid.'

'I'm coming home. I'll be five minutes.' Heather terminated the call. Euan was looking at her with concern, her friend again.

'Treeny's had a fall. I'll have to go to her.'

'I'm coming with you.'

Euan grabbed Heather's hand and together they hurried up the hill to Thistle Cottage.

⤶

They were there in a few minutes. Heather had been a little drunk on the mulled wine, but anxiety and the bitter cold quickly wakened her up, her senses on red alert. As they opened the gate and ran up the path, she realised that they were still holding hands. She fumbled with the key and Euan took it out of her hand and unlocked the door.

'Aunt Treeny!'

Heather hurried down the hall and into the living room, Euan right behind her. Her aunt was lying full length on the hearthrug.

'God, are you all right?'

Euan was already dashing forward. He kneeled down beside Treeny and lifted her into a sitting position.

'Put your arms round my neck,' he instructed.

'Don't mind if I do,' Treeny managed to say, with a faint smile and a trace of her usual spirit. In a trice, Euan had lifted her into her favourite armchair.

'What happened?' he asked, his voice gentle as he knelt on the carpet before her.

'I'm a stupid old woman,' Treeny said. 'The phone rang and I got up to answer it without using my stick. Somehow, I lost my balance and once I was down there, I couldn't get back up. Just as well I had my mobile in my pocket.'

Heather raised her eyebrows at her aunt's finally embracing new technology.

'But you're all right?'

Treeny nodded.

'Just a bit shaken up.'

'I'll make you a cup of tea with plenty of sugar. It's good for shock.'

'And a dash of brandy,' Treeny added.

As she stood in the kitchen waiting for the kettle to boil, Heather could hear Euan making easy conversation with Treeny about a hair-raising experience his brother – the local vet – had had on Galbraith's farm.

For a while, they sat in front of the merry, crackling fire drinking tea. Heather had produced Treeny's toasting fork and they made toast and ate it piping hot, something Heather and Kirsty had enjoyed doing as children.

Finally, Euan got up to leave.

'Merry Christmas,' he whispered, as they stood by the door in the dark hall.

'Merry Christmas to you, too, Euan,' Heather said. 'And thanks.'

'See you soon.' He touched her cheek, then opened the door, admitting an icy blast of air as he left.

Heather leaned against the door for a moment. She was disappointed that he hadn't attempted to kiss her again, but the freezing cold and Treeny's fall had brought in a little sanity: if he had, she didn't think she could have stopped. The circumstances – with her seventy-eight year old great-aunt only a few feet away – could hardly be less ideal. What if they'd got it on on Treeny's candlewick bedspread? And what was going on with Rowan?

It was very late by the time she'd helped Treeny to bed. Wearily she cleaned her teeth and slathered on masses of moisturiser against the bitter easterly wind. She lay on her back, staring up at the ceiling, too wound up to sleep.

⌒

In the morning, she trudged along the beach, watching the waves roll in, the cold wind whipping her hair around. It literally was the cold light of day. Had she imagined the chemistry fizzing between her and Euan? He had certainly kissed her as if he meant it – but, then again, so had Aidan. He'd been on such a rollercoaster of emotions with Rowan – especially in recent times – that he'd probably just turned to her, Heather, to console himself. Maybe he was still upset that Rowan was shutting him out, maybe they'd rowed. Heather took a deep breath of the salty air and held her head higher as she walked on. Never again was she going to be second best, the consolation prize, the fall-back position. She'd go back to London, and by the time she returned here it would be Easter and she'd be over him, so that they could go back to being best mates again. She turned and walked back to the cottage to spend Christmas Day with Treeny, Mrs Gillies, and Miss Munro.

⌒

A few days after Christmas, it was as if the snow had never been, as it had been washed away by heavy rain. A radiant, sparkly Misty turned up at the cottage, bringing with her Christmas pies which were still hot.

'Duncan's taking me to Tenerife for two whole weeks,' she confided. 'That was his present to me. Goodness knows how many letters he had to deliver to save up for it. We're going in February. I cannot wait.' She was so excited she could hardly stand still.

Heather was happy for her, but was bleeding emotionally about the lack of love in her own life. Euan had phoned her yesterday, but instead of the sound of seabirds and surf in the background, she could hear cars and buses and buskers, and he'd told her he was in Glasgow. So he must still be with Rowan. She'd terminated the call abruptly, pretending Treeny needed her for something: it was too soon for her to go back to being just good friends. He'd called her again today, but she'd let the call go straight to voicemail – she didn't trust herself not to burst into tears or start yelling at him for messing her around.

Matilda'd phoned later to confirm that she and Ben would arrive from London the next day, along with Kirsty who was booked on the same flight, so they'd be able to go to the Laird's Hogmanay Ball together.

Heather was dreading it.

21. *Happy New Year*

Matilda walked stiffly into the living room, her toes wedged apart by cotton wool balls, as she waited for her silver nail polish to dry.

'Ain't you going to get changed?' she asked Heather.

'No, I told you I'm not coming.'

'But you have to come,' Matilda protested. 'It's the Laird's ball.'

Apart from going out for a stomach lining breakfast at Fratelli's, she and Kirsty had been getting ready all day.

'I'll look stupid without a partner.'

There would be happy couples everywhere – Misty and Duncan, Cara and Paolo, Matilda and Ben and Gregor and Robbie. Inspired by the advice of Dr La Puma, Sascha had plucked up the courage to invite fellow hairdresser Scott Grant. With his flowing blond locks, he was as camp as a row of cerise satin tents, but definitely not gay, as Gregor had found out to his cost when his gaydar had let him down. Blakey was too skint to come up to the Highlands, but, even so, Kirsty had a date for the evening – she'd met Jake Bolt skulking on the beach yesterday afternoon, and just gone up to him and asked him out.

'I know, I know. But Ben'll dance with you, won't you, babe?'

Ben glanced up from the biography of some footballer or other.

''Course I will.'

'Yeah, right, Matilda. Like I'm going to take a part-share in your boyfriend for the evening. I'd look a complete saddo,' snapped Heather, although she knew her friend meant well.

'Oh, come on, Hev. We won't leave your side all night.'

'Thanks, but I need to help Treeny tidy up the cottage,' Heather said.

'We can do that in a couple of days, when all the parties are over,' protested Matilda. 'We'll all muck in and we'll get it done in no time flat.'

'It has to be done today,' explained Heather, crossing her fingers. 'If you have a dirty house on Hogmanay, you'll have a dirty house the whole year through. It's a Scottish tradition.'

'Is this true?' Matilda asked Kirsty, who'd walked into the room, her face hard and green from the application of a face pack, her hair wrapped in a pink towel.

''Fraid so,' admitted Kirsty, taking a seat on the sofa with a mug of peppermint tea.

'Babe, what's wrong?' Matilda asked. Finally, Heather was alone with her friend. Ben was in the shower and Kirsty had gone outside for a smoke. 'I don't believe all this stuff about having to clean the house. Why do you really not want to go to the ball?'

'I've… got feelings for Euan,' Heather admitted, part of her relieved to let it out.

'Euan, as in your mate? Ooh, he's lovely,' Matilda squealed.

'Shush,' warned Heather. 'He is lovely, but he's also got a not-so-lovely girlfriend, who'll be there tonight since she's the Laird's daughter. I don't think I can face seeing them together. Not after -'

Matilda reached out and stroked Heather's arm. 'It's okay,' she said, and Heather nearly broke down at the kindness in her eyes. 'Do you want me and Ben to stay in with you? We can have a few drinks and bring in the New Year here.'

'Absolutely not. I'd feel even worse if you missed it because of me.'

'Okay.' Matilda's voice was gentle. 'I won't mention it again.'

As the day wore on, Heather washed, scrubbed, hoovered, dusted, polished and cleaned, working round Matilda and Kirsty, who were now reclining on the sofa with slices of cucumber over their eyes.

Eventually, she flopped down, exhausted, on a chair. The cottage had never looked so clean - mirrors and windows sparkled, wood gleamed, everything smelt of a synthetic honeysuckle fragrance - she'd even dusted the plants.

At last, Matilda and Kirsty came into the room to show themselves off. They looked stunning together, Matilda as fair as Kirsty was dark. Matilda wore a backless dress in cornflower blue and Kirsty one in flame coloured chiffon she'd designed and made herself. Her plentiful silver jewellery looked expensive but no doubt had been picked up for next to nothing in a Brooklyn flea market or at Camden Lock.

'Is it okay if we take the car, since you're not going?' said Ben.

'Of course.'

'Oh, listen, babe, why don't you quickly get ready now and we'll meet you there? You can get a taxi,' coaxed Kirsty.

'Yeah, you can phone us when you're on your way,' added Ben.

'It won't be the same without you,' tempted Kirsty.

'Okay, I'll think about it,' said Heather, only wishing that they would leave her alone.

Ben linked arms with both girls and they left in high spirits, Kirsty and Ben still pleading with Heather to reconsider and join them later.

Heather caught sight of her reflection in the mirror above the sideboard. She looked awful. She was wearing grey jogging pants and a faded Snoopy tee-shirt. Her face was streaked with dirt, and she could have auditioned for the musical *Hair*.

Now that the bathroom was finally free, she climbed into the shower, enjoying the feel of the hot water splashing over her. She lathered herself with Matilda's rose soap and rubbed *Curl Power* into her hair. This was a new miracle anti-frizz shampoo for wavy hair for which Bright Sparks had created a series of glossy adverts - in a few weeks it would, hopefully, if the creatives had got it right, be flying off the shelves of chemists all over the country.

Later, she sat on the sofa, sipping tea and leafing through Matilda's copy of *Hello!* magazine. *Chloé and her Mr Wright* was emblazoned across the front cover, beside a photo of the couple on the red carpet. It seemed that they were reunited and planning to marry in the summer. Treeny shuffled in from the kitchen, where she'd been baking shortbread and black bun.

'Darling, you can bring in the New Year with me, Chrissie and Grace if you like,' she said. 'But are you sure you don't want to go to the ball? It's such a wonderful party always. You're young. You should enjoy yourself.'

Heather thought about the previous New Year's Eve. She and Aidan had strolled down to the Embankment, arms round each other, to watch the fireworks, and kissed on the stroke of midnight, and her secret wish for the coming year was that nothing would change, and she would be as happy as she was just then.

'It's just with it being New Year's Eve. I don't want to be there at midnight, with everyone kissing each other.'

'Well, would you not go for just a wee while? If you're not having a good time, you can always leave.'

Heather's phone, sitting on the coffee table in front of her, began to buzz.

'Hey, Matilda,' she said, rising and beginning to walk out of the room. 'What's up?' she asked, when she was in the privacy of the hall.

'We're having an amazing time,' Matilda said. 'And Euan isn't even here. So why don't you come? You could just quickly get changed and jump in a taxi. Everyone's been asking where you are.'

'Euan isn't there? Why not?'

'According to Misty, he's covering the Hogmanay party up at that posh hotel. Some of the cast of *Fly Me to Dunoon* are there. I love *Fly Me*. It's even better than TOWIE -'

'Okay, okay, I'll come.'

She went back into the living room.

'I've decided I will go for a bit,' she told Treeny.

'Good, good. You really shouldn't miss the ball. Everyone talks about it for weeks afterwards.'

'I haven't got anything to wear,' Heather said. For the first time in her life, this statement was actually true. Everyone else had been preparing for the party for weeks - Cara, Sascha, Gregor and Misty had gone all the way to the Merchant City in Glasgow on a girlie weekend to buy their outfits.

'Nonsense,' said Treeny. 'You've got about ten black dresses. And what about the red silk you bought in Edinburgh that time? It really suits you. Or that long turquoise one you wore to your cousin's wedding - that was fabulous.'

'Yeah, but they're not much use to me hanging in my wardrobe in Bayswater.'

'Well, I'm sure we can find something,' Treeny said firmly, brooking no argument.

As Heather followed her aunt into her bedroom, in spite of herself she felt a spark of excitement. Treeny had a vintage wardrobe which would put Jackie Kennedy to shame, every garment treasured, dry cleaned and swathed in plastic. It was a treasure trove to Kirsty, who'd based several of her designs on it. Heather watched as Treeny clattered coat hangers and then pulled out a dress.

'I wore this on my twenty-first birthday,' she said, handing it to Heather. 'Try it on.'

Quickly, Heather slipped out of her bathrobe. She could feel the thickness and quality of the material as she stepped into the dress and pulled it up. It was a fifties' prom dress in a rich cream colour, strapless and tight in the bodice, but with a huge, flouncy, circular skirt. She pulled up the zip. The dress fitted perfectly, moulding to her curves, hugging her waist, subtly sexy in what it suggested, rather than what it revealed.

'You need this to get the full effect,' Treeny said, rummaging in a drawer and producing an underskirt like a tutu.

'Don't you look lovely?' she went on, when Heather's outfit was complete. 'Just like that Sarah Jessica Rabbit.'

Maybe it was the subdued lighting in the room, but privately, excitedly, Heather agreed with her aunt. She could imagine Carrie Bradshaw sashaying into an uptown Manhattan hotspot in this dress. And it suited her so well. The pale colour showed off the tan she still had from spending so much time outdoors, and seemed to enhance the green of her eyes and the red of her hair. The shampoo *was* a miracle, her hair, longer than it had been for a while, had sprung up into shining curls as it dried, with no frizz in sight.

Treeny, after hunting in her wardrobe and drawers, produced a beaded clutch bag and a sea green wrap.

'You're not going in those house shoes, I hope? They kind of spoil the look,' she said. Heather was still wearing her oversized Shaun the Sheep slippers. She darted into her bedroom and returned with the shoes – metallic, with five-inch heels and studded with rhinestones – that Matilda had bought herself as a reward when she got her promotion. They were the same size and Matilda wouldn't mind if she borrowed them; they'd always shared their clothes. She slipped her feet into them and at once felt gorgeous – tall and slim and long legged.

'Beautiful,' pronounced Treeny.

She didn't have time for much make-up but she didn't need much – her skin was glowing with health so she limited herself to mascara, grey eye shadow and some pearly lipgloss. She sprayed on masses of Allure and then, hurrying back into the living room, she picked up the phone. There was a click at the other end, then:

'Hello? Gus the Taxi here (crackle, crackle)... I'm not here at the moment (baa, baa). Leave a message after the tone (woof! woof!).' Beeeeeeep.

'I can't get a taxi,' she told Treeny, who'd followed her into the room.

'Well, it is Hogmanay. You shouldn't have let Ben take the car.'

'Okay, I know.'

'There must be something we can do -' mused Treeny. Then her face cleared. 'I know, I'll phone cousin Tavish. He's got a tractor.'

'Aunt Catriona, I am not turning up at the social event of the year in a tractor.'

'Well, have you got any better ideas?'

Just then, the doorbell rang. Treeny went out to the hall to answer it. Heather heard a man's voice.

'Come away in,' said Treeny, returning moments later with Alfie Bolt in tow.

'Hi, Alfie,' greeted Heather.

'Wow,' said Alfie. 'You look incredible.'

Heather smiled, genuinely pleased. Her ego could do with a little stoking up tonight.

'So do you,' she said. Incredible was the word. *Unbelievable.* Alfie was in full Highland dress, the Bonnie Prince Charlie regalia, including sgian dubh. As there was no Bolt clan, he wore a kilt in Black Watch tartan.

'I caught Destiny playing with this this afternoon,' he said, reaching into his dress sporran and pulling out an iPhone with a shocking pink diamanté "M" dangling from it. 'Thought it might belong to your friend. It was left in Fratelli's.'

'It's Matilda's, all right,' Heather agreed. 'Thanks. She's lost without it.'

'So, you'll be on your way to the ball?' asked Treeny.

'Yup,' said Alfie. 'It's taken the trouble and strife this long to get ready.'

This had been much the state of affairs at Thistle Cottage, Heather thought. While the girls had taken hours to prepare, Ben had grabbed a quick shower, cleaned his teeth, rubbed some wax into his hair and slapped on some aftershave.

'So you could give Heather a lift?'

''Course,' said Alfie. 'Your carriage awaits,' he added, with heavy gallantry.

Heather kissed Treeny goodbye, whispering her thanks for the make-over, and followed Alfie outside. It was bitterly cold and the earth was hard and glittery with frost. Alfie's car, a jet black BMW Z4, a mid-life crisis on wheels if ever there was one, stood throbbing at the gate, the music of the Jam belting out. Alfie jumped in the front and Heather the back. She sat in the middle, her skirt taking up the whole seat. The car was full of the scent of a discreet, extremely expensive perfume.

''Allo, darling,' said Shanice, twisting round to face her and raising her voice above the music.

'Hi, Shanice. Should be a good night.'

Alfie started up the car and roared off down the coast road, to the ear-bleeding accompaniment of *Going Underground*.

22. *Cutting a Rug*

It didn't take long to get to the castle in Alfie's powerful car. As they pulled up, Heather caught her breath. The trees in the garden were all draped with coloured lights and it looked beautiful, magical, like the illustrations in her favourite fairytale book when she was a child. Again, she felt a spark of excitement. Now she was glad that Treeny had persuaded her to come.

'You girls go on, and I'll find somewhere to park.'

Heather followed Shanice up the stairs to the huge wooden door, stepping carefully in her high heels. Shanice rattled the heavy brass knocker, and the door swung open. Inside, the warmth wrapped round Heather like an electric blanket and she could hear the crackling of a real fire. Shanice took off her floor-length fake fur and hung it on a nearby antler. At fortysomething, she was an extremely glamorous woman. She coloured her hair a rich chestnut, and her eyes a deep violet. Her lips and nails were fire engine red. Her black dress plunged front and back and was slit up the sides, adorned only by a few simple gold hoops. She had a superb figure, but Heather suspected the appliance of science. She had that glossy, polished, lacquered look that only very rich women have. She linked her arm through Heather's and together they made their way down the black and white tiled hall, past some suits of armour that dated back to the Battle of Bannockburn. In a flagstoned side room, a group of older people were drinking mulled wine. Heather breathed in the cinnamon laden, fruity smell, always so evocative of this time of year.

The ballroom was large and with a beautifully restored natural wood floor and wood panelling. A large fire burned in the grate and the air was heavy with the scent of the wood, Shanice's perfume, and a spicy punch which was being served. At one end of the room, a wide staircase swept up to the first floor balcony and a massive stained glass window. The ceiling rose up and up, like that of an ancient church. A Christmas tree reached as high as the balconies, which were swathed with holly, ivy and white fairy lights. Bunches of mistletoe hung from every chandelier.

'Check the Ugly Sisters,' said Shanice suddenly, nudging her as the current dance ended and the bagpipes screeched to a halt. She threw back her head and laughed. For such a sophisticated looking woman, she had a wonderful, loud, abandoned laugh, which seemed to come from right down in her Blahniks. Heather followed her gaze and also burst out laughing. Gregor and Robbie were dressed up as the girls from Abba. Gregor, in electric blue satin, silver platform boots, a blond seventies' wig and a replica of the iconic blue cloche hat, was Agnetha, while Robbie, as Frida, wore a brunette wig and a metallic pink catsuit with a heart cut out of the navel, along with the inevitable platform boots, his in white.

The music started up again and Misty, slender and pretty as a daisy in sheeny grey, grabbed Heather's hand and swept her into a whirling eightsome reel. Next, she was claimed by Gregor and Robbie for the Dashing White Sergeant, then by a succession of ruddy Young Farmers. She waved over at Kirsty who, too cool to dance, was sitting on a striped chaise longue with Jake Bolt. They were talking seriously, their heads close together. After six months in Kirklochy, Heather could cut a rug with the best of them. She watched as Alfie and Shanice danced expertly past. Rumour had it that they had been secretly driving to Inveralan twice a week for lessons.

After the ceilidh, supper was served – traditional fayre consisting of cullen skink, Balmoral chicken and cranachan, a delicious dessert made with cream, oatmeal, raspberries and whisky. Despite Heather's misgivings, it was a wonderful evening, enchanted, magical. Maybe it had something to do with the punch, which was lovely and surprisingly potent. The castle was so beautiful and the men looked so glamorous in their kilts. Separately, the women's dresses were pretty and bright, but together they made a kaleidoscope of colour on the dance floor. To add to the magic, Katie, very excited to be allowed to stay up for the bells, was wearing her favourite fairy outfit, the skirt shaped like petals, sparkly wings on her back, a glittery wand in her hand and a tiara nestling in her dark curls. With her two front teeth missing, she'd never looked so adorable.

There was Cara walking towards her in the simple dusty pink shift she'd bought in Glasgow, her shiny hair piled up on top of her head. She handed Heather a cup of coffee and they both leaned against the wall, sipping slowly.

'Such a wonderful evening,' Cara said.

The local councillor for Dreichndrookit gave a brief speech, thanking the Laird for his hospitality and generosity and then Katie, curtseying prettily, gave a bouquet of red roses to his wife. This was the first time Heather had seen Rowan's father. It was easy to see why Treeny had said that he had a touch of James Bond about him – he had the height, breadth of shoulder and suave appearance of Sean Connery circa *Dr No*. Miranda Wood, Rowan's exquisite actress mother, looked even more lovely and ethereal in the flesh than she had on screen.

Jake Bolt was mooching sulkily alone nearby; Kirsty was standing in the midst of a circle of Rowan's friends – the Golden Youth. One of them was reaching out and touching her dress.

'Heather, honey,' she cried, a few minutes later, rushing over. 'You look fabulous.'

She seemed rather exuberant. Heather guessed she'd had a few punches too many, and she could also detect the faint but unmistakable smell of cannabis in her hair.

'What did they want?' she asked.

'Dresses,' said Kirsty. 'Someone asked me where I'd got mine. I said it was my own design, then it just snowballed. I've given out all the business cards I brought with me. They all want something unique to wear at some May ball they're going to at Cambridge.'

'Everyone else'll be in the same old same old, I guess: Donna Karan, Versace, Vera Wang –' Heather said. It was hard to imagine anyone living a life such as this.

Heather put her arms round her sister, holding her close, rocking her slightly.

'You'll be the new Stella McCartney, Kirsty.'

Kirsty rejoined Jake Bolt, who was, by now, looking seriously annoyed. Heather waved over at Misty and Duncan, who were standing apart from everyone else, talking in low voices.

Suddenly, Cara burst out laughing.

'Trust Rowan to upstage us all,' she said.

Rowan, in a gold dress that Kate Moss would die for, was walking across the floor towards them. She looked stunning, her copper hair set into ringlets. No one could match her energy, her vitality, her style and her charisma.

'Aunt Cara, come with me. I've got something to show you.' Katie was pulling at Cara's hand. In turn, Cara grabbed Heather's and the two women followed the child up the staircase and along what seemed like miles of corridor to another, narrower staircase. Katie stopped at a circular room, the inside of a turret. Standing in the doorway, Heather and Cara gasped. There was a huge brass bed covered by a white counterpane, which was strewn with red roses. Tea lights flickered on every other surface, reflecting again and again on the windows and mirrors. Outside, the night was clear, with a full moon and sparkling starscape.

Paolo, standing alone in the middle of the room, raised a hand above his head and snapped his fingers theatrically. Katie dashed forward and then the room was full of the sound of Lonestar's *Amazed*, impossibly corny but wonderfully romantic all the same. Heather felt tears spring up in her eyes, and, realising she shouldn't really be here, stepped back into the shadowy corridor.

'Cara Fraser,' Paolo said, dropping onto one knee. 'Will you do me the very great honour of becoming my wife?'

'Of course I will, of course I will.' Heather could hear a sob in Cara's voice, as she also fell to her knees. The ring caught the light for a moment as Paolo slipped it onto her finger.

'Does this mean you'll be my real uncle?' That was Katie, as she ran forward to be enfolded in a three cornered embrace.

Heather turned away and began to tiptoe back down the corridor. From another room came the sound of soft, sensual voices, then a woman's tinkling laughter. She ducked in the next open door and snapped on a light, revealing a small bathroom. Pulling out her mobile phone, she managed to contact Gus the Taxi, and asked him to pick her up just before midnight. She'd probably have to pay him golden time for that, but she didn't care.

Somehow, she managed to negotiate the corridors and find her way back to the balcony that overlooked the ballroom. Various couples stood in intimate conversation under a chandelier. She averted her eyes from the unappetising sight of Jake Bolt with his tongue down her sister's throat and leaned on the balcony, looking down at the dance floor below. The ceilidh band, Swinging Shepherds, had finished their set, to be replaced by a more sedate type of band. Matilda and Ben were dancing together, but barely moving, just stepping from foot to foot as they gazed into each other's eyes. Matilda had been unusually circumspect about this relationship – usually she was flicking through bridal magazines and choosing the hymns for her wedding after the second date, but Heather felt that, together, she and Ben had something lasting. Misty and Duncan weren't dancing, but were sitting on the chaise longue earlier vacated by Kirsty and Jake, his arm round her and her head resting on his shoulder.

Gregor and Robbie, on the other hand, oblivious of the few other couples shuffling around the floor, were giving a virtuoso performance which wouldn't have been out of place on *Strictly Come Dancing*. Even the bitchy judge with the ridiculous name would have been impressed. Heather watched in admiration. She remembered Gregor telling her that he'd been mercilessly teased by the macho local boys when he decided to take classes in ballet, tap and ballroom dancing, and again, later, when he began training to be a hairdresser. But now, here he was, being himself and hugely enjoying it.

It was nearly time to go. In a few minutes, everyone would gather downstairs for the bells and *Auld Lang Syne*. Then the party would carry on through the night until breakfast was served. Heather turned towards the stairs, nearly crashing into someone. It was Sean.

'I was hoping I would see you,' he said, grabbing her arm to steady her.

'I was hoping I would see you,' agreed Heather. He wasn't wearing Highland dress but black trousers and a pewter grey shirt, and it suited him. In her high heels, Heather must be touching six feet, but she still felt that she could lean on him and feel protected. She breathed in the familiar smell of lemon soap and white spirit.

'I hope next year'll be a better one for both of us,' she said.

'I think so,' said Sean. Something in his tone made her look him full in the face; he sounded so definite.

'Has something happened?'

Sean shrugged.

'Not really. I just feel better, as if I've turned a corner. Maybe it's to do with thinking I could've lost Katie, maybe it's being so busy with work, maybe it's none of those things but just time passing, but I feel as if the depression's lifted, and I can move on.'

'I hope so,' Heather said. 'I really do.'

She hugged him tightly.

'I should apologise to you,' Sean said, into her hair.

'Oh, please don't,' protested Heather, 'because then our entire relationship would be based on perpetually apologising to each other.'

'No, I should,' said Sean. 'I just, I don't want you to think that you were only ever a substitute for Megan.'

He stroked back some hair behind her ear.

'I really liked you. Really like you. You're funny and kind and a hell of an artist. And you look beautiful tonight. It was just... timing.'

'Thank you, Sean,' said Heather, just as Katie came rushing up, threw her arms round her father's waist and began bubbling excitedly about Paolo's proposal and how Cara had asked her to be her flower girl.

'Let's go downstairs,' she said, then. 'It's nearly time for the bells.'

'I have to go,' said Heather, glancing at her watch. 'It's nearly midnight.'

'Why? Will you turn into a pumpkin?' asked Katie.

'No,' said Heather, with a giggle. 'I've got a taxi booked.'

They all went downstairs together, Katie running on ahead, her sparkly wings dancing on her back.

'Hello, Euan.' Heather heard her shrill voice say in delight. She froze, ducking behind a pillar. Her heart was racing so hard, she felt quite sick. Seeing him and Rowan kissing on the stroke of midnight, looking forward to another year together, was just what she had been trying to avoid.

23. *Honesty*

'Euan, Euan, guess what?' cried Katie, waving her wand around in her excitement.

Good call, Katie, Heather silently applauded. Maybe she could make her escape while the child acted as a decoy.

'You'll… use your magical powers to turn me into a frog,' Euan guessed. Heather peeped out from behind the pillar, watching as he crouched down before Katie, so that their eyes were on a level.

'No!'

'A prince, then.'

'No,' Katie said again, beginning to giggle. 'Aunt Cara's getting married to Paolo and I'm going to be the flower girl.'

'Well, I'm sure you'll be an amazing flower girl,' Euan said, his voice now grave. He was good with kids, Heather caught herself thinking. This only made her love him more, as she thought what a great dad he would be. But she had to be strong. She'd had her heart broken once, and Euan had healed it: now she had to protect herself from further pain.

Suddenly, the corridor seemed deserted. Sean had spotted Cara and Paolo in the throng and stopped to congratulate them and everyone else was streaming towards the ballroom for the countdown to the bells.

'Katie, you haven't seen Heather tonight, have you?' asked Euan.

'Yes. She was with me and Daddy.'

'It's all right,' said Heather, stepping out from behind the pillar. 'I'm here.'

'Heather! At last,' said Euan. 'Thanks, Katie,' he added, and ruffled her hair before getting to his feet.

'You look beautiful,' he went on.

'Thank you,' said Heather. 'But I've got a taxi waiting, so I need to go –'

'But, Heather,' said Euan, a puzzled frown on his face. 'It's nearly time for the bells, and I want to talk to you.'

'I can't do this, Euan. I'm sorry. I just can't,' Heather said.

'What do you mean? What can't you do?' Euan now looked even more perplexed.

'I can't be your consolation prize. I can't be second best.'

'What do you mean, second best?'

'Oh, come on, darlin', give him a chance,' came Shanice's voice. This village! thought Heather, not for the first time. Shanice had just emerged from a small cloakroom on the left and was now leaning on the wall, sipping champagne and watching the scene with frank interest and amusement.

'If you don't, I will,' she said, raising her glass to Euan in an appreciative toast.

Not this side of hell, thought Heather.

'Yeah, give him a chance,' echoed Katie. 'I like him.'

Dong! Dong! Dong!

The bell in the castle, perfectly synchronised with that in the church, began to ring out for New Year's Day. Heather marched past Euan and pushed open the heavy wooden door, stepping out into the freezing night.

'Heather.' Euan was behind her, his voice like a gunshot. Holding her head high, she began to walk down the steps to where the taxi was parked, Euan hurrying to keep up. It would have been a sweeping, dramatic exit, but for the fact that Matilda's shoes weren't that easy to walk in, especially down a deep flight of stairs. She lost her footing and went flying, fortunately into the arms of Gus, who was waiting for her. When she'd tripped, her left shoe had gone sailing into the bushes by the side of the stairs. Matilda would kill her, but she didn't have time to worry about that now.

'Heather, let's talk, please,' Euan said.

'Should auld acquaintance be forgot, and never brought to mind –' sang a hundred voices from inside.

‘Oh, my goodness, dear, what's the matter?' asked Treeny, as she let Heather into the cottage.

‘I think I'm in love with Euan,' Heather blurted, weakening at the sight of her aunt's sympathetic face and unable to keep her emotions in check any longer. 'But he's in love with Rowan. It's like Aidan and Savannah all over again.'

‘Heather, come here a moment,' said Treeny, leading the way into her bedroom. Heather limped after her, still wearing only one shoe. For once, it was warm in the room, and she sat down beside her aunt on the candlewick bedspread.

‘If you love Euan, you should tell him,' said Treeny. 'Don't let anything stand in your way. I was in love, once, and I –'

Treeny's face was deadly serious.

‘You were in love?' Heather said softly, the only sound bagpipes coming from the next room.

Treeny nodded, barely perceptibly.

‘I was engaged.'

‘Who were you engaged to, Treeny?' Heather's voice was barely more than a whisper. Treeny hesitated, as if, even now, she wanted to keep her secret.

‘Treeny, it's me. It's us. We've always been able to talk.'

Treeny nodded again.

‘Jack Buchanan.'

‘Euan and Callum's grandpa?'

‘Yes.'

Heather realised now that the "fit older guy" that Matilda had seen looking at Treeny at the fayre must have been Jack. Maybe he'd secretly carried a torch for her all these years, thinking about what might have been.

‘So, what happened?'

‘We started going out on the night of my eighteenth birthday party,' Treeny explained. 'There'd been a ceilidh in the village hall and he'd walked me home. We sat outside talking until the small hours. But our parents didn't really approve, with us being Catholic and his family being in the Free Church.'

Heather nodded. In her limited experience, the last word she would use to describe the Free Church was "free".

'But that made it all the more exciting and romantic.'

'Go on.' Heather took her aunt's liver spotted hands.

'Then, when I was twenty-one, Chrissie decided to go to Edinburgh to train as a teacher. I was young, and I wanted to see something of the world before I settled down to life as a farmer's wife. I decided to go, too. So I wrote to Aunt Jenny to ask if I could stay with her –'

Treeny swallowed, but managed to regain control.

'…Jenny said I'd be welcome. I thought Jack would wait for me. It was just something I needed to do. But he was very angry. He said that my place was with him and we had a huge argument, but I decided to go anyway. I hated him ordering me about. Too feisty for my own good.'

Treeny was trying to smile but Heather caught the glitter of tears in her eyes.

'He didn't wait for you?'

Treeny shook her head.

'After a while, he said it was best we called the engagement off. He said he'd found it very difficult with our families not getting on, and all the arguments there'd been. In the end he married Fay MacLeod. Her father owned the farm next to theirs, you see, so it meant that, when he retired, both farms could be joined together.'

'And there was never anyone else?' Heather asked.

Treeny shook her head.

'No one who mattered.'

She was crying now, dabbing at her eyes with a lace hanky.

The doorbell rang.

Quickly, Treeny composed herself and went out into the hall, Heather following.

'Euan,' she cried, as she opened the door. 'How wonderful to have a first foot who's tall, dark and handsome.'

Heather glowered at her aunt's cardiganed back. Euan wasn't Treeny's first foot – *she* was. Treeny'd been right about the tall, dark and handsome bit, however. It seemed that Shanice, Katie and Treeny all counted among his admirers - a wide cross section of the female population.

'Hi, Treeny. Happy New Year.'

Euan stooped to kiss her aunt's cheek and Heather noticed that he was holding a rhinestone studded metallic shoe. Sulkily, she sank down on the phone seat and allowed him to slip it on her foot – it didn't do much for her dignity to be hopping around.

'Why don't you go into the kitchen and get Euan a drink?' suggested Treeny, with a meaningful look at Heather. Wearily, she made her way through the living room, Euan following. Mrs Gillies, Mrs Peden and Miss Munro were chattering and drinking sweet sherry. They were "a wee bit tipsy" as Treeny would say, i.e. absolutely trolleyed.

'Hi, ladies. Happy New Year to you,' Euan said.

'Happy New Year, Euan,' chorused the "girls". They all, even Mrs Gillies, gazed at Euan like a bunch of teenagers in the front row of a Justin Bieber concert. Heather led him into the kitchen and they sat down on either side of the table, as if they were at a job interview. As a child, Kirsty had scratched her initials in the wood, and they were still visible despite several coats of varnish.

'I don't understand,' Heather ventured after a moment. 'Why aren't you up at the castle, bringing in the New Year with Rowan?'

Euan took her hand across the table.

'Rowan and I've split up,' he said, his expression grave.

'Again.'

'Again and for good this time,' Euan said.

'But you were in Glasgow just the other day. I thought... I assumed you'd gone to visit her.'

'I was in Glasgow the other day,' Euan said. 'But not to see Rowan.'

She was aware of a suppressed excitement under the gravity.

'Okay, Euan,' she said. 'Why did you go to Glasgow? I know you're bursting to tell me.'

'I was doing an interview,' Euan said. He paused. 'With Skye Friel. The only journalist she'd talk to.'

'Oh. Oh, my God. Your big break. But how on earth –'

Euan's eyes danced.

'It was just luck, really. Well, not for the poor dog, I guess.'

Despite herself, Heather giggled.

'What dog? What are you going on about?'

'Skye's got this labradoodle she dotes on. When the mutt cut her foot on a trap, she got her housekeeper to call the vet –'

'Callum?' squealed Heather.

Euan nodded.

'He took the chance of asking her if she'd give me an interview and she was so grateful to him for patching up poor old Ruby that she said she would.'

'Oh, my God,' said Heather, again. 'What a star your brother is.'

This was more like it. Heather felt as if the awkwardness which had built up since the kiss had melted away, and they were just buddies hanging out again. The kiss. She ignored the tingle which went through her at the thought of it. Was it her imagination, or had the Scottish country dance music in the living room stopped?

'Anyway, I didn't come here to tell you about how I'm the new Jeremy Paxman.'

'You didn't?'

Euan shook his head. His expression was again serious, his fingers entwined with hers.

'I came here to tell you that I love you.'

'But I don't –' Heather could feel her face flushing in a mixture of ecstasy and panic.

'You don't feel the same?' Euan's eyes never left hers.

'No. No. I do feel the same –' Heather cried.

'Then what? What's the problem?'

'Because I love you so much and I want to be with you. But I can't bear it if you're on the rebound, or you go back to Rowan –'

'Heather, I'm not going to go back to Rowan, and I'm not on the rebound. I think it's been over between us for a long time now, but I felt as if I should give it another try because we were both hurting about the baby. She finally opened up to me and I thought it should've brought us closer. I didn't want her to have to cope on her own after all she'd been through. But she said she just wanted to cheer herself up, get on with her life, focus on work, forget about everything and have some fun. So, every weekend, we'd be out living it up at clubs and parties and posh restaurants and all I could think about was how I'd rather be with you.'

'You would?' Heather's voice was low.

'Yes. You're my best friend. You make me laugh. You get me. And I know you really care about me.'

'Of course I do.'

Heather could feel happiness and well-being coursing through her. She felt free, light and airy in a way she never had in the past six months.

'Are you certain you're over Rowan?' she asked. 'I mean, she's so beautiful and talented and she's got loads of charisma and –'

'Oh, yes,' Euan said. 'She's got all that. And she's wild and exciting and challenging. But I want more than that now. I want a girlfriend who's also my soulmate and my friend. And that I fancy something terrible.' His face broke into a grin. 'Namely you, Heather, if you want me to spell it out.'

'Do you really mean it?' Heather said, feeling as if this couldn't really be happening to her.

'Heather. I spent the whole of Saturday afternoon at Devonshire Gardens with Scotland's top supermodel, and I still couldn't stop thinking about you: how much I missed you and wished you were there.'

'When did you realise?' Heather asked, a huge smile stretching across her face.

'The day you had your accident on Ben Lochy,' Euan said at once. 'I was so worried about you. That's when I realised how much I cared but I was still trying to sort things out with Rowan.'

'I love you,' Heather said. She leaned over to kiss him just as a cheer went up in the living room. Jumping to her feet, she pulled the door open. Mrs Gillies was standing just outside, no longer spritely enough to leap out of the way.

'Chrissie was just going to make us all a cup of tea,' improvised Treeny.

'Tea, my arse. You were listening,' protested Heather, but she was too happy to be properly angry.

⤹

'I feel kind of sorry for Rowan,' she admitted later. She and Euan had gone out for a walk. The moon hung like a paper lantern over the sea and the sky glittered with stars.

'I know,' Euan said. He stopped walking and kissed her on the forehead. 'But she's doing really well in the soap, she's had a call back for a part in a detective drama and she's got a new boyfriend. She's dating Ross Carmichael.'

'No,' squealed Heather. 'I don't believe it. Okay. I definitely don't feel sorry for her.'

Euan's arm was in what felt like its rightful place – round Heather's waist. She reflected that both she and Rowan had had their time in the darkness, and wondered if they had both learned from it.

'You're surely not suggesting that "the sexiest man in Scotland" is better looking than me,' Euan teased.

'Never,' agreed Heather. 'So, what's next for your stellar career?' she asked, as they strolled along the deserted promenade.

'I've been offered a column on the *Herald* magazine,' said Euan.

'In Glasgow?' said Heather.

'Nope – I'm staying right here. It's all agreed. I'm a writer: I can work from anywhere.' Suddenly, his voice was urgent. 'Heather, don't go back to London – stay here with me.'

'I will,' Heather shouted, frightening a seagull. She knew for sure now that Euan really loved her. She kissed him, and the kiss went on and on until a bunch of teenagers mooching along the road began to cheer.

Epilogue

Gregor McPherson and Sascha le Chevalier won the Highland Region Colouring Championships and will now go forward to the next round, to be held in Forres.

Chloé Marsden and Ryan Wright married in the summer in a beach ceremony in the Seychelles. *OK!* Magazine paid £1m for sole rights to the wedding photos. "Well placed" sources "close" to the couple say that they are blissfully happy/on the verge of a break-up. A baby girl is predicted, although Chloé isn't actually pregnant.

Catriona McAndrew is currently holidaying in Rome with her good friend, Chrissie Gillies.

Kirsty McAndrew © has opened her own boutique – Pink Sunshine - in Camden Passage.

Rowan Galloway has been nominated for a Scottish BAFTA, for her portrayal of Lady MacBeth. She is currently romantically linked with TV's Ross Carmichael, dubbed "The Sexiest Man in Scotland" by readers of the *Daily Record*.

Cara Fratelli is expecting the first of what is confidently anticipated to be many bambini.

Following a successful exhibition of his recent work in Edinburgh, Sean McAllister was featured in both the *Herald* and the *Scotsman* weekend Arts supplements. He has completed his portrait of Heather, which is now hanging in pride of place above the fire in her and Euan's cottage.

Katie McAllister won first prize – a £10 book token – in the children's art competition in Inveralan. She has a new pet, a hamster called Speedy, and has forsaken Hairy McLairy and Zachary Quack for Louis out of One Direction.

Craig Peden and his band have recorded their first demo tape *Thanksgiving* (the title is ironic) in his bedroom. Both sets of neighbours have contacted Dreichndrookit Council regarding a council tax rebate.

Nadine Jaye is currently in rehab. On release, she intends to retrain as a beautician.

Matilda Jaye is still going out with Ben Walker. They are deliriously happy but, after a recent promotion, she is too focused on her career to think about marriage.

Dr Paul Walker has recently completed his Phd in Astrophysics.

Euan Buchanan's career as a journalist has gone stellar since he published his much praised exclusive interview with elusive supermodel Skye Friel, but he has no plans to leave Kirklochy.

Jessica Lomax has achieved her burning ambition to become a WAG. Her current boyfriend is Championship League footballer Shayne Potts, but she hopes to be promoted to a Premier League player in due course. She now writes a column in *Closer* magazine about her wardrobe and celebrity lifestyle.

Dr Brandi La Puma's book, *How to Find Him and Keep Him*, has been translated into 17 languages. She is now firmly established as America's favourite relationship guru and has recently appeared on both the Leno and Letterman shows.

Skye Friel has disappeared from the catwalk and is happily living with her dog in her Highland castle. Sources close to the supermodel (i.e. her gardener) say that she has opted out of the rat race to enjoy a better quality of life.

Heather and Euan got married in Florence and lived happily ever after. While Euan pursues his career in journalism, Heather paints in her studio overlooking Kirklochy Bay.